PEOPLE WHO
WALK IN DARKNESS

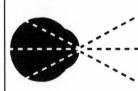

This Large Print Book carries the
Seal of Approval of N.A.V.H.

PEOPLE WHO WALK IN DARKNESS

STUART M. KAMINSKY

WHEELER PUBLISHING
A part of Gale, Cengage Learning

GALE
CENGAGE Learning™

Detroit • New York • San Francisco • New Haven, Conn • Waterville, Maine • London

GALE
CENGAGE Learning

Copyright © 2008 by Double Tiger Productions, Inc.
An Inspector Porfiry Rostnikov Mystery.
Wheeler Publishing, a part of Gale, Cengage Learning.

ALL RIGHTS RESERVED

Wheeler Publishing Large Print Hardcover.
The text of this Large Print edition is unabridged.
Other aspects of the book may vary from the original edition.
Set in 16 pt. Plantin.
Printed on permanent paper.

LIBRARY OF CONGRESS CATALOGING-IN-PUBLICATION DATA

Kaminsky, Stuart M.
　People who walk in darkness / by Stuart M. Kaminsky.
　　p. cm. — (An Inspector Porfiry Rostnikov mystery)
　ISBN-13: 978-1-59722-874-9 (alk. paper)
　ISBN-10: 1-59722-874-5 (alk. paper)
　1. Rostnikov, Porfiry Petrovich (Fictitious character)—Fiction.
2. Police—Russia (Federation)—Fiction. 3. Large type books. I.
Title.
PS3561.A43P46 2009
813'.54—dc22   2008039326

Published in 2009 by arrangement with Tom Doherty Associates, LLC.

Printed in the United States of America
1 2 3 4 5 6 7 12 11 10 09 08

To Barbara and John Lutz.
We couldn't ask for better friends.

We shall find peace. We shall hear the angels, we shall see the sky sparkling with diamonds.

— ANTON CHEKHOV, *Uncle Vanya*

CHAPTER ONE

Luc O'Neil was lost.

He wasn't particularly worried.

His cell phone wouldn't work down in the labyrinth nine hundred feet below the frozen layer of earth, but the homing device required of everyone entering the mine was glowing bright green. The pipe, the vein of rock that contained the diamonds, was a reasonably rich one. Nothing exceptional but productive, small, brown gems that would go mainly into industrial tools and the vast stockpile of the Russian diamond monopoly Alorosa, which in turn sold its holdings to DeBeers.

Twenty percent of all diamonds mined worldwide were from Russia and all of the mines, Luc knew, were located in Siberia. If they dared, which they would not do because there would be no profit in it, Alorosa could challenge DeBeers and flood the market with relatively inexpensive diamonds of all quality levels. It was a standing, unspoken suicidal threat, a doomsday scenario for the diamond market. The price paid by the world for diamonds allowed Russia a preferred seat at the table.

The value of diamonds, as Luc knew, was not dependent on their rarity, but on the ability of the diamond cartel to control their flow and price. Luc was well aware that diamonds are nothing but pieces of compressed carbon found not only in Siberia but in Botswana, Australia, South Africa, and, to a smaller degree, all over the planet.

But production was down in this mine. Or at least that was what Luc had been told. His job was to find out if the mine was so tapped out that it would not pay to keep it operating.

Luc was a geologist with a good underground sense of direction. But if that failed him, he could always follow the dull yellow lights that glowed indifferently every fifty yards or so on the jagged walls of the tunnel.

He was contracted with and well paid by the Canadian company that owned a piece of this operation. And so, screw 'em. He had a job to do, plain and simple. He would get it done and get out of here, e-mail his report to London, let DeBeers deal with it, and get the hell back to Toronto. Luc had missed his son's birthday only two months ago, when he was in Australia. Collette had not bothered to reproach him. What was the point? Let the boy know what kind of father he had, she had said. Well, she was right.

Luc scanned the walls for signs. He had been doing this for a decade. He didn't have to think about what he was looking for. It either felt right or it didn't. The diamond sense was a part of him. He was a human detector.

Dobson had told Luc he had been selected because he had more experience in this sort of thing. What sort of thing? Going into underground diamond mines, finding out why production was down, and determining if the mines were finally tapped out?

Dobson was at a surface mine in Botswana. Hundreds of thousands of tons of fickle rock did not threaten above Dobson's head.

Dobson could get to Capetown in less than three hours from even the most distant company mine in Southern Africa. There were places in Capetown, good food, warm beds, and warmer women ranging from pale, ghostly white to dark, smooth ebony.

11

And then Dobson would be stopping to meet with diamond cutters in Tel Aviv where, in spite of the slight threat of suicide bombers, he would stay overnight in a luxury suite in the Dan Tel Aviv Hotel. Luc, on the other hand, would spend the night in a visitor's room in the four-story concrete block that housed the mine's middle-management workers here in Devochka.

Luc knelt next to the wall to his right. He had insisted on coming this way, even climbing over the dust-covered yellow machinery and down the slight incline. There was a feel of something this way.

His guide, an old night-duty mine watch-man, Boris Antonovich, had told him that this shaft needed shearing up. Boris, tall, sullen, hulking, and bearded would not have been Luc's choice as a guide, but Boris had one advantage. He could speak a little French.

Luc had not even bothered to answer when Boris issued his warning about the shaft. The geologist had simply gone down the tunnel, examining the walls, taking samples, seeing nothing of great interest, going deeper and deeper, farther and farther. And then he had noticed that Boris was not behind him.

Probably back there sulking because Luc

had come this way instead of to the tunnel to the right that Boris had suggested.

"This is an old shaft," Boris had said. "It's not worked anymore."

Luc had known this.

"It is dangerous," Boris had said.

"Danger is relative," Luc answered.

"Physical danger is absolute."

A Russian philosopher in Siberia. Just what Luc needed.

"I'm going in," Luc had said.

Boris had shrugged and shook his head.

The large tunnel was arched, with a craggy roof and wall and an even, flat floor. Rubber-reinforced trucks, with beds that could hold 10,000 tons of ore, had ample room to rumble into the darkness at the end of the yellow tunnel.

Boris's arguments for not going into this particular shaft were very persuasive, but not in the way the Russian desired. The more Boris warned, the more determined Luc had been to go this way. In a battle of wills between a Russian and a Canadian, the man with the money and the gun will always win. Luc had a gun.

Luc was no fool. He had started carrying the weapon at first because of the stories others had told about being threatened, attacked. Rumor was that an Australian geologist who worked for the company had been beaten to death at a mine site in the Outback.

Luc, on his third trip to a site, had been attacked by a black mine worker in Namibia. The man was tall, lean, his open shirt revealing taut muscles, his face revealing rage, his mouth spewing, cracking with a babble of language Luc didn't understand.

In the man's right hand had been a rock. He had run at Luc, who was aware of voices, dark faces behind the man with the rock. Luc had fired. Once. The lean man fell to his knees, still looking at Luc, still babbling. The lean man didn't die. He had attacked Luc because he was the only white man present. He had attacked Luc because the man's wife had died and the man didn't have enough money to bury her properly. He blamed the mine, the humming, dark, maddening tunnels. He blamed the managers, the vague sense of the mine's white owners.

The doctor who operated on the crazed man to remove the bullet told Luc that his patient's babbling had been a rant ending with, "It is alive. It breathes. It waits."

So Luc carried a small but effective gun in the leather bag over his shoulder.

He knelt. He looked. He focused his laser flashlight on the wall in front of him. Someone had covered a four-foot section of the wall with dirt that almost matched the rest of the wall. Most people wouldn't have noticed.

Luc rubbed at the dirt-covered wall, took out a chemical spray, and washed a section. Even before the spray finished its work, Luc could see what had been hidden, a wooden panel about three-feet square. The panel had been carefully covered with chips of rock and dirt to simulate the surrounding wall.

Luc removed the panel and placed it against the tunnel wall. Then he shined his light inside a cave that extended about six feet into the rock. Luc crawled into the cave, coughed, and examined the walls around him.

He could see immediately. He needed no tests. An untrained eye would see nothing. Luc saw everything. He chipped away a small outcrop to his right, just above his head. Bits of rock rained down on his head and back. He examined the rocky ore in his hand and decided. It was, if he were not mistaken, a reasonably rich outcropping.

Considering the size of the cave and the quality of what he had in his hand, Luc concluded that someone had removed millions of rubles worth of uncut jewelry-quality diamonds from the —

Someone was singing.

Luc, still holding the rock sample, crawled back out of the small cave and took out his gun. He sat with his back against the tunnel wall and listened.

It sounded like the voice of a child, a child singing in Russian in a beautiful, clear voice that echoed sweetly through the tunnel, a funereal cathedral echo.

The voice was coming closer.

Luc got to his feet, dropped the rock into his case, and ripped the filter mask from his face.

The tunnel lights went out.

Luc was not a whimpering baby. He had served in the army, saw combat in Bosnia, had his share and more of barroom fights. Someone was playing games in the darkness. Fine, he would play too.

Luc turned on his flashlight and aimed it down the tunnel. The child's voice came closer and Luc could see a flickering light heading toward him, casting shadows on the tunnel walls.

He waited, cursing his heavy breathing.

It was definitely the voice of a child, sing-

16

ing a Russian song he thought he had heard before.

"Who are you?" he called out, his voice determined, strong, echoing.

The child kept singing.

Then she appeared. Alone. Small. Hair brushed down, dark, streaming over her shoulders and down the front of her white, white dress. In her left hand was a lamp, an old oil mining lamp, a kind that, Luc was certain, had never been used down here.

The child stopped. She was no longer singing.

Luc could see no one behind her.

The diamond thieves probably thought he wouldn't shoot a child. Maybe they were right. But there had to be adults not far behind her. He could simply walk past her, gun in hand, at the ready, and make his way back down the tunnel.

Did they know he had a gun?

Did they know he had found the small cave?

And where the hell was Boris?

The child smiled at him showing unexpectedly clean and even small white teeth. Russians did not have clean, even white teeth, not even the children.

Luc inched his way along the wall looking for trouble, ready for trouble, deciding not to send a warning shot into the darkness, deciding not to let them know he had a gun.

He was even with the child now. She had watched him move along the wall, scraping his head on the jagged rocky surface. She couldn't have been more than ten or eleven years old. The light from the lamp in her hand cast shadows on her face, her eyes showing clear and blue.

She looked at his gun and kept smiling.

A sound down the shaft. Luc turned his flashlight toward it. There was nothing there. He sensed a scuffling, turned the light back to where the girl had been standing. She was gone. He aimed the beam toward the cave he had uncovered. The girl was standing before it, her lamp now held low. The shadows had turned her face hooded and skull-like.

Luc was afraid, undecided. Should he leave her and run? Should he shoot her? Should he take her hand and lead her out of the darkness?

No. He couldn't bring himself to touch her.

The hell with it. He hoped he had enough bullets for whoever was waiting in the black oblivion. He turned his back on the girl, aimed his flashlight toward wherever disaster was lurking, and took a step.

Behind him the girl started to sing again.

It struck him in the dark of a diamond mine in Siberia that he had never heard his five-year-old son sing. Luc wondered if he ever would.

CHAPTER TWO

"What do you know of diamonds, Porfiry Petrovich Rostnikov?"

They were seated in the office of Igor "the Yak" Yaklovev, Director of the Office of Special Investigations. Compared to the offices of other departments and bureaus in the central police headquarters on Petrovka Street, the Yak's was modest. It had a small conference table with eight chairs near the door, and a desk rumored to have belonged to Lavretiy Pavlovich Beria, chief of the Soviet police under Stalin. When Stalin died, his successors executed Beria, and his office furniture, like that of many of his colleagues, was divided by the grabbing hands of middle-level *apparatchiks*.

"They are mostly white when cut. They are valuable as jewels and for industrial use. We have diamond mines in Siberia," Rostnikov answered.

"That's all?"

Rostnikov shrugged. The two men looked at each other over the desk. The Yak was lean, fit, and reported to occasionally engage in martial arts exercises with Vladimir Putin, with whom he had served in the old KGB in St. Petersburg. He was well aware that he was called "the Yak" behind his back. He did not mind. The wild yak can weigh more than 2,000 pounds and survive in extreme cold. It is wary and fast.

Behind the Yak, and on the wall just above his head, was a modest black-and-white photograph of Putin almost smiling. When the Yak had been appointed to head the Office of Special Investigations, it had not been considered a prize for an ambitious man. The Office was part of the 15th investigative division of the Investigative Directorate. The Directorate was itself a unit of the Moscow Criminal Investigation Division. The Office of Special Investigations was at the very bottom of the Moscow police force. The Office had been created solely as a receptacle in which to dump unsolvable and politically sensitive cases filled with a high likelihood of failure. The Office's first director, Colonel Ivan Snitkonoy, whom the Yak considered a pompous, uniformed ass, had seemed blissfully unaware that he had been dumped into a

21

job whose present and future promised only oblivion. But something had changed. And the change had come with the man who sat across the desk, Porfiry Petrovich Rostnikov.

Rostnikov had been demoted from the procurator's office to life under Snitkonoy, the Gray Wolfhound. Rostnikov had brought his own team, all of whom, like Rostnikov, had left after Procurator Anna Timofeyeva had her second heart attack and was forced to retire — along with the protective cloak, which she had provided the far too inquisitive Rostnikov.

Like Yaklovev, Rostnikov had a nickname: the Washtub. He was squat, compact, and heavy, with a dour Russian peasant face. He seldom smiled broadly. His voice was a soft, bearlike growl, but not a frightening one.

At the moment, Porfiry Petrovich Rostnikov was not thinking of diamonds, but of his left leg, which was made not of flesh, blood, and bone, but of metal, plastic, and wood. His other left leg, the one that had been replaced, the shriveled one he had dragged behind him since his childhood, was floating in a very large jar in the second level below the ground floor of Petrovka, in Paulinin's laboratory. Paulinin, agreed by the detectives of Petrovka to be a forensic genius and a lunatic, who talked to the corpses he worked on and far preferred their company to that of the living.

As the Yak continued to talk of diamonds, slowly coming to the point where Rostnikov would have to pay attention, the Chief Inspector was trying to decide on an issue of great importance. Should he take the shoe off of his left foot before climbing into bed each night, or simply leave it on when he removed the leg? Since getting the leg, he had been taking the shoe off, but what was the point? His wife Sarah told him simply to be comfortable. The bed was large. It made no difference to her.

Rostnikov considered bringing up the question to the Yak, but knew he would not. The Yak's mind was on diamonds, and he had no sense of humor or irony and little curiosity. All of these attributes contributed to Rostnikov's appreciation of the man. Anything the Yak said converted to how his words might be exchanged for political, economic, or social advantage. Rostnikov, however, always considered the irony of human existence, engaged in uncertain acts of humor, and was eternally curious about everything from whether a man should take the shoe off of his artificial leg when he went to sleep to who might kill a drunken policeman in an alleyway, not that anyone had recently killed a drunken policeman in an alleyway.

This train of thought reminded him that Russia, even with the passing of Communism, was still among the three countries in the world with the highest rate of alcoholism.

"You will learn," said the Yak leaning forward, folding his hands on his desk and meeting his Chief Inspector's eyes with a practiced, unblinking look that caused at least a drying of the mouth in everyone — everyone except Rostnikov.

Rostnikov blinked, adjusted his leg, and looked back at the Yak. Rostnikov nodded. He was not sure whether the Yak was issuing an order about diamonds or warning him that he was going to be in a situation in which his survival might be at stake when the lesson came. Rostnikov pursed his lips and nodded his head as if he knew what the Yak was talking about. And then the connection came.

"You are going to Siberia, to a diamond mine where a man, a Canadian geologist, died two days ago. You will determine if he was murdered. If he was, you are to tell me who killed him."

"When am I leaving?"

"Tonight. There is a supply load of medication for the mining town, Devochka, leaving at nine by plane. You will be on it."

"I will take Karpo."

"Take whomever you wish. Pankov will arrange for a car to pick you and Karpo up at your home and get you to the plane."

Pankov was the sweaty, frightened little man who sat at a desk outside of Yaklovev's office, listened at the doorway when he considered it safe to do so, and did what he was told with nervous dispatch and an impressive number of contacts who owed him for small favors.

Rostnikov nodded again, considering the oddity of the name Devochka, a man's name that meant "little girl." Why had it come into being and why had a mining town in Siberia been given such a name?

Rostnikov started to rise, no mean trick for a box of a man with an artificial leg. The Yak held up a hand to let him know that the conversation had not ended. Rostnikov eased himself back into the chair and looked at Yaklovev. Was the Yak enjoying his Chief Investigator's discomfort? Perhaps.

The two men had an uneasy and mutually beneficial alliance. The Yak protected Porfiry Petrovich, and the small band of investigators working under him, from political pressure on the outcomes of their investigations.

He protected them well and with keen sincerity. In return, each success by Rostnikov was another potential step upward for the Yak. Except at the moment, he did not want to step upward. He gathered information, evidence, tapes, confessions, and indiscretions and locked them away in a safe hidden in his apartment.

Thanks to Rostnikov, when the time was right, the contents of that safe would secure Igor Yaklovev's future, a future that would move the Yak far above his present office.

Rostnikov knew all this. It was the way of the world.

In a system in which the old laws had been thrown out and new ones still not fully defined, Rostnikov addressed puzzles, found the answers to questions, met people, and, when possible, engaged in the dispensation of justice, something the courts did only on occasion.

His was a fragile and questionable pursuit, but one he had accepted and in which he did well enough to survive.

"Your lesson," said the Yak, handing Rostnikov a file folder.

Rostnikov took it.

"Devochka is one of the oldest diamond mines in Siberia. It dates back to 1887 when the Tsar ordered the exploration of Siberia for precious metals. It is estimated that as many as 40,000 people died looking for jewels in the ground that could be polished to fit into the rings, tiaras, bracelets, and precious little jewel boxes and precise gleaming eggs of the nobility. Aside from those who supervised, most of the workers were convicts, criminals, and political prisoners. They died, as many as twenty-five a day at the site of Devochka, where they began to mine. And then the mine was abandoned for lack of success after four fruitless years, but remained a prison camp."

The Yak pointed at the report.

"The mine was and is not the most productive and profitable. The rocks containing the tiny gems are reluctant to give up their treasure."

Rostnikov didn't ask the Yak why he was telling him what must surely be in the report. He knew the Director well enough to know that there was a point — not historical, but very much in the present, and possibly the future.

"The mine has always been the bastard stepchild of Siberian diamond mines, almost closed when Stalin ordered new exploration for Siberian diamonds in 1957. Geologists and a new generation of convicts, political and criminal, died in the digging in numbers greater than those who had died at the mine in the service of the Tsar. Diamond pipes, veins of diamonds, were discovered. New mining machines were brought in, modern techniques employed, but Devochka kept steadily producing in a small stream. It was and is a mine and a town passed by time, its residents a congregation of generations of criminals and outcasts."

And then Rostnikov knew why the Yak was telling him about the diamonds. He looked at the man as he spoke and saw a dreamy glaze in his eyes as if he were looking somewhere at something that didn't exist. It was the first time Rostnikov had ever seen a hint of imagination in the Yak, and it had been brought on by a vision of diamonds or what diamonds could give him.

The Yak went silent. Moments passed. Rostnikov spoke.

"I see."

But what I see is not what you are seeing, Rostnikov thought. *You want me to deliver to you the key to control a crumbling diamond mine and the possibility that one more vein will be struck and bleed.*

Rostnikov started to rise.

"Wait," said the Yak, coming out of his reverie.

He turned his head not to see if Rostnikov

28

had noticed his weakness. The Yak was certain that he had. The question was how he would handle this instant.

Rostnikov pretended not to have noticed.

"We are taking on two other cases related to this investigation. Assign who you will to them and have those doing the investigation report to you and only you. You, in turn, will keep me informed on a daily basis."

"From Siberia?"

"From Siberia. The connection of sorts between the cases," said the Yak, "is not a coincidence."

Two more folders appeared in the Yak's right hand. He passed them to Rostnikov.

"The cases must be resolved in nine days," said the Yak, "one week from Tuesday."

Rostnikov looked for a sign in the man's eyes or the movement of his fingers. There was none.

"You know who General Mihail Franko-vich is?"

"Yes," said Rostnikov.

Frankovich was Director of the Division of Murder in the Investigative Directorate. The joke in Petrovka was that Frankovich was well qualified for the job because he was reported to have murdered at least two suspects who had refused to confess. Frankovich was not of the KGB old-boy network.

He had risen from the ranks in the Army as his father had done before him.

"General Frankovich would like to incorporate the Office of Special Investigations into the Division of Murder," said the Yak. "We have been too successful. This office has moved, at least in the eyes of some, from being a dark hole to being a small diamond."

Rostnikov nodded.

"Nine days from now there will be a meeting of the Moscow Criminal Investigation Commission," the Yak went on, carefully watching the emotionless face of his Chief Inspector. "General Frankovich will bid to take over this Office. It is possible he will succeed, unless . . ."

"You present evidence of a success so great that the General will have to withhold his bid," said Rostnikov.

"Precisely," said the Yak. "I do not intend for the Office of Special Investigations to be lost."

That was not exactly the truth. The Yak's plan was far more bold. He had prepared for it over the past four years, gathering information about the failures of the Division of Murder and the weaknesses of General Frankovich. The Yak had his own plan to take over the Division of Murder, employing concise reports of failure and

Loyalists were defeated. Though desperately in need of volunteers, they had been happy to see the sadistic young man depart. This newest member of the Montez family seemed to have inherited that homicidal streak.

"You cannot stop your heart from beating," said Kolokov, reaching down to place his right hand on George Umbaway's chest. "It is a lie detector."

Kolokov turned his head slightly to the right as if listening in the air for a heartbeat. Smoke curled into Kolokov's eyes. He squinted.

"Remarkable. You might have a heart attack before I can get your answer. What *is* your answer, by the way? You've forgotten my question. Who supplies you with the diamonds, and when and where are you getting another delivery?"

George willed his heart to slow down. He was sweating even though it was cold in the room. He thought about his wife, Marie-Marie, and his children. For no reason he wondered, not for the first time, why his wife's left arm had been refusing to function. She would need to be sent to England for evaluation and possible surgery. George trusted neither white nor black doctors in South Africa or Namibia or Botswana.

private documents that might uncharitably but accurately be labeled blackmail.

"Frankovich has his own loyal staff," the Yak continued. "It is unlikely he would retain the personnel now working in this Office. You and your detectives would be reassigned, as would I. You understand?"

"Perfectly."

"Good. You have provided for me in the past, Porfiry Petrovich Rostnikov. It is vital that you do so once more."

The Yak had delivered what the Americans called "a pep talk." It lacked the emotion one might expect at halftime from the coach of the Dynamo Soccer Team. The Yak may have felt emotion, but he was incapable of conveying it. Besides, Rostnikov didn't need a pep talk.

While he did not know what the Yak's plan was this time, he knew it was more than simple survival. One did not survive in Russia at the Yak's level, particularly in the police hierarchy, just by protecting one's rear. One had to tear a painful, bloody chunk out of the rear of the enemy as well.

While he did not welcome the prospect of losing his job, Porfiry Petrovich did not mind having a deadline, a clock ticking over his shoulder. He knew he had a tendency to sit back and listen rather than advance. He was a man of great curiosity. He was not in the least ambitious, which was one of the reasons Yaklovev trusted him, or came as close to trusting him as the Yak was capable of.

"That's all," said the Yak.

He was rubbing the thumb and a finger of each hand together as if he were about to count a stack of money. The movement was small. It didn't escape Rostnikov.

Porfiry Petrovich Rostnikov rose with difficulty, tucked the three file folders under his arm, and looked at the Yak. Their eyes met. There was a warning in the eyes of the man behind the desk under the photograph of Vladimir Putin. Rostnikov was to ask no more questions.

When Rostnikov had moved slowly across the room and out the door, Yaklovev removed from his desk drawer a more detailed copy of the reports he had given his Chief Inspector.

There were many things in the reports he had not mentioned, though he had included the tale of the ghost girl. It was part of the peasant fabric of lore that built up around every small town and most of the large ones throughout Russia. Russians could be ignorant and superstitious. It was one of the many weaknesses in the national psyche that

a careful, ambitious man could exploit.

"I am of mixed minds about what I want you to do. Are you listening? You don't look as if you are listening."

The lean black man didn't answer and didn't look at Vladimir Kolokov. He stared straight ahead to the single dirty window in the concrete basement.

Kolokov was a man of average size and build, neither thin, nor fat, nor athletic. His hair was a mop of brown-yellow, his face a forty-three-year-old mask of indifference.

Kolokov was smoking an American cigarette. He had offered one to George Umbaway. George had refused.

Two of the other three Russians in the room were also smoking. The two lounged against the wall where George, were he to turn his eyes but slightly, would be looking directly at them. There was nothing of interest about the two men except that they might be called upon to kill George and his companions in another room. It was the fourth man who did frighten George. The man, Pau Montez, was the youngest of the quartet. He was lean and muscular, his neck thick. His head was shaved and he wore a permanent smile. Pau's grandfather had fled Spain for a welcoming Russia when the

"What do I do with a man like this?" Vladimir said with exasperation, looking at the Spaniard for an answer he was certain he would not receive.

The Spaniard smiled.

"Alek, Bogdan?"

The two men in the corner stopped talking when they were addressed. The younger of the two, Alek, looked at the older for an answer and got none.

Kolokov shook his head.

"Then I will have to rely on my own resources. I want the information you have, the answers to my questions, but I am of two minds. I also want to torture you. I want to see the extent to which a man, or woman, will undergo agony before they are broken. I must admit that I've never had the opportunity to torture a black man before. I understand that black people have a very low level of tolerance for . . ."

"Just do it, Vlady," Bogdan called out.

Kolokov spun around and flung his cigarette toward the man. Bogdan held up a protective arm and the perfectly flung missile bounced to the floor. Kolokov pointed a finger at the man and said, "Do not tell me what to do, ever. Suggest. Do not tell me."

"But you . . . ," Alek began and changed his mind.

The Spaniard was smiling more broadly, enjoying the exchange.

"You have made up my mind, African," said Kolokov, fishing a fresh cigarette from his shirt pocket and lighting it as he moved to a table against the wall where George could see something white next to a cardboard box.

Kolokov's voice had risen.

Now George could see what was on the table and became truly afraid.

Kolokov turned back to George, adjusted the sleeves of his white surgical jacket, and said, "I wear this to keep the blood from my clothes, my body. And also, between us, it makes me feel like a doctor or a scientist doing important research, which, in a way, I am. If I am ever caught, I can give them vivid reports on the effectiveness of each session. All right, George, here is what we are going to do. It was a method used on my father by the NKVD. He survived. You may. He didn't have the option of giving information or confessing to anything. They just wanted to torture him. Maybe it was a slow day. Are you hungry?"

Now George turned his eyes to the man who was either mad or pretending to be to frighten him.

"We're going to feed you. We are going to

put a feeding tube down your nose. Wait, I'll show you."

Kolokov moved to the cardboard box on the table and pulled out a coil of plastic tubing.

"I think it's too thick," Kolokov said with a sigh. "But it will have to do. When it was done to my father, blood gushed from his nose, but they kept pushing until the cartilage cracked. He couldn't scream, not with the pipe in his throat. And breathing was . . . you can imagine. He remembered wheezing until the pipe was in his stomach. Then they . . . am I boring you?"

Kolokov leaned forward so that his eyes were looking directly into those of his prisoner.

"You should listen. It is interesting. Watch."

He retrieved a screw-top jar from the cardboard box. It was filled with a thick liquid.

"Looks like shit, right? Don't worry. It's not. It is a healthy, if perhaps somewhat rancid, thick broth rich in carbohydrates and proteins. You'll be a healthy man if you survive."

Kolokov held the jar in front of George's face. The liquid in it was a murky brown with small pieces of something languidly floating in it.

"We will hold you down for half an hour so the food will be absorbed and can't be vomited. Then we will remove the tube. Then you get another chance to talk. And if you don't, we repeat the feeding for as many days as it takes and, according to my father, who went for ten days before falling into a coma, it is more painful each time the pipe goes down the raw passages. I've always wanted to see what my father suffered. I may finally be getting my chance. And if you die, we still have your two friends to feed. I would like to be extremely wealthy, rich from diamonds, but I'll gladly accept the alternate option of torture and, who knows, I may get both."

Kolokov held the tubing and a funnel in one hand and the bottle in the other. The Spaniard crossed his arms. George knew which option he wanted.

In the company of madmen, one's best refuge is to go mad oneself.

"Well?" asked the Russian.

There was no doubt what Vladimir Kolokov wanted. George was not about to grant it to him, even if it meant death. George was shaking now. He could not help it. He was shaking too much to speak but he did make a gesture with his head that left no doubt of his response.

He shook his head no and tilted it back. Kolokov looked disappointed.

Oxana Balakona stood near a wall in the North Station of the Kiev Railroad Station. In her right hand was a small suitcase, plain, faux leather, black. People hurried past her — more than 170,000 passengers came through the station every day — but she was not unnoticed.

Oxana was a model — a beautiful, thin, dark model in demand as a mannequin for sultry clothes, a sly smile on her red lips.

Women glanced at her. Most men, even the old ones who only harbored the memory of a libido, stared at Oxana as they moved by.

Train arrivals and departures were announced by a calm baritone voice. Children cried and whined.

Oxana was aware of the attention she brought, but at the moment it was of no interest to her. In fact, her looks were a threat to the reason she was here.

She checked the large, modern, metal clock at the second level of the open area.

The woman was late.

And then Christiana Verovona appeared, as unimpressive as Oxana was striking.

Christiana was about Oxana's age, no more than twenty-five, but she looked at least ten years older. Oxana had a fair description and an old photograph of the woman, but that was not how she recognized her.

Christiana Verovona was carrying a suitcase exactly like the one in Oxana's hand.

No time to waste. Oxana hurried through the crowd on the polished gray-on-charcoal colored floor toward the bizarre lobby display next to which the other woman stood. The display was encircled by a knee-high polished stone wall topped by a low fence of clear plastic tethered to low posts. In the center of the circle were four fifteen-foot-high palm trees whose trunks were made of see-through plastic and whose fronds at the top were bright green plastic.

The beautiful woman under the palm trees saw Christiana coming now. Christiana had simply been told that someone would appear by the palm trees, place a duplicate suitcase next to hers, take Christiana's suitcase, and walk away.

Christiana, who had come from Moscow, was not totally without the virtue of good looks, but they had been squandered. It made no difference to Oxana who made the exchange, saying only, "Have a nice trip back to Moscow."

"Yes," said Christiana.

And then the woman who had taken Christiana's suitcase was gone. Christiana looked up at the clock. She would have to hurry. The new suitcase was about as heavy as the one she had exchanged. She picked it up and hurried toward the long, high-ceilinged, broad walkway that led to the trains.

Christiana had only a flicker of hope that she would succeed. Not that anything had gone wrong or appeared as if it might go wrong. She told herself, as she hurried through the crowd of jostling people going in both directions, that all would be fine. Georgi had told her that it would be fine and she wanted to believe him, wanted to deliver the suitcase, be handed the money, more money than she had ever made in a year. Then she wanted to go to her room and lie down and sleep curled up facing the wall.

She held out her ticket showing it to anyone who wore a uniform. Finding the right train was easy, but her car was far down the track. The train was making loud noises as if it were about to leave without her. She held the handle of the suitcase with two hands now and tried to run. The suitcase bounced against her knees, drumming as she walked.

Christiana was in no shape for running.

Money. Think of the money. She would put all of it away. Well, almost all of it. She would go off somewhere for a while and give up the drugs. Georgi would not try to stop her. He really didn't need her anymore, which was good.

She saw a conductor still far down the train looking toward her.

She thought of the beautiful dark woman with whom she had switched bags. Was *she* doing it for the money? She must be. If Christiana looked like her, she wouldn't be running down a train platform with a suitcase assaulting her. What if it came open? It could. Christiana had not packed it.

Almost there.

She had given up the vodka. It hadn't been so bad. She still had the heroin and the pills. One step at a time. All she needed was a little time away.

The conductor was motioning for her to hurry. She tried.

And then she thought about Alaya. She did not mean to, did not want to. Alaya was gone. Christiana did not know where. Georgi had convinced her that he could not afford to raise a child. She was a prostitute, a prostitute who, with the help of a smile and well-applied makeup, could still bring in a reasonable price. And so she had handed over Alaya after being told the infant was headed for the home of a rich candy importer. Georgi had kept all the money. Christiana had not wanted any.

Christiana showed the conductor her ticket.

"Compartment four," he said.

She climbed up the steps and into the train car pulling the suitcase behind her. It was painfully heavy now. The muscles in each arm were knotted and aching.

Georgi was definitely not bad, not a pimp like so many of the others. He had linked her up with businessmen, some from Moscow, some from as far as Argentina, and quite a few from China. He did not care about the tips they left her. And most of them were kind. She did her best to please. Georgi was more interested in gambling and business deals than sex. She was now, and for months had been, companionship, nothing more. The few dollars she brought in were meaningless.

All the seats on both sides of the aisle were full. The train lurched forward. She tried to hold the suitcase high, failed, and apologized when she grazed the shoulder of a dark, fat man with a thin, trim beard. She found the compartment, slid the door open, pushed the lock, and stood for a few seconds catching her breath. Christiana put the suitcase on the seat and looked around. The train rattled forward, heading back to Moscow.

Georgi would be at the station to meet her. Everything would be fine.

A knock.

"Yes?" she asked.

"The door is locked," came the voice of a man, an almost musical tenor.

"Yes," she said.

"This is my compartment," said the man through the door.

The train was picking up speed now, rumbling through the station and the train yard.

"No," she said. "You are mistaken. I have the whole compartment."

"This is car seven, compartment four?"

"Yes," she said.

"That is what my ticket says. You can take a look. We will have to ask the conductor for an explanation."

Christiana moved the three steps across the compartment and unlocked the door. The man was about her height, willowy, with a boyishly good-looking face, though he was no boy.

He wore a long black soft leather jacket, dark slacks, and a white shirt. His thin dark hair was brushed straight back. He smiled apologetically and stepped in, sliding the door closed behind him and locking it.

"I have been waiting for you to get on," he said, motioning her back toward the window. "You almost missed the train."

The smiling man, she was certain, was there to get the suitcase. There was no doubt about that. She would have to explain when she got back to Moscow, and Georgi would know she was telling the truth, but it would make no difference. She looked at the suitcase.

"You made the exchange. Where is the other suitcase?"

Christiana had a lifetime of being the object of violence from men. Something about her invited it. But this man was not interested in sex or the pleasure of inflicting pain. Something as cold as dry ice, as white as diamonds was in him and she was afraid.

"I do not know. A beautiful woman has it, an actress or a model, I think.

"A model, I think," she said again feeling her left leg begin to twitch. "I think I've seen her before, in magazines or on television."

"And?"

"Nothing. That's it. Believe me."

Now there was a knife in the hand of the man's delicate fingers. He rolled it, spun the blade back and forth.

"You do not know any more, do you?"

The train lurched on noisily. Metal screeched on metal.

"No," she said.

"Then, *izvi'neete,* I'm sorry to say that I have no use for you."

He skipped one step forward and twisted her to him by the wrist. Before she could scream, he had a hand over her mouth and the knife blade entered her neck expertly, deeply.

"Now that did not hurt, did it?"

He was right. It had not hurt. Christiana would not have to make excuses to Georgi in Moscow now. She would be dead, and, given her life, there were worse things. She slumped forward, and the man guided her falling body into the seat. It was an almost elegant move, balletic, professional. He had not a drop of blood on his shirt, slacks, or jacket.

He wiped the knife blade on her not-quite-shabby coat, moved her gently so that her head rested on the window, picked up the suitcase, and left the compartment after putting up a DO NOT DISTURB sign. He went back to his coach seat for forty-five minutes, chatting with a young soldier before the train pulled into the first station down the line.

He said good-bye to the soldier, got off the train with the suitcase he had taken from the dead woman and one of his own. He waited for the train to pull out of the station. As it moved past, he looked up and saw the dead woman, eyes open, mouth open, and contorted against the bloody window. He pulled a cell phone out of his pocket and quickly aimed it at the dead woman. He clicked off two photographs. Then the train was gone.

He moved casually toward the depot to buy a ticket back to Kiev.

After leaving the Yak's office, Rostnikov sat at his desk reading the information in the folders he had been given. The words that held the three cases together were 'diamonds' and 'nine days.'

He was reasonably certain that the Yak had told him the truth about almost everything — except his motives. He was reasonably sure that in nine days the meeting would be held to determine the fate of the Office of Special Investigations.

He called his squad in, and in the cramped office he gave out the assignments. Iosef and Zelach would investigate the torture-murder of two black South Africans whose bodies were found seated in a cemetery. The dead men were both former workers in a Botswanan diamond mine. Both were suspected by Interpol of smuggling diamonds. Both, along with an unknown number of others, were known to have been in Moscow. The South African, Botswanan, and Namibian governments had asked the Russian government to watch the two men. Now they were dead. Now they were the concern of the Office of Special Investigations.

The other case involved a murdered woman found in a train compartment when it pulled into Moscow from Kiev. The woman was alone in a first-class, two-bed compartment. She was a known prostitute. She had been stabbed once. There was but one mention of diamonds in the report on Rostnikov's desk. On a yellow Post-it the Yak had carefully printed the word 'diamonds.'

The Office of Special Investigations did not normally delve into the murder of prostitutes. Nobody really delved into the murder of prostitutes. But this Moscow prostitute had been found murdered in the most expensive private car on a train. This prostitute, Christiana Verovona, had purchased a ticket to Kiev and another almost immediately back to Moscow.

Rostnikov gave the case to Sasha Tkach and Elena Timofeyeva.

Rostnikov said little at the meeting. There was little to say, and whatever was spoken was certainly being listened to by Pankov or the Yak. Rostnikov and the others in his squad knew where the microphones were planted in the wall here in Porfiry Petrovich's office and in the room where all of them had their desks.

They met outside of Petrovka when they wanted privacy. They met inside Petrovka when they wanted the Yak to know what they were saying. The Yak knew that all of them were well aware of the microphones. He did not hope to suddenly hear priceless snippets of profitable information. He simply wanted them to be aware of his presence and to have all conversations of even the slightest possible consequence taped and recorded on CDs for his own protection. The Yak was very good at protecting himself.

"Questions?" asked Rostnikov.

There were many. All went unasked.

Sasha Tkach wondered for an instant if he

had been selected by Rostnikov because his wife Maya had taken their young daughter and son to Kiev for an indefinite stay. Sasha, the tinge of boyish, innocent good looks now maturing into brooding handsomeness, was on official probation from his wife. Sasha was often selected for undercover work that brought him into contact with women who were available and found him willing in spite of his fragile resolve. The case promised to take him to Kiev. He wasn't certain how he felt about that. He was certain that he would be happy to get away from his mother, Lydia, with whom he was temporarily living. Lydia was nearly deaf, a retired bureaucrat who held strong opinions on everything from Putin's smile to the influx of Muslims in Khazakstan. She spoke loudly with a shrill voice and harbored ambitions for her son that had nothing to do with being a policeman.

Sasha was also certain that he wanted to see his children, particularly Pulcharia, who was now six. He wanted to see Maya and his son very much, but he felt that Pulcharia somehow held the key to his sense of possible salvation, since he had first seen her moments after she was born.

Kiev was not on the mind of Elena Timofeyeva who had been assigned to work with Sasha. She had babysat Sasha before. She did not look forward to doing it again. She had other things to worry about.

Elena was the only woman in the Office of Special Investigations. She had gotten the job because she was an experienced police officer, but also because her aunt was Anna Timofeyeva, the former procurator for whom Rostnikov had worked for twenty years. Now, though a sometimes troubled relationship, Elena was engaged to marry Iosef Rostnikov, who sat next to her in the cramped, hot office of her future father-in-law. Elena knew she was a healthy, plump, clear-skinned woman who would, like her aunt, mother, and the rest of the women of her family, be forever destined to battle a tendency to become significantly over-weight. To overcome heredity, Elena had to live on a near-starvation diet, which made her irritable. That irritability could easily erupt if Sasha behaved irresponsibly. One thing Elena could be counted on for was a sense of loyalty and responsibility. She would do anything short of death or self-mutilation to avoid disappointing Porfiry Petrovich.

Iosef and Zelach, on the other hand, were a perfect pair of investigators. The hulking Zelach, who lived with his mother though he was forty-three years old, was devoid of imagination. He had the kind of slouching body on which no clothing ever looked right — no clothing except for the policeman's uniform he no longer wore.

Iosef, who'd had a brief career as a playwright, had an abundance of imagination. And all clothing seemed to have been designed for his tall, solid body.

Iosef was given to irony. Zelach did not recognize it when he heard or encountered it. Zelach's bland courage was recognized and appreciated, as were his occasional revelations, which delighted Iosef. Over the past three years, Iosef had discovered that Zelach's eclectic talents included tested ESP abilities, a talent for kicking a soccer ball long distances, and an almost encyclopedic knowledge of Russian, Lithuanian, and German heavy metal bands.

"You will report daily to me or to Emil Karpo," said Rostnikov. "We, in turn, will dutifully report to Director Yaklovev. Should you require funding for your investigation, I'm certain that the always-cooperative Pankov will supply it instantly."

The last, as they all knew, had been said for the benefit of Pankov, who was or would be listening to their conversation.

"One more thing," said Rostnikov. "There

is an urgency about these cases. It is necessary that closure is achieved within nine days from today."

Only Zelach considered asking why there was a nine-day deadline, but there was a great distance between considering and asking. Zelach knew enough not to ask.

"And," said Rostnikov, "there is nothing more."

That ended the meeting.

CHAPTER THREE

The two little girls looked forward to the nightly ritual. Laura and Nina Ivanovna stood solemnly next to each other in the Rostnikov living room as Porfiry Petrovich moved the padded knee-high bench from the corner.

The girls' grandmother, Galina, was in the little kitchen off of the living room talking to Rostnikov's wife Sarah. Galina, the girls, Sarah, and Porfiry Petrovich all lived in the same one-bedroom apartment on Krasnikov Street where the Rostnikovs had lived for more than three decades.

Laura, nine, and Nina, seven, had been abandoned by their mother, Miriana. Galina had tried to take care of them on her pension and odd jobs. She had endured and then, while working at night at a bakery, she had asked the manager for a stale bread to take home to the girls. He had loudly refused. It had never been clear, but somehow Galina had shot the manager with his own gun during a struggle over the bread. Galina was sixty-four, accustomed to a life of hardship, and reasonably strong.

Rostnikov had accepted the case, though the Yak thought it not worthy of the attention of the Office of Special Investigations. Galina had gone to prison. Sarah and Porfiry Petrovich had taken in the girls. And when Galina got out of prison, she joined them.

It was tight, but Sarah and Galina were extremely good at making the space work with a minimum of claustrophobia. Sarah and Porfiry Petrovich had the bedroom. Galina and the girls slept in the living room, Galina on the couch, the girls on a soft mattress on the floor.

"Do you know why I do this each night?" Rostnikov said, moving the weights from the cabinet near the apartment door.

Laura shook her head no. She had no idea, but she knew it was a sight worth beholding.

"I do it to commune with my inner self, to lose Porfiry Petrovich Rostnikov in a meditation that transcends my body."

Both girls looked puzzled as Rostnikov put out the weights and set up the rack on which he could place the bar so he could do his presses. He wore a gray sweat suit with the letters "FSU" in red across the chest. Under the letters was the faded image of the head of an Indian with a colorful feather in his hair.

"Really?" asked Nina.

For months after they had first come, the girls had said little to nothing, held each other's hands, sat on the sofa watching television, and gone to school quietly. For the past four or five months, they had begun to feel as if their world might not be ripped open. They trusted Sarah and Rostnikov, though they could never be sure when he was serious or just trying to be funny. They were still unable to allow themselves to laugh.

"No," said Rostnikov, sitting on the bench and reaching down for a fifty-pound weight with which to do curls and arm lifts. "That was nonsense. You recognized nonsense. Good. I lift these weights because they are old friends who welcome me, test me, challenge me. When I'm not with them each night, I miss them. It is the same way I feel about you. Am I telling you the truth now?"

"Yes," the girls said together.

Sarah and Galina looked across from the kitchen to see what the 'yes' might mean, but Rostnikov was silent under the strain of the weight in his right hand.

"Coffee?" asked Sarah.

Rostnikov grunted his assent and looked at his wife. He never stopped worrying about her. Two operations, both successful, for lesions on her brain. No guarantees that these invaders would not return. Her hair was still red, but it no longer flamed, and the strength in her face he so admired, while still present, was touched with a weary strain.

"Chocolate?"

Both girls said "Yes" without taking their eyes from Rostnikov. Soon he would be perspiring. Dark, uneven spots would appear against the gray sweat suit. Rostnikov put the weight down and lifted it with the other hand.

"Change mine to chocolate," Rostnikov growled.

Galina moved to start the chocolate. She worked in a grocery and often came home with small tokens of gratitude. The Rostnikovs would not accept any of her meager supply of money. They urged her to set aside whatever she could for the girls, and that is what she had done and would continue to do.

"Mrs. Dudenya stopped before you got home," said Laura.

"What did she want?" asked Rostnikov.

"Her toilet is backing up and making strange noises," said Sarah from the other room.

Sarah did not understand her husband's fascination with plumbing, though she tolerated it. He clearly enjoyed getting his tools out of the closet in the bedroom and heading cheerfully out the door to engage the rusting maze of pipes and the reluctant and fickle valves in the old building.

"It will have to wait till I return from Siberia."

"Why are you going to Siberia?" asked Nina.

"To talk to a ghost."

"You aren't telling the truth again?"

"Yes, I am," said Rostnikov, picking up the fresh towel he had placed on the bench and wiping his face and neck.

The television set was off. Rostnikov didn't like it on when he was with his weights. Often he played music on the small CD player atop the table on which the weights rested. His musical taste was eclectic. Recently he had discovered a soothing, dreamlike group of young females called Destiny's Child. But he never abandoned Credence Clearwater and Dinah Washington.

"Question," said Rostnikov in the process of arm lifts, holding his hand at his side, gripping the weight, and then lifting it straight out from his side to shoulder level and holding it there till his arm trembled and he could hold it out no longer.

When he did this, his face turned red and his eyes closed. This was the most solemn moment of the evening display.

"Should I take the shoe off of my artificial leg at night when I put it next to the bed or leave the shoe on?"

"Leave it on, but change the socks every day," said Laura.

"Why?" asked Nina. "A wooden leg doesn't sweat and smell."

"It isn't wood," said Laura.

"I'm inclined to take off the shoe," said Rostnikov after setting the weight back down and lying on the bench.

"Why?" asked Laura.

"Some habits of a lifetime are difficult to break and there is no reason to do so. Others should be broken no matter how long a lifetime has been."

"I don't have bad habits," said Nina.

"You pick your nose," said Laura.

"I don't, much."

"I advocate doing such things in private," said Rostnikov. "In fact, I advocate doing most things in private. The moment you share them with others is the moment they feel they have the right or obligation to advise you about your ideas or behavior. You understand?"

"No," said Laura.

"No," said Nina.

"Good," said Rostnikov, putting down the block of chalk that he had rubbed into his palms. "At your ages, it would be dangerous to understand."

He reached up, gripped the bar, and with an explosive grunt lifted the three hundred and fifty pounds from the rack and held it steady. Working without a spotter was a bad idea, but he had little choice. If there were a problem, no one in the household could control the weight. No, the challenge was Rostnikov's alone.

Years earlier, when Iosef was in his teens and already broad and strong but far better looking than his father, Iosef, who had been mistakenly named for Stalin in a misguided moment of nationalistic zeal, had spotted for his father.

Iosef never had his father's interest in the weights. He had been a contentious soldier and a failed playwright before he became, with his father's support, a policeman.

Now Iosef worked under his father in the

Office of Special Investigations and seemed to enjoy it with one exception. He had little tolerance for the intrigue, the cautious politics that went on inside Petrovka. He was particularly incensed by the perception, quite true, that Igor Yaklovev was self-serving, disinterested in justice, and quite corrupt.

"That's too many," said Laura counting his repetitions.

"Yes," said Rostnikov. "I was thinking."

"What about?" asked Nina.

"Diamonds," said Rostnikov.

Later, when the girls and Galina were talking quietly in the kitchen alcove, Rostnikov, with an ancient, much-traveled suitcase in hand, stood at the door waiting for the driver. Sarah stood at his side touching his arm, and said, quietly, "Siberia is cold."

"Not so much in November," he answered.

Porfiry Petrovich had been known to become absorbed in thinking about everything from the case at hand to the possibility of distant planets, and walk out coatless in freezing winter. He had, in fact, suffered frostbite on several occasions.

She had packed his things, including his fur-lined hat and coat and his boots, though she too knew that Northern Siberia at this time of year was not quite at the edge of the impending winter.

"You have your book?"

He pulled a new paperback novel from his jacket pocket. It was the last of the *87th Precinct* novels written by Ed McBain before the author died. Rostnikov had savored the book, held off reading it until now. It was his Siberian treat. He feared he would weep when he read it and said good-bye to old friends on the pages.

"You spoke of a ghost to the girls," Sarah said.

"Yes."

"You were talking about him?"

"I was," said Rostnikov.

"I'd almost forgotten that he exists," she said.

"I have not."

"You are certain he is alive, that he is there?"

"His name is in the file I was given by Yaklovev."

"No ghost," Sarah said, more to herself than Rostnikov.

"Not a real ghost, but can a ghost be real? Certainly not as satisfyingly real as Mrs. Dudenya's toilet. If he were a ghost it would, by definition, not be real."

"You will be careful?"

"I am always careful," he said.

"We define 'careful' differently," she said. "You are more curious than careful."

"Are the two necessarily exclusive?"

"I always hope they are not," Sarah said as they heard the knock at the door. "Call."

Rostnikov kissed his wife's cheek, picked up his suitcase, waved back at Galina and the girls, and went through the door.

Emil Karpo stood at the window of the single room in which he had lived for more than twenty-five years. There was nothing to see of any great interest from the window — a street lamp, a five-story warehouse, the passing of seasons marked by the appearance of weeds and grass in a small patch next to the warehouse, a swirl of snow and its accumulation in the winter. He was satisfied with the view. Some things did not change, and that was how he felt most content. He did not feel comfortable. Comfort was the enemy of progress. It allowed time to pass without accomplishment.

Inspector Emil Karpo, as lean as a leafless birch tree, as erect as the street lamp outside his window, his face with the pallor of one who shuns the sun. His nickname, never spoken to his face, was "the Vampire." He had others, but that was the one that had stayed with him.

Only Mathilde Verson had dared, with a smile, to use one of his nicknames, "the Tatar," to engage in occasional teasing of the man who had started as a client and finished as a lover. Before she died in the crossfire between two gangs on the streets of Moscow, she had made it clear that she no longer wanted him to pay for her services.

"You are a tough town, Emil Karpo," she had said pursing her lips, meeting his dark eyes with her own green eyes, smiling.

For almost all of his life, even as a boy, Emil Karpo had seen people turn away from him. This served him well as a young man and as a policeman dedicated to a belief in the Utopian possibility of Communism. He had served the possibility well knowing that the ideal had to be met by dedicated men and women who were imperfect animals.

When Communism had failed, Karpo had dedicated himself to the law — the uncertain, malleable law left behind by a failed hope. He had endured the transition without complaint. He had Porfiry Petrovich, in whom he could believe. He had Mathilde, with whom he could begin to do what he was uncertain about accepting — feel. Now she was gone.

He turned back into the room illuminated by a lean wrought iron lamp in the corner, its shade a compromise of two tones of sober blue selected by Mathilde to complement the single light in the ceiling, muted by a simple white glass cover. Karpo's eyesight was perfect in spite of the nighttime hours he spent at his desk against the ceiling-high shelves. The shelves were filled with reports carefully handwritten in black notebooks, meticulously checked, on every case in which he had ever been involved.

He had a computer. It sat on the simple wooden desk before the shelves. He did not fully trust the computer. He knew it could send his words into oblivion, wipe out his carefully prepared observations. He had transferred much of what he had written in his notebooks to the hard drive and backed it up, but it was the notebooks on which he relied.

There was a bed with its head against one wall. It was little more than a cot. The blanket he had laid out would meet the taut requirements of all but the most sadistic noncommissioned Army officers. The blanket was a dark blue one, with which Mathilde had replaced a khaki one.

A dresser, three drawers high, stood against the wall near the door. Inside, neatly laid out, were underwear and socks. After packing, what remained in his closet were three pairs of black slacks, two black business jackets, four black turtleneck shirts, four white shirts, and three ties, one black, one blue, and one with red and green stripes, a gift from Mathilde that he had worn once.

Coat over his arm, Emil Karpo waited, valise on the floor next to the door.

He knew only that Porfiry Petrovich had told him that they were going to Siberia, to a diamond mine where a Canadian had been murdered. When he needed to know more, he would be told.

There was a scratching at the door. Not a knock. A scratching sound. Emil Karpo took no chance. The journals on shelves over his desk were filled with the emotionless accounts of crimes petty and abundant, sad and horrific. And there were those who harbored grudges for the ghostly detective who had sent them to prison or into hiding or exile.

Karpo, hand on his weapon, opened the door.

The lean black cat that walked slowly in stretched as she moved, her left paw betraying a long, imperfectly healed injury. The cat ignored Karpo and leapt onto the cot.

Karpo put his weapon away and moved to the cot to pick up the cat. When he was a boy, his brother had a cat not unlike this one, which did not object to being lifted. Karpo put him outside the door and watched the cat saunter down the darkened hallway.

Something, the smell of the cat, the feel of its fur, the pulsing of its purr, evoked a sense of childhood. It was not unpleasant.

"I am about to be very rich."

He lay beside Oxana in the bed, grinning, his hands behind his head, his mind savoring a simple but expensive list of indulgences — a dacha on the Black Sea with a modest boat including a cabin with a large round bed that gently rocked to the melody of his body and that of whatever young or not-so-young woman he had invited aboard. But there would be more. Yes, the clothes, like James Bond, but what he dwelled on most was the notion of food. He would stuff himself through the beak like a pampered goose, bred to produce the finest fois gras. He would drink fine wines from France and Spain. Maybe he would have enough to buy an English soccer team. He had no idea what they cost.

Maybe a great many things, though he was

smart enough to know that he would have to keep a very low profile for years and hold onto a job he really didn't mind.

"We," Oxana Balakona said.

She shared this apartment in Kiev with another model who was away on an ad shoot in Cyprus. Oxana also had a small apartment of her own in Moscow.

"We?"

"We will be rich," she explained. "You said 'I.' "

"Of course, 'we.' "

"If there were to be only you before I receive my share of the money," she said, "some people would be enlightened about what happened to their diamonds."

"The diamonds do not belong to them," he said, happily turning to look at her profile. She had a lovely profile, aquiline, her skin almost white. "They stole the diamonds from someone else, who stole them from a mine in Africa. I paid for them with euros confiscated from a band of Estonian smugglers."

"Still, some people would be interested in what happened to the diamonds," she repeated without looking at him, wanting to reach for her cigarettes on the table next to the bed, knowing he did not like it when she smoked in bed.

They had not known each other long, but he had not been shy about making his wishes clear. He was not bad looking and Oxana had a reasonable if not excessive sexual drive. The problem was that he was an animal, a smart, careful animal driven by an almost constant desire for immediate gratification. For him, sex was quick, self-indulgent, filled with lust, growls, and grunts instead of words.

It wasn't bad. Oxana was an animal too, but she considered herself a sleek, calculating, protective cat. He was a wild bear. They were not a bad match.

"You are a greedy creature," he had said when he had approached her about the diamonds.

She had smiled the knowing smile that had appeared in several hundred ads, magazine layouts, and on runways in eleven countries. She was not greedy, but she had no intention of explaining that to him. Yes, she made lots of money, but she had many expenses and, as one very gay German designer had once said to her, "Models have a limited shelf life."

Oxana would eventually no longer be the product which could sell illusions to women who had no hope of ever looking like her and to men who would dress their wives and mistresses with the clothes Oxana modeled. Both the men and women hoped they could buy a little of the illusion, that it might be slightly transferred with the silk, cotton, and cashmere.

Oxana had five or six years more as a model. Then a battle she could not win against weight and age would begin, or end. She had no intention of letting herself go when she was rich, but she wanted the pleasure of knowing that she was maintaining her beauty for herself and not for others.

"What are you thinking?" he asked.

"You really expect me to answer that?"

"Absolutely not. I expect you to lie. I expect to look at your beautiful face, at your little smile, and delight in watching you lie."

"I was thinking about what I will do with the money."

"We," he said. "What we will do with the money."

"We won't be together," she said, reaching for her cigarettes, no longer able to wait.

"Why not?" he said with a grin, his hand on her lean thigh.

"Truth or lie?" she asked.

He considered his options and said, "Your choice."

"We'd grow tired of each other. Very

quickly."

"Are you already growing tired of me then?" he asked, getting out of bed.

His body was not hairy. His features were strong, rugged. He bore a small white scar right on his left eyelid and several others, one the size of a baby's fist on his right arm.

"No," she lied.

"Good."

She lit her cigarette, inhaled with satisfaction, and allowed herself a small smile for the future.

"A shame you have to stay so thin," he said.

"You don't like it?"

He shrugged. "Given what I am looking at, I would be a fool to complain."

He had pulled a chair to the side of the bed and propped up his feet near her. He was wearing nothing.

"Given what I can see from here," she said. "You are far from complaining."

"Shall we?" he asked.

She surprised herself by putting out her cigarette and saying, "Why not? A celebration."

"It's too soon to celebrate," he said, climbing on the bed and reaching for her.

She held up a hand, palm extended.

"Lie down," she commanded.

He laughed.

"You're giving orders? I like that, but not too often."

As she straddled him, Oxana considered, but only for a moment, when it might be best to kill him. He knew the contact in Paris. When he told her, the opportunity would arise. She was certain he did not plan to share with her, and she could not let him live to hunt her down.

She knew he was almost certainly thinking the same thing about her.

"What is your name again? Forgive me for . . ."

Vladimir Kolokov's face was inches from the face of the black man in the chair. The Russian's eyes were open wide, his head tilted very slightly to the right as if he were paying very close attention to the black man.

"James," said the man in the chair, his voice dry, cracking.

"No, no," said Kolokov with a laugh, turning to face the other three men in the room, sharing the joke. "No, I know your name is James. It's your last name I have trouble with."

"Harumbaki."

"Harumbaki," Kolokov repeated. "James,

I am sorry to tell you, your friends are dead."

James knew this. The Russian had let him see their bodies before two of the men in the shadows had dragged them off.

"But you, you and I are partners," said the Russian.

He patted the shirtless black man on the shoulder. James tried not to cringe, but a slight movement betrayed him.

"Have I hurt you?" asked Kolokov, himself looking hurt by the movement of the man in the chair.

"No."

"Your Russian is a little weak, James," Kolokov said. "You'll have to speak up."

"No, you have not hurt me."

Kolokov, who relished the scene, turned away to face his audience of three, and then he turned back suddenly, inches away from James's face again, spit spraying his prisoner's face.

"But I could, could I not?"

One of the men in the shadows, Alek, laughed.

"Yes."

"Then we are partners," said Kolokov. "We have a fair split. I get everything and you get to live."

"Yes."

"You tell me who you sell the diamonds to and when, and you and I go and make the transaction, and we all part company with a drink and a tear for fallen comrades."

"Yes," said James, not believing it for an instant.

Believing this lunatic was not really an issue. The diamonds were gone. When they had encountered Kolokov, James and the others had been on the way to their courier, a stupid Russian drug addict who had not been of James's choosing. James and the others had been informed of the theft of the diamonds and the murder of the prostitute who had been carrying them. A drug addict and a prostitute. If he survived, which was not likely, James planned to find out how two incompetents could be selected to transport millions in diamonds.

Kolokov leaned even closer and whispered into James's ear.

"I am sorry. I cannot treat you too nicely. You understand how it is. My friends here would not understand. They would be jealous. They would think, or maybe even say, 'Vladimir, you have a new friend. You have abandoned us.' You understand, James Hakimkov?"

James did not correct him. Instead he said, "Yes."

With that Kolokov pulled a small screwdriver from his pocket and shoved it deeply into the side of the man in the chair.

James gasped.

"Are you all right?" asked Kolokov with mock concern. "I'm sorry. I had to do it."

James couldn't speak. The pain was searing, throbbing, screaming.

"Are you all right, James?"

James shook his head yes.

"Good."

Another pat on the shoulder.

"We'll clean that up. It's not deep and I rinsed the screwdriver earlier today. Fresh bandages. Pau's mother was a nurse, is that correct, Pau?"

"Yes," came a voice from the blurred darkness.

"Partners," came Kolokov's voice as James started to pass out.

CHAPTER FOUR

"You've come to visit your father's leg,"
Paulinin said, stepping back to let Iosef and
Zelach through the reinforced door.

Paulinin's laboratory was two levels below
ground in Petrovka. It was an anomaly. A
bureaucracy bustled or shuffled in the
sparsely furnished rooms above, but Paulinin's laboratory stood alone as a testament
to a time long gone if it ever existed at all.

"Among other things," said Iosef.

Paulinin, dressed in a white laboratory
apron spotted with something that was
probably more unpleasant than blood,
looked at Zelach who was decidedly uncomfortable.

"The man who slouches," said Paulinin,
adjusting his glasses.

Zelach immediately straightened up. There
was much in the laboratory that made
Zelach uncomfortable — the seemingly
random jars of specimens arranged in no

apparent order, the unmatched desks covered with books and towers of reports that threatened to tumble over, the laboratory and autopsy tables under bright lamps.

But what made Zelach most uncomfortable was Paulinin himself.

The lean, bald man was clean shaven. His ears were large, as were his teeth. He spoke quickly, softly, and often burst out loudly with a "Don't touch that" or an "Are you paying attention?"

But, as the scientist led the way around the desk toward the low music from a CD player or radio, Zelach saw that there were two naked black bodies on adjoining autopsy tables.

"Over there." Paulinin pointed with his left hand as they moved.

"I know," said Iosef, looking at the leg of his father floating in a large jar.

Zelach looked too.

"I don't talk to it enough," Paulinin said almost sadly. "Too much to do. Chopin."

He had turned his head and was looking at Zelach who was puzzled. Did the mad scientist call Rostnikov's leg Chopin?

"The music," Paulinin said as they moved between the two autopsy tables. "Chopin."

Akardy Zelach knew little about classical

music. Heavy metal, fine. Jazz, fine. Classical, no.

Iosef, Porfiry Petrovich, and Karpo had long assured Zelach that the scientist was brilliant. Detectives and even members of military law enforcement came to him, but most police avoided him, preferring mediocrity in their investigation to the prospect of having to deal with the man who now patted the arm of the dead man on the table.

"What has he been telling you?" asked Iosef.

"Ah, this one does not speak Russian very well, and my other guest speaks no Russian."

"How do you . . . ?" Zelach started and then stopped himself. Too late.

Iosef folded his arms and waited patiently.

"This one was tortured. Slowly, slowly. His mouth, throat, lungs, vocal cords were unharmed. Someone wanted him able to speak. In his pocket were receipts, notations. No rubles. The money was taken. I know because he was well if not expensively dressed, very good serviceable English shoes. He would not be walking around without money. He was a man who didn't have to be bereft of funds. His friend . . ."

Paulinin turned and patted the arm of the other dead man reassuringly.

"His friend here had no rubles either, no notes or bills or receipts in Russian. He relied on his friend for all necessary conversation and transactions with Russians. He was not tortured, only murdered, which shows that a knowledge of the Russian language is not always a blessing."

Paulinin seemed to be waiting for confirmation.

"It is not," agreed Iosef.

Zelach wanted to get out of the alcoholic and chemical smell, the dark corners, the glaring specimens enlarged by the glass bottles that surrounded them, the two dead men to whom Paulinin spoke.

"Can you imagine what it would be like to have a tube forced down your nose, rubbing the lining raw and bloody all the way to your stomach, and have food forced down the tube?"

He was looking at Zelach.

"No I cannot," said Zelach.

Paulinin shook his head and scratched his neck.

"Old KGB torture," he explained. "Many are the afflicted who were feasted so inside Lubyanka, but a long walk or a short Metro ride from where we now stand."

"Our torturer is former KGB?" asked Iosef.

"Perhaps still secret police," Zelach tried.

"No, they know how to rid themselves of bodies."

"Anything else?" asked Iosef.

"Small, very sharp knife. The torturer was not tall, maybe five feet and eight inches. The tortured man was seated. See his ankles, the rope burn around his groin. The highest wounds indicate the man's height. Other wounds indicate that our man with the knife was nervous, attention deficit disorder or something like that. He kneels, stands upright, crouches, keeps moving. His hair is dark brown and long. He is alcoholic."

"How . . . ?"

Zelach again.

"Hair samples on both bodies. Not the victims'. DNA," explained Paulinin. "I called in favors. The men and women in the DNA laboratory owe me. There is a faint but detectable smell of alcohol on both of my guests, though neither of them has the slightest trace of alcohol in his stomach."

"Did your guest talk to the Russian?" asked Iosef.

"Oh yes. The torture stopped abruptly. The tale was told, but not the end. The end depends, I think, on the third man."

"The third man," Iosef repeated.

"What third man?" asked Zelach.

"Two blood types on the body of my guests are Type B. So, I believe, is the man who tortured them. Ironic. Torturer and victims are blood brothers. But there is a third blood type, AB, on the skin of these two men. My guess is that all three men struggled, were beaten, bled on each other. We are fortunate. The third man carries the virus for narcolepsy. The man was bitten by a tsetse fly. It is, therefore, likely that he is from somewhere in the south of Africa."

"Because tsetse flies are only found in Africa?" said Zelach.

"No, because my two friends here bear tattoos on the backs of warriors from the same Southern African tribe, a Botswanan tribe."

"Warriors?"

This from Iosef.

"Yes," said Paulinin. "Perhaps, but modern ones. These tattoos are only an homage to the past. They are like the tattoos prisoners wear to mark them as being from a particular gang."

"Anything else?" asked Iosef.

"One moment," said Paulinin, moving back into darkness, changing the CD. When he returned he looked at Iosef.

"Rachmaninov," said Iosef.

Paulinin smiled.

"There is one more thing. *Pa'smatril.* Look."

He turned the tortured dead man on his side and said, "You have to look very carefully."

Paulinin pressed his finger into a red spot on the dead man's back. His finger disappeared into the body.

"They both have them. The other one's is on his thigh, like little pockets."

"Drugs," said Zelach.

"Diamonds," said Iosef.

"Possibly," said Paulinin.

Iosef did not press the issue. He was certain. The meeting in Porfiry Petrovich's office made it clear that they were all in search of diamonds.

"Now," said Iosef, "if you can only tell us where to begin looking for this third man . . ."

"Four-seven-two-four Kropotkin Street," said Paulinin.

"You cannot know . . ." Zelach could not stop himself.

"Rent receipt in my friend's pocket," said Paulinin, touching the nearest corpse.

"*Spa'siba.* Thank you," said Iosef.

"Yes," added Zelach resisting the urge to run out of the laboratory.

"Zelach wants to know if it is true that you have Stalin's head and Lenin's teeth and eyes," said Iosef.

No, no, no, thought Zelach looking at Paulinin.

"I have treasures pathological, historical, and cultural," said Paulinin who was looking over his glasses at Zelach. "It would be unwise to share treasure. Let yourselves out."

Rachmaninov bloomed in the garden of glass, wood, and metal at their backs as Iosef and Zelach moved toward the door to the corridor.

A voice spoke cheerily behind them.

Paulinin was talking to the dead men. The scientist seemed certain that the dead men also talked to him.

And in some sense, he was right.

"Bedraggled," Lydia Tkach said, looking at her son.

Sasha was at the mirror in the tiny bathroom adjusting the white shirt under his tan zippered jacket. She had followed him before he could close the door.

Sasha, examining his face, had to agree. The unruly line of hair still came down to cover his forehead, only the hair was no longer really the color of corn. He was handsome still, but the appealing boyishness was missing. Undercover assignments were still his lot, but he could no longer pass himself off as a student or an innocent. His blue eyes betrayed him.

"Look at you."

Sasha looked at his reflection and saw sympathy in the eyes that met his. Lydia was retired, no longer the tyrant who held together a gaggle of functionaries in a government office. Lydia, long hard of hearing, tended to shout when she was displeased. She tended to shout when she was happy. Shouting was her conversational currency and Sasha had endured it for more than thirty years.

"I'm looking," he said. "What am I supposed to see?"

It was the wrong thing to say. He knew it as soon as the words had been spat from his lips, but he could not give up the small vestige of childish defiance.

"You are supposed to see a husband," she said. "You are supposed to see a father with two children, one of whom is ill in an awful, dirty city of murderers."

"The children are not ill and Kiev is neither dirty nor full of murderers."

Why could he not silence himself?

"What was I saying?" she asked, looking

at the dull green painted wall of the bath-room.

"You were telling me what I am supposed to see in the mirror."

He turned to face her. She was small, lean, strong, and reluctant to wear the perfectly satisfactory hearing aids he had bought her.

"Yes, you are supposed to see a police-man, a policeman who could be shot or stabbed or beaten on the head or run over by a car."

"Don't forget poisoned," he said, moving past her into the living room.

"You are not funny," she said, following him.

"I know. It is one of my many failings. What are you doing today?"

"I'm working at not changing the subject when I talk to my only child. Did you see someone in the mirror who has been drink-ing too much, like his long-dead father?"

"My father died in a car accident."

"Hah."

"Hah?"

"I suspected poison at the time," she said, trying without success to lower her voice in case some governmental agency thought enough of her to eavesdrop on her every word. "He was engaged in very sensitive government work."

"Yes," said Sasha, knowing that his father had been no more than a senior file clerk in the Underministry of Vehicles.

Now she followed him into the little kitchen where he opened the refrigerator door, removed the sliced brown bread and the last of the ham they had been nursing through meals for three days.

"You have never said anything about poison," Sasha said, knowing that he was lost, lost in one of those futile conversations with his mother.

"I didn't want to trouble you," she said. "Put mustard on that."

Sasha paused, plate of butter in his hand.

"Who doesn't like mustard? Let's have a show of hands," he said, holding up his free hand.

"You are mocking your mother," she said loudly with mock resignation.

"I have never liked mustard," he said, placing the butter dish on the small table.

"And that has been your downfall."

"Not liking mustard has been my downfall?"

"Being difficult has been your downfall," she said, reaching out to tear off an edge of the ham he had placed on the table.

"I am not yet hopelessly fallen," he said.

She said nothing, watched him make a

sandwich, considered giving him more culinary advice, and thought better of it.

"You should stop being a policeman," she said. "It is dangerous and you are no longer as alert as you once were."

"Which of us is?"

Now they were into a familiar conversation they had repeated dozens of times.

"I've talked to Porfiry Petrovich about my concerns for your safety," she said, folding her arms over the green dress she mistakenly believed flattered her.

"Many times," Sasha said.

"Yes, many times."

The sandwich was finished. It was a monument to distracted inefficiency. He took a bite.

"You should sit when you eat. It is bad for your digestion to eat while standing."

He moved toward the door.

"It is worse to eat while walking," she said.

She walked behind him to the door. He finished downing what he had in his mouth, paused, and turned to face her. She was a head shorter than he, which made it easier for him to lean over and kiss her head, which he did.

"I think I'll be going to Kiev soon," he said. "I will talk to Maya. I will beg, plead, promise on the lives of my children to be a good and faithful husband and father. I have no great hope. I've made such promises before."

"I know," Lydia said, taking his hand. "Tell her it is the last time you'll ask her to come back to you."

"She said last time was the last. I'm late."

He smiled at his mother. It wasn't much of a smile, but it was enough. She stood in the open door of the apartment as he headed for the stairs, eating his ham sandwich.

"Beg her to come back," she called out. "Tell her you'll stop with the women, the drinking, the brooding."

"I don't think all the neighbors heard you," Sasha said over his shoulder.

"They already know everything," she said. "Be safe."

He waved his sandwich at her and went down the stairs.

Sasha had twenty minutes to get to the address where he was to meet Elena Timofeyeva. There was no way he could make it.

CHAPTER FIVE

Porfiry Petrovich Rostnikov, Chief Inspector in the Office of Special Investigations, was airsick. The seat was small, the space for his legs — one real, one artificial — was restrictive, the ride bumpy, the smell of human bodies and tobacco cloying.

Porfiry Petrovich Rostnikov would be fine when they were on the ground, according to the young woman in a military uniform who seemed to be in charge of avoiding questions. She was also in charge of giving them each a bottle of water and a bar of whole grains held together by congealed honey.

Dubious information about the nature of his illness did not soothe Porfiry Petrovich Rostnikov. He tried to read the slightly tattered paperback copy of his Ed McBain *87th Precinct* novel.

There were two seats on each side of the aisle. Emil Karpo, erect as always, sat looking out the window at clouds. Rostnikov preferred the aisle. Actually, Rostnikov preferred not to be on any airplane at all.

There was no one to whom he could complain. He was resigned. It was not unlike most things in life.

Rostnikov closed his eyes and leaned back. Six of the other passengers on the plane were heading for Devochka. All six of them worked for the mining company. There was no one else to work for. The plane would drop them off at Devochka and then take the remaining thirty-seven passengers to Noril'sk.

Rostnikov had read the folder the Yak had given him. The security folder for Devochka had been prepared by the Director of Security at the mine. The name of the man and his signature were on the reports in that folder. Rostnikov knew the man. He was also certain that Yaklovev was well aware of Porfiry Petrovich's connection to the man.

"You are ill, Porfiry Petrovich," came Karpo's voice through the hazy pink of Rostnikov's closed eyes.

"The air."

"Here," said Karpo, putting something in Rostnikov's hand.

Rostnikov opened his eyes and looked at the pill in his palm.

"For airsickness?" Rostnikov asked, swallowing the pill without waiting for an answer.

"Yes."

"You get airsick?"

"No," said Karpo. "But I prepare for the contingency when I fly."

"Are you prepared for all contingencies, Emil?"

"No, that would be impossible. I try to prepare for those I can anticipate."

"A wise life plan," said Rostnikov. "We make a good team, Emil Karpo. You are logical and unimaginative . . . no insult intended."

"And none perceived. I see little value in having an imagination. Besides, it is not a choice one makes."

"And I am intuitive," said Rostnikov, feeling a bit better already. "Intuition can deceive."

"As can logic," said Karpo.

"You realize Emil, this is one of the longest conversations we have ever had that did not involve murder, mayhem, theft, or imminent danger."

Rostnikov was about to say something about Mathilde Verson, but he decided not to, maybe some time later when her ghost did not still stand so close to Karpo's shoulder.

"See if you can find the young lady. See if any of the passengers were in Devochka the day the Canadian was murdered. If so, I would like to talk to each of them before we land."

Karpo clicked his seat belt open and began to rise.

"Another thing," said Rostnikov. "If anything exists on this plane that resembles food, I should like very much to eat it."

"Would you like to have something to eat?" asked the man. "Soup? Ice cream?"

The child stirred in the bed and turned to face him.

"No."

"How do you feel?" asked the man.

"All right."

"Not hungry? Not thirsty?"

"No."

"You want to play chess?"

A long hesitation and then, "Yes."

The man never intentionally lost to the child, but lose he did, and with each loss he smiled and reached over to tousle the child's hair.

"You want to play here?" the man asked.

"No. We might bump the bed and turn

over the board. I can come into the other room."

"We'll have to use the timer," the man said. "I have an important visitor coming here today. I must be out there to greet him."

The child understood and climbed out of the bed.

It would be harder to smile after this game if he lost or won. It was weighing heavily on his mind that he had killed the Canadian, but the deed was done, and not for the first time had he killed.

"This time I have white," the child said.

"And I, like my blighted soul, am black. Let us play."

"Two games?"

"Depends on how long this game takes," he said, setting up the board. "The airplane will be here in an hour and there's someone on it I must see."

"Who?"

"A man named Rostnikov."

The child had a white pawn raised high.

"That's the same . . ."

"Yes," said the man as the white pawn went down on the board.

The man looked out the window in the direction of the airstrip. "It's your move," said the child. "Yes, it is my move," said the man.

"How did this happen?"

The thin, silver-haired, impeccably dressed old man sat erect, shook his head, and reached for his tea. Gerald St. James, whose name had once been Branislaw Moujinski, was not angry, though he had reason to be. Neither was he disappointed, for he knew better than to expect much of others. He had seen almost everything in the nearly forty years he had been in the diamond trade. Most of what he had done was considered illegal in the countries in which he did business. But, since he was in business with most of the countries, he had made many people rich and grateful and eager to overlook transgressions.

There was the necessity of, what was it the Americans called it, plausible deniability? This was why the old man, who longed to put a "Sir" in front of his name, was President of Monarch Enterprises, Ltd. with offices in Moscow, Antwerp, Tel Aviv, and London, where he now sat drinking tea.

Were he to turn his chair around, he could see the unimpressive DeBeers building. Gerald St. James had paid more than twice what his offices were worth just to have this view. He savored the sight of the DeBeers building and its underground vaults housing an estimated five billion dollars in uncut diamonds. DeBeers had begun storing the diamonds in 1930, stockpiling the gems to keep the market from overflowing. Periodically, privileged diamond dealers from around the world would be permitted to come to London to purchase "sights," assortments of diamonds that they could purchase with cash. There was no negotiating, no dealing, no haggling. The dealers were told what the price was for the sight they were offered, and they paid it. Refusal to make the purchase was not an option.

Gerald St. James would have killed to be one of those offered a sight. In fact, he had killed in the very hope that he would someday be among the elite purchasers at the DeBeers table. When the opportunity arose he could find a respectable dealer who would front for him.

"Chocolate?" St. James offered the woman across the desk.

She nodded and took one of the Cadbury chocolates from the crystal bowl he eased in front of her. St. James was addicted to British candy, food, clothing, and cars. He had considered buying a title. Many people already assumed he had one, and he did not correct supplicants and business associates who called him Sir Gerald.

The woman, dressed in a brown business suit, was about fifty, full figured, clear skinned, and no nonsense. She did not eat the candy but held it in the palm of her hand as she spoke.

St. James adjusted the vest under his jacket, sat back, put his fingers together in a steeple, and waited. His eyes were dull blue and unyielding. Ellen Sten felt them on her and looked up to meet them.

"Problems," she said.

"So I gather."

"Our man in the Russian mine had to kill a Canadian mining engineer," she said.

"Had to?"

"Perhaps not, but he did. It's done."

St. James reached for a chocolate and put it in his mouth without taking his eyes from her.

"And he didn't make it look like an accident?"

"He was hurried."

"Police?"

"Police," she said. "Our man will take care of it. The Russian police have never been a problem."

"I'm comforted by your confidence," he said. "Go on."

"Two of the Botswanans to whom the last

shipment from the mine was transported have been murdered in Moscow. A third is missing."

"Do we know who is responsible?"

"Not yet. Possibly a competitor."

"There's more?"

"Yes," she said. "A courier delivering a shipment to Kiev for transport to Paris was also murdered. She made the delivery and then the payment was stolen on the train back to Moscow."

"Someone is attacking our enterprise?"

"It would seem so," Sten said. "But it could be coincidence."

There were many things Gerald St. James shared with Ellen Sten, but he had survived and prospered for decades by always holding something back. St. James was well aware of who was responsible for the attack on the Botswanans.

"Coincidence is the easy dismissal of connected events to avoid the often difficult task of finding an understandable if not logical connection," said St. James.

She nodded.

"Find out," he added. "Keep in touch with our contacts in Devochka, Moscow, and Kiev."

She nodded again. It was what she had been doing for hours. St. James knew it.

"And Ellen, use whatever resources you need to clean up this mess."

His voice was calm, even. She knew that his concern was only minimally about the fifteen or twenty million dollars in diamonds and more with the threat to Monarch's entire enterprise and his wish for ultimate respectability.

"Yes," she said starting to rise.

"And if you do not intend to eat that chocolate, please put it back in the bowl if it has not already begun to melt in your sweating palm."

Balta, which was the name he had given himself, had a simple plan. He had a name, Oxana, and he knew she was a model.

After he had gotten back to Kiev having cleanly killed Christiana Verovona, Balta called the person who had hired him. He reported that he had the money and that he would find the diamonds and deliver them himself. He would cut out the middleman, middlewoman in this case, named Oxana.

Balta was not greedy. His needs were simple. Three million American dollars' worth of diamonds plus his share of the cash were quite enough. Besides, he liked his work and a future reference from his employer might be helpful in his career. He did not intend to retire.

Now, having adopted a quite different and pleasant persona, Balta sat at the Talgen Restaurant on Velyka Vasylkivska Street, leisurely eating strawberry vareniki with just a bit of sour cream.

The waiter came to the table ready to provide service. There were two reasons for the waiter's helpful approach. One had been Balta's show of a very substantial one-hundred-hryvnia bill before even ordering. The other had been Balta's engaging presence.

"Dessert?" asked the waiter, who sported a thin mustache and was doing his best to look French. "We have the finest selection of pastries in Kiev."

"Watching my weight," said Balta with a smile.

"I understand," the waiter said. "Coffee?"

"Coffee," said Balta.

"With a very small sweet at no charge?"

"What kind?"

"British. A Cadbury chocolate. Quite small."

"I believe I will," said Balta.

"Good," said the waiter, who moved away, anxious to please.

Balta liked the Talgen and was quite familiar with the quite tasteful erotic shows that went on in the next room at night.

Balta looked around the crowded restaurant. Two men in business suits were at a nearby table. One of them, no more than thirty-five, looked at him and smiled. Balta smiled back. Life was apparently good for the businessman. It was certainly, at this moment, quite good for Balta.

Life, was not, however, quite so good in Moscow for Georgi Danielovich. Elena Timofeyeva and Sasha Tkach were knocking at the door of his apartment. They were going to tell him that Christiana Verovona had been murdered on the train to Moscow. She had not been worth much as a prostitute, but income is income. No, the really bad news they were bringing without knowing it, was that she had been found without a suitcase. The money for the diamonds was gone. Whoever killed her had taken it. The very serious, well-built man from Monarch in London who spoke perfect Russian was not going to be happy. What Georgi did not know was that the well-built man from Monarch in London already knew of the theft.

Georgi opened the door.

Elena and Sasha found themselves facing a man with a flat, dark face in need of a shave and a haircut. Georgi was about thirty. He looked fifty. He was a dry, wasted man with the look of an addict both Elena and Sasha recognized.

Georgi, his eyes an interesting but not becoming mixture of red and yellow, looked at them and reached down to tuck his shirt into his pants.

"Police," said Elena.

The policewoman looked something like the second woman he had lived with and run when he came to Moscow from Tblisi. Georgi couldn't remember her name anymore, but there was little Georgi could remember in the hours, like now, after heroin.

"I've done nothing," he said wearily.

They pushed past him into the room that smelled of sweat, stale food, and cigarettes. Sasha and Elena had been in many rooms like this. They would shower tonight, and the smells, if not the memory, would be gone, though they would have to carry them the rest of this day, which was just beginning.

"Close the door," said Sasha.

It was what policemen often did with someone like this. Give him a simple order. Start the process of obedience. It worked almost all of the time. They could see it would work with this one.

Georgi closed the door, finished tucking in his shirt, pushed his hair back with the palm of his hand, and faced them.

"What's this about?"

"Your name?"

"Georgi Danielovich. What . . ."

"Christiana Verovona lives here," said Elena.

It wasn't a question, but Georgi made it one and said, "Yes, but she is away now and . . ."

"She's dead," said Sasha, walking around the room, looking at things.

"Dead?" said Georgi, not quite understanding.

He looked at the woman who reminded him of . . . yes, her name had been Olga.

"Olga," he said to himself.

"Who is Olga?" asked Elena.

"No one. Never mind. I'm a little sick. Christiana's not here."

"She is dead," said Elena.

"Yes. You told me. I forgot."

"Georgi," said Sasha, pausing in his invasive walk around the room. "Talk to us about diamonds."

"I have got to eat something," Georgi said. "I'm hungry. I'll pass out. I've got to eat."

"What do you have here that can be

eaten?" asked Sasha.

"The refrigerator."

"You can't eat the refrigerator," said Sasha.

Elena averted her eyes from her partner's. She had no intention of being a party to his odd attempts at humor.

"I didn't . . ." Georgi started.

"Go get something to eat," Elena said.

"And then talk to us of Kiev," said Sasha. "Talk to us of diamonds and Christiana Verovona."

"Yes," said Georgi. "I will talk, but first I must eat. I do not know why I am so hungry."

He moved from the chair and stumbled over to the refrigerator. It was then that Elena sensed a warning, but it was too late. Georgi reached into the refrigerator as Elena shouted, "Sasha."

Sasha was closer to Georgi than she was, but not close enough. Georgi stepped back against the wall leaving the refrigerator door open. He had a gun in his hand.

"I'm going," he said.

Elena held up two hands palms up to show that he was free to leave. No comment was necessary. The man's hands were shaking. No pacification, no provocation. Let him leave. He would be easy to find.

"When I left home this morning my mother was worried about something like this," said Sasha.

Georgi blinked and licked his dry lips as he inched toward the door. Sasha took a step toward Georgi.

"Sasha," Elena warned.

"No more," said Georgi. "Do not move."

Sasha shook his head. He was smiling.

"Put the gun down on the floor," said Sasha. "Gently. Do not drop it. Just put it down."

"I will kill you both if I have to," Georgi warned.

"No," said Sasha, taking another step toward him. "You will not. It would earn you nothing but death if you could even shoot straight enough to hit one of us. The other would kill you on the spot. Right?"

Elena, though she felt no confidence in Sasha's assessment, said, "That is right."

"And," said Sasha, taking yet another step closer to Georgi, "if you were fortunate enough and we were unfortunate enough to discover that you could shoot straight enough to end our lives, which is extremely doubtful given your shaking hand, what would happen to you? You'd be caught by policemen very upset about your having killed two policemen."

"I don't care," Georgi screamed, almost at the door.

"If you put the gun down, we talk, you tell us things, we all live happily ever after."

"Shit," said Georgi. "Shit, shit, shit."

Sasha now stood less than three feet in front of him. Georgi made a fist with his free hand and bounced it gently against his mouth.

"Now put the gun on the floor," said Sasha.

Georgi docilely handed the weapon to Sasha, who tapped the gun solidly on top of Georgi Danielovich's head. Georgi slunk to the floor holding his head and moaning, "That hurts."

"I told you to put the gun on the floor," said Sasha, kneeling in front of Georgi who was holding his head with both hands. "Now, we talk."

And, thought Elena, *later you and I will have a chat about the stupid thing you just did.* Sasha was smiling. Sasha looked happy. Sasha, she was certain, was more than a little bit suicidal.

CHAPTER SIX

Just beyond a sparse forest of what looked like leafless trees, six elk darted across the snowless tundra. In the distance there was a long range of low mountains topped with snow. No sign of man had been seen from the air for more than five hundred miles.

And then, Devochka appeared, a collection of eight identical one-story concrete block buildings with slightly pitched roofs and a wide road of cracked concrete which stretched from the concrete block buildings to a far different structure, the mine. The structure was taller, older than the town and reflected the cloud-covered sun from the few unrusted spots of its steel beams.

Next to the structure was a dark strip, perhaps three hundred yards long. Karpo could not tell how deep a bite had been taken to create the strip.

"What do you see, Emil Karpo?"

"It was a strip mine and then tunnels were

dug when the stripping ceased to yield diamonds."

"They had to go deeper," said Rostnikov, sitting back to adjust his leg before the landing.

"Yes."

"We shall have to go deeper," said Rostnikov. "Ferret out secrets, talk to people, drink their vodka, rub our hands together as they do, listen to their complaints."

"I do not drink vodka," said Karpo.

"I know. You drink no alcohol. I was speaking of us collectively. I'll drink the vodka for both of us. Perhaps they have celery juice for you."

"Water will be sufficient," said Karpo, looking out the window.

Rostnikov was not a drinker unless there was a celebration or an investigation that warranted it. He was not repulsed by alcohol and, in fact, enjoyed the occasional thrust of liquid heat and euphoria, particularly from French brandy. He got a similar and far more satisfying reaction from fixing his neighbor's maze of water pipes or from the weights in his cabinet, and with no dulling of the senses.

"They will drink and try to find our secrets," said Rostnikov, "and in trying to find our secrets, we will discover theirs."

"We have no secrets," said Karpo.

"But they do not know that," whispered Rostnikov.

"Why are you whispering?"

"To simulate conspiracy. To ready us for an inevitable duel."

"And if they do not engage you in such a duel?"

Rostnikov looked at the unsmiling man next to him and resisted the powerful urge to put an arm around the shoulders of his dour companion.

"They are Russians, Emil Karpo. It is in their nature to protect themselves even when they are not being attacked."

"I am Russian. I do not feel this need."

"You are the exception. Perhaps it is your Mongol blood or a quirk of birth, but I have always found your directness refreshing. We have always made a good team, have we not?"

"Yes."

"Prepare yourself for a surprise when we land," said Rostnikov.

Karpo nodded. He was almost curious.

The plane's low, sudden roar signaled descent. Rostnikov put on his seat belt and felt the slight pop in his ears. He distrusted statistics on airplane fatalities. They were always reported in terms of miles flown and not in terms of takeoffs and landings. Airplanes seldom simply fell from the sky, but they did run into significant problems when trying to leave the earth or come back to it, where they belonged.

The landing on the wide, cracked road to the mine, which doubled as Devochka's airstrip, was reasonably smooth, and when the engines stopped the voice of the pilot wearily announced, *"Voa ta na,"* Here it is.

They were within forty yards of the line of concrete block buildings.

Seat belts clicked. The other passengers coughed, talked, shuffled. None of the handful who rose to get off seemed particularly happy to have arrived. It was difficult to imagine that some of them called this place home, that they and many he would meet had lived their lives here and, in all likelihood, so had their parents. Inbreeding had plagued Gulag towns for generations. Perhaps the same would be true of Devochka.

The two policemen were the last to get off. Descent down the aluminum steps was an even bigger adventure than had been the ascent. Rostnikov did not know who was watching, and there was little he could do to make the maneuver anything but slightly awkward at best. He silently urged his young and senseless leg to cooperate in the venture.

When he and Karpo had reached the ground and retrieved their bags, they saw a contingent of four men stepping across the road toward them.

"Well, is it what you expected?" Rostnikov asked Karpo.

The buildings appeared to be solid, well maintained, functional, and bleak. There were many windows, wide windows letting in the sunlight, facing not just the far less modern structure of the mine, but the forest and mountains beyond.

"I had no expectations," said Karpo.

The quartet was almost on them now. The passengers had all deplaned, retrieved their luggage, and begun walking toward the closest of the buildings.

"It is not like our last adventure in Siberia."

"That was two thousand kilometers from here."

"Yes," said Rostnikov, looking toward a thick gathering of trees in the distance.

Three of the four men were not impressed by the Moscow policemen but they tried not to show it. What they witnessed was a gaunt, thin, and quite dour spectre in black and a limping, average-sized, broad man with a typical Russian face.

The engines of the airplane which had gone down to an uneven, impatient murmur, were now revving up with loud rattling noises of belching anxiety.

"I'm Yevgeniy Zuyev," said the first man, extending his hand. "I am the Chairman of the Town of Devochka. Let's go inside where we can sit and talk and complete the introductions without the sound of the airplane."

Rostnikov nodded his agreement and followed the man, who could not have been more than forty.

As they walked, Karpo observed Porfiry Petrovich's eyes meeting those of a bearded member of the group who looked back over his shoulder. The meeting of eyes was without emotion. Karpo noted the exchange and thought the man looked familiar. Emil Karpo did not forget names or faces. He was sure he had not met the man before, yet the uncertainty of recognition impelled him to keep his eyes on the man as they walked. The man was perhaps fifty years old, bespectacled with a very serious and not friendly look on his face.

"Slow down for the Inspector, Zhenya," said the bearded man.

"No need," said Rostnikov.

"Sorry," said Zhenya Zuyev, slowing his pace.

"Thank you," said Rostnikov.

The third man in the group was a tall, remarkably muscular man no more than thirty years old. His head was shaved and he wore no hat. He could have been quite forbidding, but the smile he wore looked genuine. The last man, who walked head down and looked worried, was the oldest of the group. His hair, peeking out from under a fur hat, was white, his back bent, his face furrowed with thin lines like dried up river-beds.

When they reached the closest building, Zuyev held the door open, and they stepped in behind Rostnikov and Karpo. They moved down a wide, well-lit corridor with Zuyev taking the lead.

They passed a large room to their right, with comfortable chairs facing a wide-screen television set.

"This is our primary building. Government office, security, large town meeting room, largest cafeteria. We have a large collection of DVDs," said Zuyev. "Of course, most people prefer to watch in their own rooms and apartments."

Zuyev led them into a cafeteria-style dining room where a few of the several dozen tables held teenagers and older people snacking and drinking tea or coffee.

"We serve three meals a day, every day," said Zuyev. "Of course, most people prefer to eat in their own rooms and apartments."

"You said that," said the old man impatiently.

"Do you have a weight room?" asked Rostnikov.

The bald young man with a smile said, "An outstanding weight room, eleven machine stations and a full range of free weights."

"Viktor is bench press, snatch, and clean-and-jerk champion of Siberia," said Zuyev, skirting the tables and going through a door into a small private dining room. "He is training for the Olympics. We are very proud of him."

"I should like to see the weight room later," said Rostnikov.

"You lift, don't you?" said Viktor.

"Yes," said Rostnikov.

"I knew it," said the young man.

They sat around the table with white mugs and matching white plates set before them. Two platters of cookies stood on the table, along with insulated pitchers that Zuyev identified as Brazilian coffee and black tea.

It seemed to Rostnikov, who reached for the coffee, more like an informal party than the beginning of an investigation into the death of a foreign visitor.

"You've met Viktor Panin," said Zuyev, nodding at the bald and smiling young man. "He, and the rest of us, are on the governing board, in addition to which Anatoliy Lebedev," he nodded this time at the old man, "is the Alorosa mine director."

Which left . . .

"Fyodor Andreiovich Rostnikov," said the bearded man, looking at Karpo. "Director of Security in Devochka and in the mines."

There was a silence in the room, a waiting for someone to say what had to be said. Now Karpo knew why the bearded man looked familiar.

"Fyodor Andreiovich and I are brothers," said Porfiry Petrovich.

"Ask."

Iosef looked at Zelach and reached for a sticky apricot and mince pastry on the plate between them.

"Ask?" Zelach repeated looking around the room.

There were seventeen people at the tables. All of them but the two policemen were black.

"Ask," said Iosef.

"What are we doing here?" asked Zelach.

"Being very conspicuous," said Iosef, drinking some of the thick, dark tea from the blue mug in front of him. "Have another one of these. They're delicious."

Zelach took a pastry. It was his third. They were delicious. He would have liked to take one home for his mother but it would be awkward to ask and difficult to transport for the rest of the day.

They were being examined. Some of the black men — there were no women — looked at them directly, with reasonable curiosity, others were more furtive. Four men at a table got up to leave.

"It is my understanding from Titov . . . You know Titov in the foreign visitors section?"

"Yes," said Zelach.

A pair of men in their late twenties now rose and departed.

"He says this is where Botswanans gather. There are places where Ghanaians do the same, and many other black Africans have their own niches."

"But . . ."

"Our goal is to sit here and drive away customers by our very presence," said Iosef.

"Why?"

"So that someone will eventually come to us, if for no reason other than to try to get us to leave."

"There is no other way?" asked Zelach.

"Lots of other ways," said Iosef, "but we only have nine days. Subtlety and discretion are not options. With each departure of customers, we come closer to . . . ."

He paused as their waiter approached. He appeared to be the only waiter for the dwindling gathering. The man was very dark, hair cut almost to the scalp and showing a frost of gray. He had a thin mustache, which also showed signs of gray, and a smooth, youthful face that defied the hint of age.

"Finished?" the man asked pleasantly reaching for the platter.

Iosef stopped him by placing a hand over the plate.

"What do you call these pastries?"

"Vetkoek," said the man.

"Deep fried dough filled with mince?" asked Iosef.

"Yes," said the man, glancing over at another pair of departing customers. "And we add apricots. If you wish, I can wrap some for you to take to your home or place of work."

Zelach wanted to speak, but held back.

"No, thank you," said Iosef with a smile. "We'll take our time and eat these here. You are the owner of this establishment?"

"I am."

"Your name?"

Iosef had removed from his pocket several of the white index cards he carried for notes. He paused, clicked his pen, and waited.

"Maticonay."

Iosef wrote the name.

"I . . ."

"Business is good, Mr. Maticonay?"

"Fair."

"We are policemen," said Iosef.

"Yes," said the man, looking at the low, sagging ceiling above him as Iosef put his cards and click pen on the table. Another two customers left.

"We want to ask you some questions, and if we like the answers we will leave and recommend your place to other policemen."

"I would rather you did not recommend."

"Then we will not."

Iosef carefully withdrew an envelope from his inside jacket pocket. The man watched as Iosef removed two photographs and a drawing and placed them on the table.

"You know these men?"

The photographs of the two dead men on

Paulinin's autopsy tables were reasonably clear — clear enough to make it evident that the two men were dead.

"No," said the man.

Iosef looked at Zelach who shook his head no.

"That's not true," said Iosef. "My partner is psychic, or maybe just sensitive to such things. If he says you are not telling the truth, then you are not telling the truth, Mr. Maticonay."

"I've seen them."

"I would appreciate their names and where they lived. In addition, I would like the name of their friend, a third man."

Now Mr. Maticonay put his palms together, placed the tips of his fingers against his lips, and closed his eyes. When he opened his eyes, he found himself looking at the drawing of the tattoo that was on both of the dead men. Mr. Maticonay's knees were unsteady.

"Please sit," said Iosef.

"No."

"Then . . ."

"I have six children."

"And?" asked Iosef.

"They would like to know their father when they are grown."

"We live in difficult times," said Iosef.

"All times are difficult," said Mr. Maticonay. "I cannot answer you."

"Too late," said Iosef. "You've been talking to us. You look distressed. We are being watched by the few of your customers who remain. If the people who wear this tattoo are like all gangs throughout the world, you are going to have a problem unless we help you."

"You would have helped me by not coming into my shop and not changing my life," Mr. Maticonay said. He sighed and continued. "Two men sitting back there, by the kitchen door."

"Yes?"

"They wear this tattoo. It's not a gang tattoo. It is a tribal marking."

"You have only one word to say to me and you should be perfectly safe," said Iosef. "The word is 'no.' I will get up and shout now and you will answer 'no.' "

Iosef suddenly rose pushing back his chair, and shouting, "If you don't tell me, we will have this placed closed by tomorrow."

"No," said Mr. Maticonay.

"You two," said Iosef, looking at the two men near the kitchen who had risen from their table. "Where are you going?"

Zelach was up now, too.

"No one leaves," Iosef continued. "For those who have not yet figured it out, we are the police. We want to talk to all of you. If you try to leave, my partner will be forced to shoot you."

Zelach was up now, and Iosef whispered to him,

"The door."

Zelach slouched quickly to the front door, blocking it with his body.

The two young men who had been seated at the table near the kitchen were up now. One of them reached for the kitchen door. Iosef had his gun in hand now.

"You will stop," he shouted at the two men as customers went to the floor, hands covering their heads.

Both of the men at the kitchen door took out guns of their own and began firing as they pushed into the kitchen. Iosef and Zelach fired back. Mr. Maticonay, who had not gone to the floor, was on his way to it now, a bullet in his neck.

"A back way," called Iosef to Zelach, who understood and went out into the street in search of a rear entrance.

Iosef glanced at Mr. Maticonay who sat stunned on the floor, his hand to his neck to try to stop the bleeding.

"Someone help him," Iosef shouted as he

ran toward the door to the kitchen.

The kitchen was small, almost nonexistent. There was no one in it. The rear door was open. Iosef moved toward it, gun held level, gripped in both hands. They could be waiting. They could count as well as he. Two policemen. Two men with tattoos who had something to hide. They could be waiting.

Iosef stepped into the sunlight, looked to his right and then to his left, where Zelach stood and shrugged.

"Look for them," Iosef shouted and ran back through the kitchen and into the shop where a man was kneeling over Mr. Maticonay.

Iosef went to his knees, holstered his gun, and examined the wounded man.

"It's not bad," said Iosef. "Just bloody. I'm sorry."

Mr. Maticonay gurgled something. Iosef leaned close to hear what he was saying. The man's eyes were closed.

"Cowboys," he said.

Iosef understood.

"Too many guns," the man said.

"Black," said Georgi Danielovich, "from Africa."

"Where in Africa?" asked Sasha.

They were sitting in a coffee shop, dim

and dark and dusty, but far better than the horror which was Georgi's one-room apartment.

Georgi needed a shower, a shave, a haircut, and a change of clothes, but most of all he needed whatever his drug of choice might be.

"I don't know," said Georgi, reaching for the cup of something tepid and brown.

"Two of them approached you," said Elena.

"Two, that's right."

"Their names?" asked Sasha.

Georgi shrugged and said, "Who remembers?"

"And this was the first time?" asked Elena.

The shop was empty except for the two detectives and the addict, head in his hands, who was very quickly coming apart.

"Could you identify these two men?" asked Elena.

Georgi looked up with what was supposed to be a smile but looked more like a pained grimace, which, perhaps, it was.

"They were black," he said. "They could walk through that door right now and I would not know them. My head hurts. I need a doctor."

"You do not need a doctor," said Sasha, leaning toward him. "But you will if you do not start remembering things right now. We are in a hurry. We have nine days."

"Nine days?" asked Georgi in confusion. "We have nine days for what?"

"No," corrected Sasha. "*We* have nine days, but you have only a few minutes. You need to drink your coffee, maybe have something to eat, use the toilet, and you also need another clump on the head."

Georgi didn't have time to protect himself. Sasha's knuckles came down on the same spot where the gun had raised a throbbing welt.

"Sasha," Elena warned as Georgi screamed.

The man behind the bar watched with interest but no sympathy.

"You are boring me," Sasha whispered.

"My head," cried Georgi. "Brain damage. You're giving me brain damage. A doctor."

"You don't use your brain anyway," said Sasha. "If you did, you'd be helping us find out who killed your girlfriend."

"I just wanted to make a few rubles," said Georgi. "Is that so bad?"

The question was addressed to Elena.

"Just tell us everything," she said.

Georgi tried drinking the dark liquid.

"This is terrible. Can I get . . ."

"Talk," Sasha warned. "I'm not only bored

and impatient, I'm in a hurry. Maybe you're like one of those *butchka* toys. You tap it and it runs in circles."

To Georgi, the good-looking policeman definitely looked insane. The plump pretty policewoman looked sane, but it was unlikely she would intervene.

"My luck," sighed Georgi. "The first chance I get to make real *kapusta,* money, and this happens."

"Christiana Verovona's luck was worse."

Georgi shrugged and brushed back his dirty straight hair.

"I should have kept the diamonds," he said. "Run with them, but where do you sell diamonds?"

"I don't know," said Sasha.

"You see?" said Georgi. "You see? And one of those blacks looked even crazier than . . ."

He stopped and looked nowhere.

"Talk now," said Sasha, placing the gun he had taken from Georgi on the table.

"They gave me the diamonds in a briefcase," Georgi said, "told me not to open it, not to take a single diamond. They said I was to take the train to Kiev, go into the lobby of the station, stand by some palm trees there, and give the briefcase to a woman, who would give me an identical briefcase."

"But you sent Christiana," said Elena. "Why?"

"He was afraid," said Sasha.

Georgi gave a shrug that said what's-the-difference-now.

"The woman in Kiev?" asked Elena.

"They told me she would be white, young, very beautiful. They said I would probably recognize her."

"You would recognize her?" asked Sasha.

"Yes. He said she's a model. Television ad. He mentioned a television ad for soap. Clover Soap I think. No, something else."

"After you made the exchange with this woman, then what?" asked Elena.

"I was to get back on the train to Moscow. There would be just enough time. They gave me a ticket to a compartment. They said when I delivered the briefcase with the money, I would be given a very generous amount of it."

"You believed them?" asked Elena.

Georgi tried to laugh. It came out as a throaty gargle.

"We were to make the exchange at four o'clock today in front of the toy store across from Lubyanka Prison."

"Your idea?" asked Sasha.

"Yes. They would not do anything to me

there, and I planned to take whatever money they gave me and go immediately to Odessa in case they were planning to kill me. They said they would use me again if all went well, and I told them that would be fine, but I did not believe them for a second. Georgi Danielovich is no fool."

Both detectives thought quite the opposite.

"Do you have some way of reaching them?" asked Elena.

"No. Lubyanka. Four o'clock."

"And you were planning to go there and try to explain?"

"I do not know. They would not believe me. And I have no money to run. I do not even have a gun anymore, to rob a drug dealer with."

"We feel for your plight," said Sasha. "You will be in front of the toy store at four today with a briefcase that you will be given. We will all go buy it. When the Africans come to make the exchange, we will arrest them and you can walk away. You might try walking to Odessa. The weather should be good this time of year."

"You will let me go?" he asked, looking at them both.

"You are paperwork, and a very bad odor," said Sasha.

CHAPTER SEVEN

It was a warm night in Moscow, more than forty years ago. A warm night. The policeman, burly and resigned, sat on a rock tented by two slabs of concrete which might well have given way to crush him. Unfortunately, this was the only reasonable cover while he watched the truck.

The building was going up slowly, typical of projects in the Soviet Union, where no incentive existed for workers to put in a full day of hard work. Appeals to the abstract love of a nation that needed more buildings were to no avail. The workers did not define themselves as Soviets. They considered themselves Russians, Georgians, Chechens, Lithuanians, or whatever.

And so they had no reservations about stealing from the State as the State had no reservations about taking from them. At least, that was the way most of them thought. It was something the policeman understood.

An inventory by the project director and the Communist Party representative at the site had revealed a serious loss of valued equipment and wiring. The conclusion was theft by employees. The solution was the placement of a policeman in the shadows.

And so he sat as he had for the past two nights, a cheese sandwich in his pocket, his holstered gun resting familiarly against his right thigh, the flashlight on his belt pressing against his left leg.

He was hungry. He slowly, quietly unwrapped his sandwich and took a large, satisfying bite.

And then he heard them coming.

He did not know what time it was, could not read the face of his watch in the darkness, but it was definitely past midnight.

They came, three of them, whispering, climbing on the rear of the truck, opening it with a key, their shoes producing a metallic echo as the door swung open. Two of the men stepped into the truck. The third remained on the ground to receive the equipment handed to him. It looked as if they had planned to take no more than they could carry.

The policeman set aside his sandwich and

slowly eased his way out of the concrete tent.

The man on the ground was leaning over to place a metal box near his feet when the policeman approached.

As the man got up to receive something else from the two in the truck, the policeman stepped to the rear of the truck, slammed the door closed, and threw the bolt to lock them in.

The thief on the outside took it all in and began to run. He was much younger than the policeman, and much lighter. He would have gotten away had he not tripped on a coil of wire he had taken from the truck.

The policeman had his gun out and pointed at the man on the ground, who realized that it was all over. The two in the truck obviously realized the same thing. They were making no noise, not crying to be let out. They sat and waited.

An hour later, the policeman led all three of his prisoners into the stone shack that served as the local police station. The shack, with temporary cells in the rear, was at least a century old. Not a single renovation had ever been done.

It was not the policeman's job to talk to the prisoners. He was just there to catch them, turn them in, and go home while the

KGB decided what to do with traitors to the Revolution.

And then, within an hour after he had caught the thieves, she appeared.

The policeman did not know how the woman found it. Somehow people knew. Someone would see an arrest taking place or hear a name mentioned by a clerk who worked in Petrovka, or a talkative young jail guard. No matter. She found out.

She was pretty, with healthy country skin and corn blond hair. She had been sitting, waiting, worried about her husband, the man who had tripped over the coil of wire, when she had found out what happened.

Relatives were not allowed into the police station. This was a place of little hope and the province of those who had learned indifference.

She confronted him when he stepped out of the police station into the early morning light. "What has happened to my husband?"

And that was how it had begun.

The policeman never denied to himself, and he could not hide it from his wife, that if ever he were to suffer a downfall, it would be because of a woman or women. He could not help it. In spite of his less-than-handsome features and bulky frame, there was something comforting about him, something sad and peaceful. He recognized this and let it happen.

And that was how it had happened this time.

Her name was Klara. She was a Pole. She did not love her husband, never had, but he had promised the pretty young girl security and love. He had delivered neither. It was not that he did not want to. He was simply incapable of doing more than being a full-time laborer and a part-time thief.

Klara worked in a glass factory, in terrible heat, for little pay. Now her husband was in jail. That would end his income. She might have to go back to Poland, to a family that did not want her and could not afford to have her.

So the policeman and the factory girl became lovers. It lasted for five months. Her husband went to a *Gulag.* The policeman helped her even though he had little money and a family of his own.

And then she became pregnant.

And that was how Fyodor Andreiovich Rostnikov, half brother of Porfiry Petrovich Rostnikov, was born.

James sat at the table, a blue metal cup of stale, cold coffee in front of him with a dent in its lip. On the side of the cup was an emblem. It looked a little like a coat of arms. He was curious, but not enough to ask Vladimir Kolokov, who sat across from him.

The table was planked wood with rickety legs. Every time James lifted his heavy arms or dropped them back on the planks, the legs of the table rattled against the uncovered concrete of the floor.

"Tell me," said Kolokov, examining him, "are you smart?"

Wanting to stay alive and hoping for an opportunity to escape before the day of the exchange, James calculated and easily came to the conclusion that he should say, "I'm very smart."

Kolokov grinned. It was the right answer. A moderately clever man would have said that he was dumb, stupid, perhaps the most densely stupid creature that ever placed foot inside of Russia. A truly smart man would realize, as James did, that the possible path to some hope of survival lay in pretending to be a fool who thought himself smart. James had learned well from his six years working with these strange people, the Russians.

"Very smart," Kolokov repeated, looking at the bald man, named Pau, who was the only other person in the very dark, windowless room.

An incongruous floor lamp, heavy wrought iron with elaborate glass panels, provided illumination and something at which to glance.

"The clothes fit you," said Kolokov.

James looked down at the shirt he was wearing. One of the other Kolokov men, Bogdan or Alek, had given James these clothes, told him to strip and dress. The rough, warm, long-sleeved khaki shirt did fit, as did the badly faded jeans whose legs had to be rolled up. He had been given no belt.

James ached. His face, neck, head, arms, body, and legs all ached in various degrees of pain that worsened when he moved. James used two hands to drink from the blue metal cup.

"You understand that I had to kill your friends?"

James nodded.

"And I'll have to kill you if you lie to me?"

James didn't respond.

"That was a question."

James nodded. And then he decided. There was really no hope in playing the fool. There might be something for him in engaging the man in conversation, flattering him. What he would really have liked to do was throw the remaining coffee in the Russian's white, smirking face and then shove the cup in a sharp thrust against his nose. That would have been suicidal, but that's what he wanted to do. Instead, he said, "Why did you need to kill them?"

Kolokov's mouth opened slightly, and then closed as he smiled. The black man had said this in perfect Russian, and had said it without a trace of the fool.

"I need two things," said Kolokov. "I need to feel danger, physical, immediate danger, for me or for others created by me."

"It's a need?" asked James calmly.

"A need," Kolokov said. "I am definitely a borderline psychopath. At least that is what the psychiatrist at the prison said before I gouged her eyes out."

"You didn't gouge her eyes out," said James.

Kolokov regarded his prisoner very seriously now.

"No, I did not, but I wanted to. The way you want to gouge my eyes out right now. Calling me a psychopath gives my actions a name, but a label explains nothing."

Kolokov leaned back, reached into his shirt pocket, removed a package of American cigarettes, put them on the table, and didn't open them.

"You smoke?"

"No," said James.

"Suit yourself."

Kolokov opened the package, removed a cigarette, and lit it.

"You need money," James said.

"I'll amend that. I want money. I want to be rich. I want things. I want people to do things to, to do things for. I want a very big bathtub with constant hot water, steaming water, clear, clean water."

"Women?" asked James.

"When I want them."

"Yes."

"You understand all this?"

"Yes," said James, forcing a smile with bruised puffed lips.

James was thinking of a home and family he would probably never see again. Well, that was premature. Kolokov leaned forward across the table and whispered, "I'm surrounded by fools. That doesn't mean I'd want someone like you with me. Too smart. Can't trust people like you, but I do like matching wits with them."

"Honduras," came the voice of the bald man.

Kolokov turned toward him and said, "What the fuck are you talking about?"

"Honduras," the man repeated.

"Does something go with that observation?" asked Kolokov.

"Remember Honduras," said the bald man.

"Honduras?" repeated Kolokov, looking at James for a possible answer to the question.

James had no answer.

"The man from Honduras," said the bald man. "Three years ago."

"Hon—" Kolokov repeated. "I don't remember any — Guatemala. He was from Guatemala. How did you come up with Honduras?"

"I got it wrong."

Kolokov looked at James and sat back, smoking and remembering. The Guatemalan had been a tiny man, the color of a pecan shell. He was no more than thirty-five and had fallen under Kolokov's umbra during a street robbery. On little more than a whim, Kolokov had brought the man, Sanchez, to an apartment, and was about to do something particularly painful to him under the guise of getting him to tell how he might provide ransom money.

Sanchez had worked him perfectly, claimed to be a member of the Guatemalan mission in Moscow, talked Kolokov into a partnership to steal ancient artifacts from

Central America and sell them to dealers in Turkey. Kolokov let the man go after they shook hands on a partnership that promised to make both men rich.

The problem was that Sanchez had lied. He was not a diplomat. He was a visiting poet. He knew nothing about artifacts. He knew much about making up stories.

"You really know where there will be a delivery of diamonds?"

"Yes," said James. "They will be delivered to three Russians who will take them to various cities, where they will be exchanged for cash."

"I don't believe you," said Kolokov.

James was impassive.

"I'm telling the truth."

"I'll kill you painfully if they do not appear where you say with the diamonds."

"I understand."

Kolokov rose and began to pace the room. If this black man were as smart as he appeared to be, he knew that he would be dying as soon as Kolokov had the diamonds.

"What will you do with the diamonds when you have them?" asked James.

"Sell them?"

"Where? To whom?"

"I know people," said Kolokov pausing, wary.

"People who can handle millions in diamonds or low-level gluttons who deal in wristwatches and seal skins?"

Kolokov didn't answer.

"You need to know who can pay for the diamonds," said James. "You need to know the people who can take the diamonds west to Germany, France, England, the United States, Japan, the people who will pay you for the diamonds when you have them."

"And you will tell us who they are?"

"Yes."

"You'll have to trust me."

"No," said James. "Once you have the diamonds we go to someplace very public where it will be impossible for you to kill me without getting caught. In this public place I will tell you who the contact buyers are."

"You might lie?"

"We stay in public till you or your people make the first contact," said James. "I will give you three names. You pick whichever one you like."

"Sounds good," said Kolokov, knowing full well that he would have to find a way to kill this smart-mouthed black once he had what he needed. It should not be too hard.

"Guatemala," warned the bald man.

Kolokov shook his head and smiled at

James with a shrug. If it were like Guatemala, at least he would be ready for it. It was also a promising sign that the bald man had not said 'Honduras.'

"Are you a chess player?" asked Kolokov.

"Yes."

"A good one?"

"A good one."

"So am I. Let's play a game or two."

"Guatemala," came the voice from the shadows.

Kolokov grabbed the blue cup from in front of James and hurled it in the direction of the bald man. He hit the man in the face. The bald man made no sound.

"I'll get the board," said Kolokov. "Play your hardest, Botswanan."

"I will."

James had decided to see what kind of player Kolokov was before devising a strategy that would convince his captor that he was doing his best while letting the Russian win the game. He did decide that, while he would lose the first game, he would surely win the second, but lose the third. Kolokov would sometimes be even, but he would never lose.

James Harumbaki was not the best chess player in Botswana. He was the second-best player. He was confident that he could manipulate the Russian. The best player in Botswana was an Indian who owned four pawnshops. The Indian had finished fourth in the world the previous year.

"Watch him," Kolokov said, leaving the room to get the chessboard and pieces.

When he was gone, the bald man in the shadows stepped out. His cheek was gushing blood from the cup Kolokov had hurled at him. He calmly looked at James Harumbaki and said, "Honduras."

Balta had a simple plan for finding the model.

The city was not exactly overrun with modeling agencies and beautiful models. There were some, even a few small offices of agencies with their primary headquarters in Paris or New York. No, finding the model Christiana Verovona had described on the train before she died should not be difficult.

Balta had a list of names he obtained from the agencies. He also looked at photographs. None of the agencies would give him the addresses or phone numbers of any of the women they represented. They didn't want to risk being cut out of their share of a job.

There was a daily newspaper ad calling for beautiful young girls who were looking for a career in modeling. Balta knew it was a scam, but he called the telephone number in the ad and made an appointment.

When he arrived at the office of the Parisian Modeling Agency just off of a busy street, he was ushered through a reception-waiting room where a girl of no more than fourteen sat on a chipped metal chair next to a woman in her forties.

Balta was taken to a small office where a lean man wearing an unimpressive wig to cover his bald head made a show of rising. He was ridiculous. Dressed in crimson slacks, a blue blazer, a puffy white shirt, and a crimson scarf that almost matched his slacks, he made a show of adjusting his jacket as he sat.

"I am Anatole Deforge," he said in a French accent which did not disguise his Slavic origin. "And you wish . . ."

"To find an old friend I've lost track of." Balta continued smiling.

"An old friend. Then you are not interested . . ." he said with disappointment.

"Not at the moment," Balta added, leaving the door open to what the man who called himself Deforge might be planning to offer.

"Well," Deforge said with a shrug. "Perhaps . . ."

"Perhaps," said Balta. "I'm looking for

141

Oxana Balakona."

"Which of us isn't?" said Deforge.

"You know where she lives?"

"I can find out if she has a residence in Kiev. I know she works here from time to time. I've never had the pleasure of representing her."

Oxana Balakona was far above the aspirations of this little man, but Balta knew how to deal with little men.

"You've been very kind," he said. "I'll certainly urge her to see you."

"Would you?" he asked.

"Yes. Perhaps I could get her to come with me to see you later in the week."

Deforge could not keep himself from clasping his hands till his knuckles were white.

"My door will always be open to both of you."

"Her address?" said Balta.

Deforge held up a finger to indicate that he would take care of the matter. He picked up his phone and made a call without looking up the number.

"Nina," he said. "I need the phone number and address of Oxana Balakona . . . No . . . Yes. Of course, my sweet. If anything comes of it, you will be involved."

There was a pause. Deforge looked at

Balta and smiled. His teeth were false, large, and slightly yellow.

"Ah yes, Nina, fine. I will."

He hung up and scribbled on a square yellow sheet he tore from a pad.

"You want me to call the number for you?" Deforge asked, holding out the sheet. "It would be no trouble."

"No, thank you," said Balta, taking the sheet from him. "I think I want to surprise her."

The train pulled into the Kiev station. It had been on time. Lydia had packed for Sasha. She had done it quickly, efficiently. Everything had been fitted neatly into the blue cloth duffel bag. The price he had paid for her help had been a twenty-minute speech on life, loyalty, the need for caution, the sad demise of the Communist Party, the end of the benevolent Soviet Union, her certainty that Elena Timofeyeva would try to seduce him, his responsibility to her, his wife, his children, and the uncertainty of Porfiry Petrovich Rostnikov's motives.

Sasha had listened, or pretended to, without the usual exasperation and arguments. Lydia had tried with increasing perseverance to get her son to react, but he was having none of this. His lack of response worried her far more than her fear that something might happen in a backward place like Kiev where people marched in the streets over elections.

Adding to her concern was the fact that he leaned over and kissed the top of her her head before he left the apartment.

She had decided that she would have to talk to Rostnikov about Sasha as soon as the Chief Inspector returned from whatever ludicrous expedition he had undertaken in Siberia.

Elena's packing had taken no more than five minutes. It consisted of putting her small zipper bag of makeup, toothbrush, and tooth powder into the brown leather suitcase that she always kept ready under the bed.

She had ceded the window seat to Sasha so she could watch him during the train ride. His behavior in Georgi Danielovich's apartment, his taking away the addict's gun, could have been brave or suicidal. Elena considered the latter to be more likely. His smile did not reassure her. It made her more suspicious.

"You want to go see Maya and your children when we get there?" asked Elena as they walked to the exit where a Kiev detective was to meet them.

"Yes," Sasha said.

Good, Elena thought but did not say.

"Maya has a cousin, Masha, a model," he said. "Maybe she can help us find the model we're looking for."

The four o'clock meeting in Moscow with the Africans who had given Georgi the diamonds to deliver to Kiev had been a bust.

Georgi had been there, suitcase in hand, pacing in front of the toy store, glancing furtively at Lubyanka Prison, looking as conspicuous and obviously addicted as he was. Elena and Sasha had been watching from inside the toy store. People had passed Georgi, even a young black man in jeans and a blue T-shirt, but the man had not stopped.

After ten minutes Georgi had suddenly stopped pacing. He looked around as if listening to something and then reached into his pocket and pulled out a cell phone, which he held to his ear. He listened, began to say something, and stopped. He put the phone back in his pocket, went up to Elena and Sasha, and said, "They know you're in here."

"What did they say?"

"They want their money. I wanted to tell them that I did not have their money," he said woefully. "But they knew that too. They want me to find the person who killed Christiana and took their money. Shit, I cannot even find my way to the fucking toilet half the time."

"We will find whoever killed Christiana and took the money," Sasha said.

"But you will not give the money to the black guys who gave me the diamonds to deliver."

"No," said Elena.

Georgi chewed on his lower lip and said, "What do I get out of this?"

"With a little luck, you get to Odessa and you stay alive," said Sasha.

"That is something," Georgi said.

Now, in Kiev, Sasha and Elena were in search of a thief and murderer and millions of rubles in diamonds. They had eight days left and the promise of help from the Kiev police unit that dealt with illegal traffic and theft of diamonds and other precious jewels.

There was a chill in the air and a gray sky, which was not particularly welcoming, but the man standing next to the blue and white police car was. He wore dark slacks, a pale blue shirt, and a tan zippered jacket. He was about forty, and to Elena he resembled the Australian actor Russell Crowe.

"Timofeyeva and Tkach?" he asked, holding out his right hand.

"Yes," said Elena. "Elena Timofeyeva."

"Sasha Tkach."

"Jan Pendowski, Detective Inspector."

They shook hands.

Pendowski opened the car doors. Elena got in the front passenger seat, Sasha in the back. Pendowski got in the driver's seat and looked at Elena with the approval of a man who was confident of his appeal.

"My wife is here with my children," Sasha said.

"I know," said Pendowski. "I'll take you to her. And?"

"We are looking for a woman, a model, a very beautiful model who has been in television ads. She took a suitcase containing diamonds from a woman who was then murdered on a train back to Moscow."

"Yes, I know all this. I think I can help you," said Pendowski with a grin as he started the car.

And he could help them. And he would help them, but not nearly as much as they wished and not in the way they wished.

Jan Pendowski could, if he wished, drive them directly to the apartment of Oxana Balakona. He knew it well. He had recently spent the night next to, on top of, and under Oxana in her bed. And he could certainly take them directly to his own small apartment where, locked in a small, extremely heavy steel safe with very thick walls, was the decorated wooden box into which he had transferred the diamonds.

Jan Pendowski's plan was to be pleasant and helpful to the Moscow officers, particularly the pretty and not model-thin woman. Jan had grown tired of the thin Oxana whose bones he could feel when his body was pressed against hers. The firm flesh of Elena Timofeyeva was very inviting. She was seated close enough for him to smell. Her scent was pure and natural, a welcome change from the sweet and artificial scent of Oxana Balakona.

The next few days promised to be interesting and very rewarding for Detective Pendowski. He had many circles and dead ends for the Russians before he killed Oxana and delivered her to them.

CHAPTER EIGHT

The office of Fyodor Andreiovich Rostnikov, Director of Security, Alorosa Mine, and the Town of Devochka of the Siberian Territory, did not match his title. It was not tiny, but it was small, about the size of a freight elevator. There was one wall with a window. The window faced an open plane of tundra and a distant vision of *taiga* — a vast forest of birch, pine, spruce, and larch. Occasionally, if the season was right, there was a chance that a reindeer would appear in the distance, and lemmings ran free and multiplied and multiplied. Few other animals inhabited the perpetually frozen hundreds of thousands of acres of land permafrosted to a depth of 4,760 feet.

The town was built on steel legs driven into the permafrost and heated by huge pumps. This kept the buildings from freezing in the winter, when the temperature went down to about 100 degrees below zero, and sinking in the summer, when temperatures rose well over 100 degrees and a sickly rotting smell permeated everything. When the first buildings had been constructed in 1950, the warm air they gave off caused the permafrost beneath them to soften. The buildings sank.

Fyodor Rostnikov looked out of the lone window in his office. Behind him bookshelves covered the wall. File cabinets were lined up on the right. On the wall to his left was a single piece of art, a realistic painting, as tall as a man, of a steel girder in a field of green grass. A very small man was craning his neck back and holding onto a workman's cap as he looked up at the top of the girder, where a glittering, white, multifaceted diamond glowed.

"My wife did it," Fyodor said, looking at Porfiry Petrovich, whose eyes were on the painting. "Her name is Svetlana. We have two children, a boy, eighteen, and a girl, ten. The girl has what they call mild autism."

"When did you come here, Fyodor?"

"You may call me Fedya."

They were seated in wooden chairs in front of the steel desk, cups of tea within easy reach on little wooden mats that looked Japanese.

"Fedya."

"My mother and I came here forty-two years, four months, and eight days ago to be with her husband. I was raised in this very building."

Fedya looked around as if he had never noted his surroundings before.

"He is dead, mining accident. She died of cancer just two years ago. Anything else you want to know?"

He ran his flattened fingers over the right side of his bearded chin.

"You no longer hate our father?"

"I'm not venerating his memory," said Fedya.

"And me, you hate me?"

"I did for a very long time and then I realized one day that what he had done to me and my mother was not your fault. I resented, yes, but no more. It took too much time and energy."

Porfiry Petrovich nodded and drank some tea. Both men knew why the information was being provided. The brothers had to work together for a few days. Actually, it had to be seven days at most because of the deadline the Yak had given him.

"The murder," said Rostnikov.

"Which one?"

"There have been more besides the Canadian?"

"Hundreds that I know of. There may have been more. There's no way of knowing the total number of people who simply died in the mine or while constructing the mine and these buildings. Record keeping was terrible. We're not Germans. All the possible murders are buried with whatever records exist. Mind if I pace?"

"No."

"Would you be more comfortable removing your leg?"

"Yes, but it's not worth the effort of taking it off and putting it back on. It supports me but it does not comfort me. I was able to talk to my old, shriveled leg."

Fedya nodded in understanding and began to pace, pausing from time to time to look out the window.

"Tsar Nicholas ordered diamond expeditions to Siberia in 1898. No diamonds were found. Every one of the eighteen men who came to the Yakuntia Basin perished. It was not till Stalin ordered expeditions back to Siberia to find diamonds in 1947 that some success was achieved, but the cost was great — not that Stalin cared. Your only son is named Iosef?"

"Yes."

"For Stalin?"

"Yes. It was a mistake. I have made and continue to make many of them," said Porfiry Petrovich. "My son is not one of those mistakes."

"He could change his name," said Fedya, looking out the window.

"Stalin did not own eternal rights to the name."

"What does Iosef do?"

"He's a policeman. He works with me."

"Runs in the family. Our father, you, me, and your son."

"It's possible."

"The winters," Fedya said, resuming his pace. "Then as now, seven months of winter. Steel tools became so brittle that they broke like dry kindling. Oil froze solid. Rubber tires exploded. Then, when that first summer came, the top layer of permafrost melted, created a muddy, fly-infested swamp as big as half the countries in Africa."

"And people died?" said Porfiry Petrovich.

"Hundreds. And all of them and all of us, until the fall of the man of steel, were happy to be here. We had a doctor, medical supplies, books to read, a job to do — a very dangerous job but a job — but most of all we had . . ."

"Food," said Porfiry Petrovich.

"Food," agreed his brother, almost spilling what remained of his tea. "And warm bedrooms."

"Murders," Porfiry Petrovich said.

"Madness, fights, jealousy," said Fedya.

"Isolation here can be maddening. In 1953 a man, a small man, went mad in the mine. He had a pick. He screamed and imbedded the tool's sharp point in the head of three people, the back of two people, the stomach of another and, worst of all, he came out of the mine and used his pick on two children, one a little boy and the other a little girl. The alcoholic security guard shot the madman. The children were on the way to wait for their father, who was the wild man's first victim. You know where this is going, don't you?"

"The ghost girl," said Rostnikov.

"The ghost girl. She began appearing in the mine a month or two later. She's been seen at least nine times since 1963, probably more. There may have been people who did not want to be ridiculed, but ridicule would not have come easily to those who claimed to have seen her."

"She killed people?"

"Let us say, she was proximate when people died."

"You believe in this ghost girl?"

Fedya stopped pacing and sat in the chair facing his brother. He lowered his voice and said, "No, but that is said only in the relative privacy of this office which, as far as I can tell, is clean of microphones. In here, I'm an atheist. Out there with the people who live here and work the mines, I am an agnostic. Some of these good and not-so-good people have families that have been here four generations. They are the families of criminals sent to this Gulag. They have developed their own lore. I respect it or I cannot do my job. So, as someone said, 'Sometimes the prospect of two and two equaling five has a definite attraction.' "

"Dostoevsky," said Porfiry Petrovich.

"I know," said his brother. "You want to talk to more people or you want to go into the mine?"

"Both. People first. Mine later."

"I have from time to time kept track of you," said Fedya. "Curiosity. Even in so remote a spot as this, it is remarkable what a security officer can access with a computer — even information about a Chief Inspector of Police in Moscow."

"And I, I confess, have from time to time kept track of you. It is remarkable what a Chief Inspector of Police in Moscow can, with a telephone, discover about a security officer at a remote mine in Siberia."

"Yes, the mine. We must not in our nostalgic journey forget about why you are here. Your man Karpo is down there right now. Would you care for a slice of apple square or a Gogol Mogol?"

"Very much."

"Good," said Fedya. "Let's see what they have in the cafeteria."

Oxana did not trust Jan Pendowski. There were many reasons. First, he had the diamonds now. Second, he was a policeman, a corrupt one to be sure, but the police, she believed, were divided into only two groups, the ones with devious minds and the ones who took the most direct approach. Oxana had known both. Jan was devious, but not nearly as clever as he thought himself to be. Oxana was certain the diamonds were in his apartment. She was certain he meant to go with her to Paris, let her sell the diamonds, and then kill her. It was the only reasonable thing to do. They were very good at pleasing each other in bed or on the floor, but they were not in love.

And so, Oxana meant to get into Jan's apartment, find the diamonds, and then kill him.

Meanwhile, the gods of her great grand-parents looked down at her. Her agency had called. An editor of *Paris Match* was going to be in Kiev for a few days to set up a layout. The editor, Rochelle Tanquay, wanted to meet Oxana for dinner to discuss featuring Oxana in a spread, at least six photographs, to be shot in Paris in a week.

That was why Oxana was ushered to a table at the same restaurant where Balta had dined the night before.

And Balta was there again at this most interesting meeting.

Rochelle Tanquay was slim, elegant in a dark dress, hair cut in a Louise Brooks bob, perfect makeup. She was extremely pretty, perhaps thirty-five, maybe a bit older.

"I speak French," said Oxana.

"And I speak some Russian, but I'm sure your French is better than my Russian," said the woman with a smile, offering Oxana a cigarette, which Oxana accepted.

"I brought my portfolio," said Oxana.

"Not necessary," Rochelle said with a wave of her hand. "I am familiar with your work."

"You are a model?"

"Was," said Rochelle ruefully. "Do you know that man over there?"

"Man?"

Oxana turned her head. There was a lean man of about forty who turned his head, pretending to admire the not-very-interesting plaster figures on the wall.

"Yes, I see. It's not unusual for men to give me furtive glances," said Rochelle, "but this one seems particularly interested in you. He has the look of a stalker. I should know."

"You have had the experience?"

"More than once," said Rochelle, rolling her eyes toward the ceiling. "Shall we order first or begin talking?"

A waiter would approach soon. Ukrainian waiters were gallingly slow and inattentive, but not to women who looked like these two.

Balta watched, smiled.

"We want you for a new line, Givenchy all-purpose evening wear. I think you would be perfect. The photographer who will be doing the shoot thinks you are perfect."

A waiter approached, hovered, offered wine suggestions, told of specials he recommended. They ordered.

"I have negotiated a price with your agency. I am sure you do not want to talk money. Neither do I. I do want to talk schedule. Could you be ready to leave for Paris two days from today?"

"Yes," said Oxana.

Rochelle noticed that the man at the nearby table was still watching them.

"I have some business to take care of here," said Oxana. "The day after tomorrow would be perfect."

Rochelle touched her chin with an elegant finger and said, "A man?"

"Yes. I just need the right moment to let him know that I will no longer be seeing him."

Rochelle nodded and said, "Make it soon."

"I will," said Oxana. "Very soon."

Both Rochelle and Oxana ate lightly, a salad of beets and carrots, and drank moderately, a French wine. Rochelle picked up the check. It was what Oxana expected. This was a business meeting, and *Paris Match* could certainly afford it.

When they rose, so did the man at the nearby table.

Balta had seen enough, heard enough. Patience. When the time came to kill Oxana Balakona, and it would surely come soon, he had a very nice surprise for her.

At ten thirty-five on the second night of the investigation, the person who had murdered the Canadian geologist Luc O'Neil, put a knife deeply into the side of Anatoliy Lebedev.

Lebedev was old, a brittle collection of scarred sinew and bones. He had not wanted to go into the mine at night. He did not want to go into the mine at all. He had spent enough time in that coughing, cold darkness of muffled echoes and distant cries.

He did not believe in the ghost girl. Never had believed, even as a very young man, when he was known as Tolya. No one had called him Tolya for many years. There was no one still alive who even remembered when he was Tolya.

The second thrust came, far less painful than the first. This one entered on the left side of his neck and pointed downward.

"I am sorry," the killer whispered.

Lebedev could barely hear him. It was time. He wanted to sleep forever now. The intrigues of the living were pointless. They only thought they were doing something of importance to anyone. Lebedev had stopped telling stories of his youth, stopped declaring the triumphs and losses of his boyhood. No one cared.

The irony was that the person standing over him in the green glow of the lights in the mine was one of the few, the very few, who had shown any interest in Lebedev, except to court his vote on the Board.

"You understand?"

160

The face was inches from his. Lebedev wanted it gone. *First you murder me and then you let my last image be that of someone who needs mouthwash?* The smell of garlic, cheese, tobacco, and something else rancid and sweet would be his last memory.

There was no hereafter.

There was only the unpleasant smell of the slayer, the knife wielder, the assassin, the killer. Unpleasant.

He said something so low that the man who had killed him had to lean forward, ear inches from the mouth of the dying man.

As Lebedev died, the killer whispered, "*Da svi'daniya.* Good-bye, Tolya."

Anatoliy Davidovich Lebedev smiled and died.

At ten thirty-five on the night of the second day of the investigation, Emil Karpo sat, book in hand, at a table in the cafeteria. He was situated, as he had wished, where he could see people come and go. He intended to sit here until one a.m. — he had been told the cafeteria never closed — and then go to his room to sleep till six o'clock. He needed no more sleep than this. Karpo's nights were without dreams, always had been so except for the few weeks after the death of Mathilde Verson. Mathilde, smiling, full of life, then full of death.

A trio of men in clean green uniforms stepped into the cafeteria, talking and arguing. Their voices were almost at the level of rage as they debated the pros and cons of starting a colony of humans on Mars, a colony that they would never live long enough to witness.

One of the men, the shortest, was not speaking. He was shaking his head to indicate that both of his fellow workers were wrong. It was this short man who noticed Karpo looking up at him. The short man stopped in front of a table of clean, heavy white platters.

The other two men noticed that their colleague had stopped and they did so too although they tried to keep talking.

The policeman from Moscow made them instantly uneasy. It was not that they were guilty of anything. At least nothing very much. No, the policeman scared all three of them. He just sat there, back straight, unblinking, dressed in black from shoes to shirt. The three men left the cafeteria saying nothing to each other, having decided not to eat.

Five minutes later the manager of the cafeteria, a heavy, lumbering man came out of the kitchen and went to sit in front of Karpo.

Karpo looked at his visitor, who was clean shaven with perfectly clean, trimmed fingernails.

"May I ask you to leave, Chief Inspector?"

"I'm not a Chief Inspector," said Karpo.

"Inspector, then. You are frightening away people on the night shift who want to get some coffee, a roll maybe, and sit talking for a few minutes. You understand?"

"Perfectly," said Karpo.

"So . . ."

"I am not ready to leave."

The manager rolled his eyes toward the ceiling and went on. "All right. I get paid no more if I have one customer, you, or thirty."

"That was always a weakness of Communism," said Karpo. "A lack of incentives."

The chief started a smile and then let it go.

"Then you will leave?"

"Eventually," said Karpo.

"I cannot put this more delicately," said the manager with a sigh. "You frighten away almost everyone."

"I am aware that my face and bearing evoke no smiles."

"That is putting it very delicately," said the manager, leaning forward and whispering, "Can I tell you something in confidence?"

"Of course," said Karpo. "However, I may not be prepared to listen in good faith."

"I give up. You are a conundrum. Do you play chess?"

"No," said Karpo.

"You want another coffee?"

"Yes."

The manager, defeated, began to rise. Karpo spoke.

"The Canadian died at eleven at night. The killer was someone familiar with the mine. The killer may have come in here just before or just after the murder."

"And?"

"It is my hope that when he sees me he will betray himself."

"Or herself?"

"Yes," said Karpo.

"I will get your coffee. Do not hurry off on my account before I come back."

"I will be here," said Karpo.

It was just about then, give or take ten minutes, that the killer Karpo sought walked into the cafeteria, glanced at him, nodded, and moved to the coffee urn after first picking up a clean cup. Tolya Lebedev had been dead for less than fifteen minutes when the killer sat down in front of Karpo, coffee mug in one hand, small plate of cookies in the left.

"Do you mind?" the killer asked amiably.

"No," said Karpo.

"Well," said the killer, reaching for a cookie as the cafeteria manager returned with a mug of coffee. "Now, what shall we talk about?"

Contrary to the hope of Emil Karpo, the killer did not reveal himself.

Igor Yaklovev, the Yak, had a whiteboard with a black marker and a cloth to erase anything he might not wish to be seen. The board almost covered the top of the desk in his bedroom. The Yak had a small bottle of alcohol with which to rub down the board after erasing it. He had been assured by a forensics technician he had known in the KGB that nothing would remain that could be brought out by even the latest chemical or ultraviolet ray techniques.

The Yak used the board to get a graphic image of whatever he was working on. While he used pens, pencils, paper, and even the computer, he distrusted them, and with good reason. He had learned a great deal from the discarded writings of others. He still had Pankov go through the waste baskets and check e-mails and daily file entries.

After a few minor successes on notes written by his detectives and people in other offices who had not been careful, the Yak had ceased to check Rostnikov's garbage. This had occurred shortly after Yaklovev had taken over the Office of Security Investigation. Pankov had brought him a trio of crumpled papers. The first contained an unflattering penciled likeness of Igor Yaklovev looking into a trash can. The second paper contained an erased note in English that the Yak carefully brought up. The note read, *Do your job and you shall be rewarded.* The third sheet was an ad torn from a newspaper. It read: EXPERIENCED SCAVENGERS WANTED.

Yaklovev sat at the desk in his bedroom. A few feet to his right there stood an antique upright radio. The radio had not worked since 1943. It had belonged to the Yak's grandparents. His father had turned the radio into a shell that could be lifted. Inside the shell was a safe to which only Igor had the combination. Should anyone penetrate the safety devices in the apartment, find the safe, and open it, they would be facing neat piles of official-looking documents they could easily grab and run with.

The Yak knew this might indeed happen — the radio and the safe were but decoys. The truly important notes and valuables, audio and video tapes, and substantial amounts of cash — euros, dollars, and yen — were safely hidden in a concealed wall safe in an apartment one block away — a short walk to the Shabolovskaya Metro. The safe was rigged to explode if anyone who did not use the fail-safe code opened it.

Now, the Yak looked at what he had printed on the board:

Devochka — Diamond mine — Diamonds slowly stolen — Rostnikov, Karpo — Diamonds taken secretly to Moscow. Problem: Canadian geologist murdered in mine. Why? Because he found the thief? Probable.

Moscow — Diamonds are delivered from Devochka to Botswanan smugglers. Courier transports to Kiev for payment. — I. Rostnikov, Zelach. Problem: Two of the Botswanans are tortured, murdered. Why? By whom? Dispute among Botswanans? Someone else wants to profit?

Kiev — Courier exchanges diamonds for

cash? Courier murdered on Kiev-Moscow train. Tkach, Timofeyeva — Problem: By whom?

The Yak sat back, adjusted his glasses, and examined what he had written. The black writing held clues to profit — profit political and financial. Igor Yaklovev was not a greedy man, but he was an ambitious one.

He had survived through the end of the Soviet Union to the present by gathering information on everyone up to and including Putin. His goal was not to be rich or famous but to exert quiet power at the highest levels, even if it were from the office he now headed.

As it was, his current position of power was being threatened by a general named Frankovich, who coveted the Yak's small but increasingly influential base. The Yak was working on this. One had to work constantly to remain even and hope to gain just a bit at a time.

To accomplish his goals, Igor Yaklovev had to rely on Porfiry Petrovich Rostnikov. The Yak did not understand Rostnikov. They were as unlike as two survivors could be and yet they were a perfect match. The taciturn Chief Inspector, who always seemed amused by some inner joke, had no ambition, but he understood fully that his present and future were very much dependent on the Yak. Yaklovev provided protection for his Chief Inspector and his detectives, and Rostnikov provided information success after success.

The Yak checked his pocket watch, a gift he had given himself to mark his fiftieth birthday which he had celebrated the previous evening by dining alone on shark tail soup, pickled herring, and beet salad.

The Yak had no doubt that Rostnikov would put together what he was now erasing from his board.

Porfiry Petrovich Rostnikov needed no whiteboard or notepad. He sat in the room he had been assigned in the Devochka main building. It was sufficiently comfortable, if a bit too warm, even for the lightweight pajamas he wore. Sarah had purchased the pajamas for no reason other than that she thought he needed them and she liked them. The bottoms and tops were oak brown and covered with the names of six Russian writers — Dostoevsky, Gogol, Chekov, Tolstoy, Pushkin, and Turgenev.

He had worked out with Viktor Panin, the bald, smiling giant, in a well-equipped weight room. This had been Panin's third workout of the day and he had sweated through his gray long-sleeved sweatshirt till it was completely blackened, and his pink face looked as if he had just stepped from a shower.

Though Panin glanced down with approval as he spotted for Rostnikov, Porfiry Petrovich was well aware that, as good as he might be in park district tournaments, he was no match for this Olympic-caliber young man.

"You don't take off your leg when you work out," Panin had said while they showered.

"Nothing in it rusts or shrinks, unlike the real one next to it," said Rostnikov. "Besides, I would fall down."

"You want to know my secret?" Panin had whispered while they showered.

"I'm interested in all secrets," said Rostnikov, rinsing off soap. "It is my passion."

"I hate working out. I hate the weights."

"Then why do you do it?" asked Rostnikov.

Panin shrugged, turned off the water, and draped a large yellow towel over his shoulder.

"There is nothing else to do. I don't read. I don't watch much television. I have no close friends."

He gave Rostnikov a big, toothy smile. "Then . . . ?"

"It's the one thing I do well. Besides, something happens when I'm lifting weights. I don't know what it is, but I get lost. It's even a little frightening."

"Does it feel good?" Rostnikov said, balancing himself carefully as he dried.

"I don't know how to say it," said Panin, thinking deeply. "Not good. Not bad, but when I finish, I feel light, happy, like now."

"Meditation," said Rostnikov.

"Meditation?"

"It's just a word for what you feel. I feel it too."

"I knew it," said Panin, loudly slapping his side with a huge open palm. "That's why I told you."

"What do you want from life, Viktor?"

"More weights."

"I'm sure that can be achieved. Are you married?"

"My wife died three years ago."

"Children?"

"Two. I would like you to meet them."

"I would like to meet them."

"My parents are accountants. They are in charge of all the bookkeeping at Devochka," he said proudly.

They were both dry now and dressing.

"How did they come to be here?" asked Rostnikov.

"My father killed three people when he was a boy. They tried to take his lunch. He beat them to death with a chair. My father got very angry."

"It would seem so," said Rostnikov.

"My father was sent here instead of to prison or execution. They needed an accountant."

"And your mother?"

"He met her here. She was a bookkeeper. Her family has been here since the mine opened."

"And you have no accounting skills?"

"Ask me the birthday of any famous Russian," Panin said, popping his shaved head through the hole in his shirt.

"Maxim Gorky."

"March 16, 1868," Panin said.

"How do I know you are right?" asked Rostnikov, slowly working his way into his slacks.

The question puzzled Panin.

"Because I am. You can check."

"I believe you."

"Another one," the giant said eagerly.

"Fyodor Dostoevsky."

"October 30, 1821. You want to check?"

"No, I know that one. You are a savant, Viktor."

They were both dressed then and shaking hands.

"Again tomorrow morning?" asked Panin.

"Tomorrow evening," said Rostnikov.

Panin nodded solemnly.

That had been less than an hour ago, and now Rostnikov in his bookish pajamas waited for telephone reports from Iosef and Elena. He had the same questions Igor Yaklovev had written on his whiteboard.

He did not, however, get to think about them this night for there was a knock at the door. He uttered, "Come in" and the door opened for his brother who, if he noted Porfiry Petrovich's pajamas, did not reveal it with his eyes.

"Anatoliy Lebedev has been murdered," said Fyodor Rostnikov.

He was holding something in his right hand.

After his expected phone calls, Rostnikov had hoped to read the *87th Precinct* novel he had brought with him, but it would have to wait until much later, if at any time.

"Where?"

"In the mines. His body, cut and sliced, was found by a night guard who heard a

173

noise. The guard had trouble locating the sound, echoes in the mines."

"When?"

"Not long, maybe half an hour ago. This was found next to the body."

Fyodor held up a lamp, an old covered oil lamp with a wire handle.

"Let us get Emil Karpo and become one of the people who walk in darkness."

CHAPTER NINE

"The restaurant. It was delivered to the restaurant an hour past."

The speaker was thin, no more than thirty years old, a deep ebony color. He had been one of the men who had engaged Iosef and Zelach in a gun battle and had barely gotten away. In the middle of the table at which he sat were wadded and crumpled remains of pages from *Pravda.* Resting on the paper was a finger — the small, black finger of a left hand. The curled finger was a matter of debate between the speaker, whose name was Patrice, and the other two young men at the table. They, too, had been in the gun battle.

The other two men were looking at Patrice for guidance, orders. The problem was that the finger on the table appeared to belong to James Harumbaki, their leader. In addition, the note left with the finger had said that both Umbaway and Roger were dead. The hierarchy was clear. Patrice was in charge, a position to which he did not aspire.

"You think they have killed Harumbaki?" asked the tallest of the three men.

Of the three, Biko looked most like a leader. He was erect, decisive in his language, prepared for whatever was to be done. The problem was that he had only one solution for any problem that emerged. Kill. Biko was more than a little crazy, and Patrice well knew it. Patrice also knew that Biko had two wives and six children under the age of ten.

"I don't think he is dead," said Patrice, who had no idea if what he was saying was true.

"He is not dead."

This came from the third man, short, bespectacled, and young, the youngest of the group, named Laurence. Laurence was seventeen. He looked fourteen. He was the most battle-experienced member of the group, having been a shirtless mercenary with a Kalashnikov when he was ten. Now he had an extended family of thirty people to support.

"That's not the finger of a dead man," said Laurence, adjusting his glasses. "I've removed fingers from the living."

"You can't be sure," said Patrice.

"I can," said Laurence.

"He is sure," said Biko.

"If we don't give them diamonds," said Laurence, "they will send us a toe."

"Or his penis," added Biko.

"No, that might kill him," said Laurence.

Biko and Laurence looked at Patrice, who stared at the finger and said, "Then we answer them by leaving a message. We set up an exchange location. We tell them they must bring James Harumbaki."

"We don't have the next shipment," said Biko.

"No," said Patrice.

"What do we give them?" asked Laurence, already knowing the answer.

"Bullets," said Patrice.

"James might be killed," said Biko.

"We might be killed," said Patrice.

"That is true," said Biko.

"We will give James's share of everything for three years to his family," said Patrice. "Agreed?"

"Agreed," the other two said in near unison.

Patrice was afraid but not for his own safety. He was afraid he would be killed fighting the people who had James. Then who would look after his parents and grand-father?

"Where do we meet them?" asked Laurence.

"The park," said Patrice.

"Which park?" asked Biko.

"East Gate Park on Kamiaken Street," said Patrice.

"I do not know it," said Biko.

"We had an exchange there under some statue when I first came to Moscow last year," said Laurence.

Patrice nodded to show that this was true.

"The statue is a good place," said Patrice. "It is quiet."

"See," said Kolokov, "it doesn't hurt much."

James Harumbaki saw little point in disputing the statement. In fact, the joint where his little finger had been removed really didn't hurt very much. The crazy, parading Russian had given him two pills and a bottle of vodka. James accepted both with whatever dignity he could muster.

The bar, owned by a trio of brothers who were well established inside of one of Moscow's most entrenched Mafias, was crowded. People were laughing, drinking, smoking. Music was blaring, causing a deep headache over James's right eye. Two very large-screen television sets were on, one over each end of the long bar.

Kolokov was circling the table, balancing a drink in his hand, talking loudly over the pain, which was almost worse than the loss of a finger.

"Do not worry," the Russian said, leaning over the table. "You can always grow another finger. Oh no, I forgot. People do not regrow toes and fingers, do they?"

Kolokov laughed.

James was flanked on either side by two of Kolokov's gang, one of them was the bald man, Montez, who kept his hand upon the Botswanan's leg.

"Do they?" Kolokov repeated leaning even closer.

"No," said James.

"No, that's right," Kolokov repeated. "They do not, but they can reattach them. All we have to do is get you and your finger . . . Oh, I forgot. I sent the finger to your friends. Pau, how long will a severed finger be usable?"

"A day or so," said Montez. "More if it is iced."

"Then," said Kolokov, "we had better get you back to your friends quickly, or you may never be able to play the pipe organ again."

"We should not be here," said Montez.

"Why not?" asked Kolokov, looking around. "Our guest is not going to try to run. It would be useless and very painful. And he is not going to ask anyone here for help. Who here would help him? Do you see another single black face?"

Silence.

"Answer."

"No," said Montez.

"We are celebrating," said Kolokov. "The friends of our guest have agreed to turn over to us a fortune in diamonds to get our guest back almost in one piece."

"I don't trust them," said Igor.

"Of course not," said Kolokov. "They mean to . . . what do the Americans call it . . . double crucifix us. I would. They will try. When they do, we remove another one of the fingers of our friend here. He gets weaker. We try again. Being a criminal is not an easy job."

Some fresh music blared and a woman, pretty, in her forties, with large breasts, wearing a sleek black dress, climbed on a small stage and began to sing in Russian.

"What is that song?" asked Kolokov.

" 'Bad Moon Rising.' "

"I know it, but she is destroying it."

Kolokov moved through the crowded tables and climbed onto the stage next to the singing woman. James tested the grip of the bald man. As soon as James moved no more than a twitch, the Spaniard's fingers dug deeply into his thigh.

"No," said Montez.

James went nearly limp. His bloody finger had been rinsed with alcohol and wiped with a towel of doubtful cleanliness. The tape over a small square of bandage was clinging without conviction to his finger.

Kolokov sang. The woman in the black dress sulked as he nudged in front of her at the microphone. When he had taken the microphone, the bar patrons who were listening had hooted for him to sit down, but they quickly discovered that Kolokov was more than adequate. He was good. He tapped his foot, held the microphone almost touching his lips, and belted out the music. Hoots turned to cheers.

The three men at the table with James tried to disassociate themselves from their leader. He was a clown, a buffoon. But he was also fearless and smart — at least smarter than they were.

And then James made a decision. His arms and legs were strong, very strong. The big man at his side could probably crush him, but James surprised him with his sudden strength. James pulled out of his grasp, threw his elbow into the mouth of the man on the other side of him, and dumped the table and its contents into the face and lap of the third Russian.

Then James ran for the door, leaping over a table.

The three Russians and the Spaniard were up, but behind in the chase. No one seemed to care or notice very much. Kolokov registered the uproar but kept singing until he saw James dashing for the exit.

James felt light-headed, but he kept running. At the door, he paused for no more than a quick beat to keep from colliding with Iosef and Zelach, who had just entered. James dashed past them into the night. The pursuers were only a few steps behind.

The pursuers bumped into Iosef and Zelach, and tried to push them out of the way. Both of the detectives grabbed a pursuer. Iosef slammed Alek against the wall. Zelach punched the hip of Bogdan. Bogdan went down with a wailing groan. Montez ran into the night, followed by the wheezing Kolokov. One of the men now on the floor reached into his jacket. Iosef said, "No," and held up the gun in his hand.

Much attention was now being paid to the scene by patrons and the band on the stage.

"What's this?" said a bodybuilder type

with an accent Iosef thought might be Bulgarian.

"We're the police," said Iosef.

"So?" asked the bouncer.

"We're looking for some black men," said Iosef.

"One just ran out of here," said the bodybuilder. "If you hurry, you can catch him."

"He's not the one we are looking for," said Iosef, looking at Zelach.

Zelach shook his head no. The man who had run from the bar was definitely not one of those with whom they had the shootout this afternoon. The detectives had been to five bars based on a vague suggestion by the restaurant owner, Maticonay, who had been shot. Iosef had begun to feel that they had been lied to until they came to this place.

"Let's take these two out of here for a talk," said Iosef.

The bodybuilder shrugged. It was not his business. He did not even care if they were really the police. He was paid to keep the place relatively calm. He swaggered away as the two policemen helped the men to their feet.

"That business with the knuckles to the hip," said Iosef, "where did you get that?"

"Pressure point," said Zelach. "I've been studying a tape, practicing."

"On your mother?"

"No. On myself."

"You are a man of many talents, Detective."

"Thank you."

"We can . . ." Iosef began, but did not finish.

There was a gunshot outside, down the street. The detectives immediately abandoned their prisoners and dashed into the night. The two fallen Russians rose and went through the door after them.

"Wait," said Alek, holding out his hand.

"What? It came from that way."

"Why don't we go that way?" asked Alek.

He was pointing in the opposite direction.

"Yes," said Bogdan.

"If Kolokov gets back, we tell him we escaped from the police."

"Yes, that is what happened," said Bogdan, already believing the lie.

"Two of them," said Detective Jan Pendowski as he sat feeding seeds to big, ugly, gray-black crows from a bench on Venetsiansky Island in Hydropark.

They could hear the balls bouncing on the tables in the Ping-Pong area beyond a mesh fence a few dozen yards away. On nice days like this in Kiev, Jan liked to come out

184

and watch the college girls bouncing under their thin shirts as they swatted at the balls.

"Two," said Oxana.

She sat next to him touching a fingernail to her lower lip, where she sensed an imperfection in her makeup. As much as Jan liked looking at the young girls, Oxana Balakona liked to be looked at by males of all ages as they walked by. She had become a model because it had been what she always wanted to be: admired, looked at, wanted.

"A man and woman," said Jan. "Moscow detectives. They are looking for you."

Oxana turned to face him as he hurled a handful of seeds at a bird near his feet. The bird retreated, not sure if it was being attacked or rewarded.

"Me?"

"It appears that the woman who gave you the diamonds has been murdered."

He had her full attention now, but he did not look her way. The Ping-Pong balls and the laughter of girls beyond the fence was all-powerful.

"Murdered," she repeated.

It struck Jan, and not for the first time, that while Oxana was clever, she was not terribly smart. She frequently repeated whatever he said as if she were mulling it over or using it as a question.

"The diamonds," he said. "They are here looking for them. We must get them to Paris quickly. The two Moscow detectives will find you here. It will not take them long. I'll guide them in a long search for wild ducks but they will find you if you are here, and going back to Moscow does not strike me as a viable option. They will find you even more easily there."

"So, Paris quickly," she said, deciding to stare down a boy of no more than seventeen who couldn't help openly and longingly examining her.

"I have something to tell you," she said. "Something that is amazingly lucky."

"See that one?" he asked, pointing at a bird slightly smaller than the other dozen or so that circled before him on the ground, scurrying out of each other's way. "Lost an eye. A fight, or disease."

"Disease," said Oxana. "A fashion editor at *Paris Match* wants me to go to Paris with her tomorrow or the next day for a fashion layout. Perfect cover."

"How did she find you, this fashion editor?"

"An agency here."

"She came all the way to Kiev just to find you?"

"She was here anyway," said Oxana. "And

why would not a fashion editor come here for me? I am one of the very best."

"I know," he said. "I have my own experience of that."

She allowed herself a small smile.

"I think I should like to meet this famous editor," Jan went on, digging into the small white paper bag on his lap for the last of the seeds. "Before we send you off with her and the diamonds."

"It can be arranged," said Oxana.

"I have the Moscow detectives today. I shall run them to every corner of Kiev and back. What is the name of your editor?"

"Rochelle Tanquay," she said. "She gave me a card. Here."

Oxana reached into her small, quite fashionable red leather purse and handed it to him. On it was the name of the woman in gold script and a cell phone number.

"Call her," he said. "Set up a time. Late night at Eric's Bar."

"What do I tell her?"

"That you want her to meet your fiancé, your handsome Ukrainian police detective. What does your Rochelle look like?"

"Pretty," said Oxana.

"Better than ugly," he said. "Call."

She took a sky blue ultra-thin cell phone from her purse and punched in the number on the card Jan held up for her.

Four rings and then, "Hello."

"It's Oxana."

"Yes. Can you leave tomorrow evening? The photographer will be available most of next week, and then he has to go to Bahrain."

"Of course. Can we get together tonight for drinks?"

"I've got a dinner meeting," said Rochelle. "It will have to be late."

"Late is fine. Do you know Eric's Bar, across the street from the Kinotheater Kiev on Chervonarmiyska Street?"

"I'll find it. What time?"

"What time?" Oxana repeated looking at Jan.

He held up ten fingers and then another one.

"Eleven?"

"Eleven," said Rochelle.

"I'll bring my fiancé," said Oxana. "He's a policeman. He would very much like to meet you."

Jan nodded yes.

"Perfect," said Rochelle. "Eleven at Eric's Bar. I look forward to it."

The call ended, and Oxana returned the phone to her purse as Jan crumpled the empty white bag and dropped it into the metal trash container to his right. He got up. So did she.

Balta watched them walk down the path together. He was reclining on a blanket under a tree about fifty yards away. In front of him was a gathering of six old men watching two other old men playing chess on a park bench. They provided near perfect cover.

Balta decided to follow the man with Oxana. At the moment he looked like someone for whom he should have some concern. Balta had no doubt that he could handle the man if it were necessary or if it would help get the diamonds. And he felt that this just might be the case.

He welcomed the challenge.

The street was almost empty. The few people James Harumbaki passed were drunken men and a woman who clutched her purse as he approached from behind her. She looked over her shoulder, saw this black man with his mouth open panting behind her, and pressed herself against the wall, searching inside her oversized bag for the knife her husband had given her for things like this.

James saw the fear in her eyes and simply kept running, losing blood from the stub of his finger, leaving a red trail as he bled through the cloth napkin he had snatched from the table in the bar.

It was not easy to will the world back into submission. He tried as he trod on, no longer running, not looking back over his shoulder. There was no need.

Even with his loss of blood, the out-of-shape Russians were no match for the lean, athletic Botswanan. Still, he could hear someone coming behind him. James had no idea where he was running. His thought now was to get out of sight of his pursuer, hide until daylight, hope that he could stop the bleeding, and perhaps even get back to Patrice and the others and reunite with his missing finger.

His run was now a slow shuffle. He chanced a glance over his left shoulder. There came a large man.

The man was jogging steadily. He was not one of the three Russians who had taken him prisoner, killed his friends, and cut off his finger. This man was fully clothed and determined, and definitely not out for a jog.

James willed himself to hurry. His body did not respond. He turned and spread his legs to meet the man who was coming. Maybe he could surprise the man, kick him between the legs, break his collarbone with a blow to the neck. The options were not good, but at least there were options.

The man was closing. Far behind him, in the light from a street lamp, was another man, a slouching creature who reminded James less of a man at this distance than of a monster.

The pursuer closed in now.

Then there was the sound of a car behind the man. James saw headlights coming closer. The car screeched as it changed gears. James headed for the sidewalk.

The car almost hit the pursuing man and skidded to a stop in the street next to James. The back door of the old Zil opened.

James knew the car. He had ridden in it to the bar.

No escape. He looked at the man coming down the street and could see now that the man was holding a gun.

"*Kuda namylilsja.* Where do you think you are going? Get in now you black son of a bitch," shouted Kolokov.

"I had that audience and you took it from me. Now I think I'll take something from you."

The man in the street with a gun, no more than twenty yards away now, shouted, "Stop."

James went through the open door of the car.

Iosef fired a shot, and then another as the car in front of him took off down the street. When it had turned a corner, Zelach appeared at his side. Unlike Iosef, Zelach didn't appear to be breathing hard.

"I thought you do not work out," said Iosef, panting.

"I do not."

"Are you even sweating?"

"No," said Zelach. "Yoga."

"You do yoga?"

Iosef was looking down at the trail of blood he had been following.

"Yes. My mother, too. She taught me."

"Maybe she will teach me."

"I'm sure she would," said Zelach.

"Good. Now we must find the people in that car."

"How?"

"The Botswanans."

Sasha Tkach was afraid.

He moved slowly up the dark, narrow wooden stairway in the old three-story building that had once housed the offices of the Voluntary Collective of Sewing Machine Operators. The stairway was dark. The steps creaked with each step he took.

The building had been converted to
ments more than half a century ag
conversion had been far less than su
ful. Some of the apartments were sma
single rooms of unimpressive size.
were four rooms of varying sizes.

Sasha moved to the door he was se
took a deep breath, brushed back hi
smelled his breath against the palm
hand, and knocked.

He had left his gun in the hotel
provided by Jan Pendowski and the
Police Department's Smuggling Di
He had put on his primary change of
ing, told Elena, who was in the roon
to his, that he was going out, and ma
way to this building, to this door.

He knocked again and thought he h
woman humming. She sounded happ
sound of happiness was not a good si

"Yes?" she asked.

"It is me," Sasha said.

There was a beat. Then the door o
and there stood Maya, looking small,
a brush poised touching her long, dark

"You are here," she said.

Had he hoped for a look of forgiven
even a tiny smile of appreciation, he v
have been disappointed.

"I am here," he said.

"Why?"

"May I come in?"

She considered, let her hand with the brush drop to her side and answered, "No. Yes. Come in."

She was wearing a pale green dress he did not recognize. Around her neck was a strand of small, glittering glass pieces that looked like diamonds. Sasha had given the strand to her as one of the many peace offers made over the years for his inevitable transgressions. Was there hope in it being around her neck?

She stepped back, let him enter, and closed the door.

"The children?" he asked, looking around the room brightly lit with aluminum floor lamps and scattered with unmatched furniture.

"They are with Masha tonight. I am sorry. I did not know you were coming to Kiev."

He waited for her to offer him a seat. She did not.

"Perhaps tomorrow," he said.

"You came to Kiev to see the children?"

"And you, and because of a case. Elena is here with me."

"Give her my best."

"Would you like to see her?"

"No. I was about to go out."

"I see. Maya, I have changed."

"Into what?"

There was a bitterness in her voice he did not recognize and did not like. He had interviewed too many people, particularly women, not to recognize what she was doing.

"Who is it?" he asked.

Maya's shoulders drooped, but only slightly. She looked at the brush in her hand and then at the wall, wishing that perhaps it would provide some counsel.

"I am going to dinner with a man from my office."

"The Japanese?"

In response to his history of infidelity, a little more than two years ago Maya had begun a brief affair with an older, married Japanese executive with the company for which she worked.

"No. I have not seen him since . . ."

"Are you going to come back to Moscow with the children? I do not mean right away, though that would be . . ."

"I am not coming back to Moscow," she said softly. "You are not going to change. I don't want to spend any more years trying with you and failing."

"Would it cost so much to try once more?"

"Too much," she said. "How long are you

planning to be in Kiev?"

"Not long."

"Can you come back tomorrow morning to see the children before I go to work?"

"Yes."

"Eight o'clock."

She looked at the door again and then at her watch. He knew why she was doing both. He should have made an effort to make the situation easier for her, but he could not bring himself to do it.

And then a knock came, startling Maya who looked around for someplace to put her brush. She settled for a small round table with a surface the size of a dinner plate.

Another knock. She looked at Sasha, trying to decide whether she would choose defiance or pleading. She decided on a plea. Sasha closed his eyes and nodded in acceptance of a truce with good grace.

Maya opened the door. The man was not impressive. He was slightly shorter than Sasha, at least a decade older, his gray hair thinning significantly. His face showed weathering and suggested reliability. He wore a knowing smile and a very neatly pressed blue suit, white shirt, and a tie that hinted at old English school.

The man kissed her cheek before she

could back away and close the door.

"This is my husband, Sasha," she said, folding her hands knuckle white in front of her. "Sasha, this is Anders."

The two men shook hands, and Maya said, "I did not know Sasha was in Kiev till he knocked at the door a few minutes ago."

Anders nodded and smiled.

"I have heard a great deal about you," Anders said in only slightly accented Russian.

"I have heard nothing about you," said Sasha.

"Maya and I work together. I'm Swedish, forty-five, reasonably healthy, a lawyer, unmarried."

"And you tell me all this, why?"

"Because I want to marry your wife and raise your children."

"What has she told you about me?"

"Sasha," Maya pleaded.

"That you love her, are a fine father, and a good but immature and very unreliable man," Anders said.

Sasha nodded. The assessment was accurate. Sasha liked the man. This encounter would have been so much easier if he could see something in Anders that he could attack, but he saw and felt nothing.

"Yes," said Sasha.

"I think you should go now, Sasha," Maya said, touching his sleeve.

He looked down at her hand, willing it to stay where it was, knowing his will had no effect on her and had not for a long, long time.

"We should go too," Maya said softly. "Come by in the morning, Sasha."

Sasha nodded. He suddenly had questions that he knew he could not ask: Did she love this man?

"Tomorrow," he said, taking Anders's offered hand and then moving to the door.

When the door had closed behind him, Sasha heard their voices but he could not make out what they were saying.

Gerald St. James listened calmly to the caller and with his free hand popped a ripe, black Greek olive into his mouth. After listening for a few minutes, he said, "No more killings."

"No more are needed," said the caller.

"That is for me to determine. It was for me to determine before you disposed of, what's his name?"

"Lebedev."

"Lebedev. The policeman from Moscow? Is he competent?"

"Yes."

"Meaning he could cause a great deal of damage."

"Yes."

"But if he were killed, they would send another."

"But not one so competent, probably."

"Keep me informed, and I may revise my order."

"To . . . ?"

"Refrain from killing. This has become very messy. I don't like things messy."

The caller knew that in his younger days, when Gerald St. James was a Bulgarian street robber, killing had been very messy.

"If it is necessary, it will not be messy."

"Good."

St. James hung up. Let the caller worry about it. The entire operation was not going smoothly. The murders at Devochka were drawing too much police attention. The termination of the Botswanan connection in Moscow had run into problems. The recovery of the transported diamonds in Kiev was at best incomplete.

St. James was alone in the house in Kensington-Highgate. His very English wife was visiting friends for the weekend. One of those friends was Vikki Thorpe. Vikki's husband was Sir Charles Thorpe, former head of the British consulate in northern

Russia, the area which included all of Siberia.

Gerald St. James would get up in the morning, drive himself to pick up his wife, and conveniently run into Sir Charles. Gerald had a proposal he wished to make, a very subtle proposal which he hoped the sometimes-obtuse member of the House of Lords was capable of understanding.

Weak links, weak links, weak links. Balta was an expert in finding weak links, be they in the personalities of those he stalked or worked with or those at the base of their necks that invited the blade.

Balta didn't enjoy killing. It was simply something he did well. Other people's dying was his living. The question now, as he lay naked in bed after a hot shower, was: who was the weak link, and who might he have to kill.

Oxana would give everything up with the threat of a sharp razor stroke across her cheek. He would not even have to kill her, though if he went that way he might as well.

The policeman on the park bench, the one she was working with and certainly sleeping with, was a good choice. He was probably a pragmatist who would give up the diamonds in the hope of living another day, going on to something else or going after Balta. Balta would have to find out, meet with the policeman, probe his weakness.

It would all be decided in the morning.

He checked his watch. It was time. He had to make his call. He was sure that his cell phone was fully charged.

As he placed his call, Balta moved before the full-length mirror behind the hotel room door. It amused him to wonder what St. James would think if he knew Balta was admiring his naked body in the mirror while he talked to him on the phone.

"Yes," St. James said after the second ring.

"I'm in Kiev. I have not found the diamonds yet. Tomorrow perhaps. I do have the money."

"Where are you?"

"Premier Palace Hotel."

"Keep me informed."

Balta went back to the bed. He had peeled back the blanket and laid on the sheets still damp from the touch of his body after the shower. He would give the money to St. James, but he would report that he had been unable to find the diamonds though he had tortured and killed both the policeman and the model. He had every intention of getting the diamonds. He had no intention of giving them to "Sir" Gerald St. James. Balta would take them to Paris, where the buyer was waiting. And with his wealth, he would go to the United States, where opportunities suitable for his talents awaited him.

CHAPTER TEN

"January 7, 1951, 11:52 p.m. Report by Serge Vortz, Soviet Party Commissar, Devochka Mine."

Fyodor Rostnikov, glasses well down his nose, read from the thin black plastic-covered document.

He looked up at Porfiry Petrovich, who nodded at him across the desk, urging him to continue to read the report.

They were sitting in the same small meeting room where the Moscow detectives had sat the day before with the elected board of the town and mine. With the murder of Anatoliy Lebedev, the board was now reduced to four.

In front of Karpo who, as always, sat erect, dressed in black, ignoring the beam of sunlight that streaked past his face, was a mug of hot water. Before Fyodor and Porfiry Petrovich were mugs of strong black tea. All the mugs were white with pictures of a young Linda Ronstadt smiling up at them.

Emil Karpo had spent two futile nights in the cafeteria drinking tea, watching and listening to the few people who approached him. Though everyone acted suspiciously, none was clearly guilty of two murders.

"I was in the shaft," Fedya continued reading.

Shift Leader and Mine Safety Director Ivan Memendov was ahead of me in Tunnel Number Three, investigating a shifting of rock reported by Mining Crew Four.

Porfiry Petrovich, sharpened pencil in hand and pad of paper before him, wondered how he was going to finish the drawing upon which he was working. The drawing was of the room in which they were sitting. Karpo and Fyodor were rapidly scratched faceless images but seated upon the table a creature of no clear species crouched, ready to leap out of the drawing. Porfiry Petrovich was intrigued.

"After precisely seven minutes of waiting . . ."

Fyodor looked up over his glasses at the two detectives. It was highly unlikely that Commissar Vortz would know the precise time of waiting, which suggested to the three men that the commissar was covering his ass. If he were, it was unwise to report what happened next.

> I heard singing coming from Tunnel Number Three. The voice sounded like that of a young child, a girl. Then I heard a scream, not that of a child. I was about to enter the tunnel . . .

Another incredulous look from Fyodor. Karpo showed nothing. Porfiry Petrovich was busy with his drawing. Fyodor went on:

> . . . however I did not have the opportunity. I heard something rushing toward me from the tunnel. I assumed it was Ivan Memendov who may have been injured. I saw a light coming toward me and then saw a figure emerge, the figure of a completely naked girl of no more than ten. She was carrying an old kerosene lantern, the kind no longer used. I saw her clearly coming at me, and then she ran toward the mine entrance. She was too fast for me to catch. I have been suffering from a debilitating, recurrent injury received in the defense of Leningrad, for which I was decorated.
> Using my flashlight I went quickly into

the tunnel and discovered the body of Shift Leader and Mine Safety Director Ivan Memendov. Later examination by Devochka Physician Oleg Dubinin revealed that he had been stabbed at least eight times.

"It is signed," said Fyodor. "Commissar Vortz was reassigned to a Gulag under suspicion that he had killed the Mine Safety Director over an old feud about the provision of fuel and then made up the ridiculous story about the ghost girl because he knew the lore about such sightings."

"And there are three more reports about seeing this ghost girl," said Karpo.

"Yes," said Fyodor, "a total of six from 1963 till yesterday."

Porfiry Petrovich had finished his drawing. He held it out to look at without trying to understand what he was seeing.

"May I see the report?" he asked.

It could have been given as an order, but it was delivered as a polite request, which Fyodor honored.

Porfiry Petrovich took the report, opened it, and saw that it had been written on a typewriter whose ink roll had been reused almost once too often. In addition, the carriage had slipped and the upper third of each letter was in a red almost as faint as the black below it. He took a sip of his tea and asked, "Do you note something very strange about this report?"

"I notice very little that is not strange," said Fyodor.

Rostnikov handed the report to Karpo, who began to read.

"Why is the girl naked?" asked Karpo.

"Precisely," said Rostnikov. "Why is the beast on the table, and why is the girl running naked?"

"Beast on the table?" asked Fyodor.

"Never mind," said Porfiry Petrovich. "I am sorry. Emil Karpo asked . . ."

"Why is the ghost girl running naked?" Karpo repeated.

"Because," Fyodor said removing his glasses, "she is a ghost, or she is supposed to be a ghost, and ghosts do very strange things."

"When was the last time, before this morning, that you read this report?"

"I've never read it before this morning," said Fyodor. "It was in the retired files of the Director. You asked to see all reports of suspicious deaths in the mine and any mention of the ghost girl."

"I have a whim," said Porfiry Petrovich. "I would like a search, supervised and conducted by you, Emil, of the entire town, room by room, hiding place by hiding place."

"What are we looking for?" asked Fyodor.

"An old typewriter with a very worn ribbon."

"And you expect the typewriter on which this report was written still to be in use, or functional, and still to have the same ribbon?" asked Fyodor.

"I think it possible this report was written very recently," said Porfiry Petrovich.

"Why?" asked Fyodor.

"That I do not yet know."

But he did know. The key to two murders, he was sure, was the ghost girl.

"And what of my other requests?"

"Boris Gailov, the old man who was with the Canadian in the mine, is waiting in the hall whenever you wish to talk to him," said Fyodor, "but, as I told you, he is not a reliable witness. He's seventy-eight years old and he is more than a little mad from working in the mine for half a century."

"Then why," asked Karpo, "was he sent down to serve as a guide for the Canadian?"

"He volunteered," said Fyodor. "No one expected trouble."

"The list I requested of all girls in Devochka between the ages of six and eighteen?"

Fyodor took off his glasses, and handed Rostnikov two sheets of paper on which were written the names of seventy-two girls. The names were numbered.

"I've indicated the ages of each girl and have added lists of girls between the ages of three and five and eighteen to twenty. I've also indicated, as you can see, where each girl was at the time of the death of the Canadian. I'm still working on where they were last night when Anatoliy Lebedev was murdered."

"How many definitely could not have been in the mine when the Canadian was killed?"

"Fifty-two are completely accounted for," said Fyodor.

"Still a long list. I would like to see each girl."

"And their parents?"

"No, not yet."

"When?"

"As soon as I finish talking to Boris Gailov. What animal do you think this is?"

Fyodor put his glasses back on. Karpo turned his head to see.

"None that I recognize," said Karpo.

"Let's see," said Fyodor, biting his lower lip gently, and tilting his head from side to side. "It's a very large, hairy man with long teeth. Maybe it's a werewolf."

"Maybe," said Rostnikov. "What happens when a werewolf eats diamonds?"

"Its throat, stomach, and bowels can be torn to pieces," said Fyodor. "Or then again, nothing may happen."

"I have drawn a diamond eater," said Porfiry Petrovich.

"Shall we go out and search for him?" asked Fyodor.

He wasn't smiling. Porfiry Petrovich liked that his brother wasn't smiling. Some jests were not meant to be smiled at.

It was the third day, and the list was long. He would have to call Yaklovev shortly. As yet he had nothing to report. He looked at the drawing again and said, "Let us get back to work."

Karpo and Fyodor stood and went to the door. Porfiry Petrovich did not move. Karpo knew why — Rostnikov's leg. It had been bothering him lately. He had been moving more slowly, rising more cautiously, climbing steps more tentatively.

"Leave the door open, please, and send in Boris Gailov," he requested as the two men moved off in search of a typewriter.

Through the open door, Rostnikov could see an old man seated on a metal folding chair in the hallway. The man was pale, gray, and in need of a decision about whether to shave or grow a beard. The man, still over six feet tall in spite of his age, was lean and gnarled. His fingers were crippled by arthritis, and his back was permanently bent over.

"Boris Gailov, please come in and close the door behind you."

The old man rose slowly, entered the room, and closed the door. Rostnikov motioned for the old man to take a seat across the table.

"I am going to move to St. Petersburg," Boris said, his voice a crisp rasp.

"You have relatives there?" Rostnikov said, ignoring the non sequitur.

"No, never. That is why I want to go there. Here, I have relatives. Two sons, three grandsons, a daughter, granddaughters. I don't remember their names. I don't even remember how many there are. In St. Petersburg I can get a little room somewhere and live on my pension, just watch television, eat sandwiches, and wash and rinse my clothes."

"It sounds idyllic," said Porfiry Petrovich.

Boris looked at Rostnikov suspiciously.

"It sounds wonderful. Paradise," the detective said with sincerity.

"There is no Paradise."

"I know," said Rostnikov.

"You want me to tell you about the Canadian."

"And the ghost girl."

"There is no ghost girl," Boris said emphatically.

"I know, but you saw something. You saw a girl with a lantern."

"I did not."

"Yes, you did."

"If I say I did, I go to the asylum instead of St. Petersburg."

"No, you do not. Tell me, what does this look like to you?"

Rostnikov held up his drawing.

The old man squinted at the drawing and said,

"A large dog sitting on this table."

"You have trouble seeing."

"I have trouble picking up a spoon, but I don't complain about it," Boris said with pride.

"I have one leg," said Rostnikov.

"When I was young, men came home without arms, legs, eyes. They also came home with the teeth and bones and weapons of dead Germans."

"You came here in 1949," said Rostnikov.

"July fifteenth, a day of rain and sorrow," said Boris. "Do you know why I came here?"

"Your file says you came here because you

212

were hungry, and there was recruiting for Siberian mine workers."

"They said I was crazy," said Boris. "I was seventeen. Everyone else was being sent here for political crimes. I came to get something to eat every day. And I did. I haven't starved, and I've raised a large family."

"Which you now want to get away from," said Rostnikov.

"Yes."

"Tell me about going into the mine with the Canadian. Who picked you to go into the mine with him?"

"I do not know. A man. I got a call. Said, 'Boris, there is a Canadian needs a guide in the mine. Meet him in front of the mine entrance.' I got dressed. I did what I was told. I always do what I'm told. I hate doing what I'm told. At this point in my life, I do not like anybody."

"The ghost girl?" asked Rostnikov.

"They're all afraid to talk about the ghost girl, but why should I be? I'm ninety years old. I can say what I please."

"You are seventy-eight," Rostnikov corrected.

"And you have one leg. Let me see it."

Rostnikov slid his chair back and pulled up his left pant leg. Boris stood and leaned over, twisted knuckles on the table, mouth open.

"Like on television," said Boris.

"Just like it," said Rostnikov, having no idea what the old man was talking about. "Would you tell me about the ghost child now?"

"Why not?"

"Please."

"I take the American . . ."

"Canadian."

"Canadian, yes," said Boris. "I take this Amer . . . Canadian into the mine. My English? Not good. Canada grumbled, growls all the time. All the time. I take him to the tunnel he wants and wait while he goes in. I hear a noise."

"Noise?"

"You know. Something clanking, noise. Down there you can hear someone farting two hundred feet away."

"He farted?"

Boris looked at the barrel-shaped detective.

"No, he did not fart. All right if I continue? I am getting older with the passing of each minute. You want me dropping dead right in here?"

"Please do not drop dead," Rostnikov said politely.

Boris had not forgotten where he was in his tale.

"I hear the noise. Then I hear singing. Then I . . . see the ghost coming toward me from the tunnel."

"What was the ghost singing?"

Boris burst into gravelly song.

" 'The Po ulitse mastavoi.' *Along the paved road there went a girl to fetch water, there went a girl to fetch water, to fetch the cold spring water. Behind her a young lad shouted 'Girl, stand still. Girl, stand still. Let's have a little talk.' "*

"You saw her?"

"She hurried by me, holding her lantern at her side."

"She wore?"

"A dress, a nice one buttoned at the neck. Chaste, very chaste. I think it was blue, but in the light in the mines here it is difficult to be sure of the color. Everything looks green."

"The two men who were in here when you came in, what were they wearing?"

"Games? You're playing games with me now?"

"No," said Rostnikov. "I would like to know."

"Tall one," Boris said. "He was wearing black socks, black pants, black shoes, black jacket, and a black look, as if it were he who had seen the ghost."

"And the other man?"

"He looked like you with a beard. That was Fyodor Rostnikov, Director of Security, your brother. Everyone knows that."

"The ghost girl, did she look like any child in Devochka?"

Boris looked at Porfiry Petrovich with a compassion he usually reserved for those of limited intellect.

"She was a ghost."

"Could you identify the ghost girl if you saw her again?"

"No."

"No? Why?"

"I am not a fool," said Boris. "People take me for one, but I'm not a fool. Whoever this ghost girl is, it would not be healthy, if she is not a ghost, to identify her if I saw her."

"You could be arrested for refusing."

"And then what would you do? Send me to Siberia?"

Rostnikov laughed, clapped his hands together noiselessly three times, and then clasped them together.

"I guarantee nothing will happen to you if you identify the girl. I'll arrange for you to move to St. Petersburg."

"Just pack a bag, get on an airplane, and

get out?"

"That can be arranged."

"I will identify her if I see her, but I would have to look at all the girls here to be sure. I have not memorized the face of every child in this place. I will identify her if I see her again."

"Good," said Rostnikov, standing to alter the stiffening of his leg. "I will arrange for every girl in Devochka to be in the meeting room later today. Tell no one what we are doing."

Boris rose.

"Be careful," said Rostnikov.

Boris leaned forward to whisper, "I have a gun."

Rostnikov held a finger to his lips to warn the old man to keep that information quiet.

"One question," said Boris.

"Ask."

"Can you dance with only one leg?"

"I do not know. I have never tried."

"Try," said Boris.

When he was gone, Porfiry Petrovich gathered his drawings and stood. With the door still closed, he hummed one of the peppier Sarah Vaughan songs he listened to when he worked out. As he was humming, he attempted to take a few dance-like steps. It was not bad. He tried a few more and hummed a bit louder.

His back was to the door when it opened silently. Emil Karpo and Fyodor Rostnikov stood in the open doorway, witnessing Rostnikov's dance. Rostnikov sensed their presence, stopped dancing, and turned to face them.

"I was dancing," Rostnikov said.

"Yes," said Karpo.

"You should try it."

"I think not."

Rostnikov tried to imagine the man dancing. It was impossible except for a macabre shuffling of the feet that conjured up the image of a humorless zombie lurching slowly forward.

"I agree."

"We found the typewriter," said Fyodor.

"It must not have been well hidden. It took you all of thirty minutes."

"It was in plain sight."

"Where?"

"On my bed," said Fyodor.

He should not have let the Moscow policeman find the typewriter. He should not be playing games with this.

Did he want to get caught? No. The policeman would have figured it out in any case. He was smart, this barrel of a policeman. It would not have taken him very long to figure out that the report had not only been altered, but written completely anew. Let Rostnikov wonder why the typewriter had been placed where it could so easily be found. The question was, what was in this replacement report that would provide Rostnikov with the information he needed. It was simple, clear, right in the report. One word.

This killer had one more murder to commit and then he would stop, melt back into the community, into his work.

He would have to go back into the mine, close and seal the small cave where he had found the vein of diamonds that he had been mining and shipping to the Botswanans in Moscow. The Canadian and Lebedev had found the cave. No one else must find it.

Tonight. Late tonight. There would be but one guard. He hoped it would not be Misha Planck or Leo Kamikayanski. He liked them both. He did not wish to kill either man, but it might have to be done.

One final shipment of diamonds to Moscow.

Just one more shipment and he would tell St. James in his London tower that he would no longer steal or murder.

Just one more.

The teacher asked a question. The child had not been listening. Instead the child had been singing an internal song, the song of the mine.

"Along the paved road, there went a girl to fetch water."

The child had no idea what the question was. Other children watched. The teacher repeated the question.

"Who was Abraham Lincoln?"

"An American President."

"What do you know about him?" asked the teacher.

"He was responsible for a bloody suppression of a revolution by the southern states of America," answered the child.

"The result?"

"Darkness. Lincoln held up a lamp and frightened faces were revealed."

"Imaginative," said the teacher, "but I would prefer a more conventional answer."

The child had none.

CHAPTER ELEVEN

"Okay, let's do it this way."

Kolokov was pacing around the room. With almost every step the buckled once-yellow linoleum on the floor crackled like the shell of a Botswanan click beetle.

James was now tied to a white plastic chair. Electrical cord bound his wrists behind his back, eliminating all but minimal circulation. The faces of Kolokov and the bald man named Montez offered no sympathy.

The room was large, the former kitchen of a dacha that had once belonged to the member of the Duma designated as Commissar of Transportation. The Commissar was dead, murdered by one of his assistants, named Rasmusen, who wished to show the newly minted Yeltsin government his hatred of the Communist regime.

Now the dacha was abandoned, too close to the city to be considered a reasonable getaway by those who could now afford it, too expensive to restore for those who might consider it.

The rusting pipes groaned. The wooden walls cracked. The linoleum floor buckled.

"Do I blame you for trying to get away?" Kolokov went on, expecting no answer and getting none. "No. I would have done the same. But I must have cooperation."

He stopped pacing and looked at James, whose eyes were fixed straight ahead. He could endure his numb hands and the broken nose the Russian had given him. He could go without food. He had done it many times before, in Africa. What he could not tolerate was the smell of decay and cheap tobacco that came out of the mouth of Kolokov when he placed his face a few inches from James's, as he did now.

"Cooperation," Kolokov continued.

James gave no reaction.

"Are you listening? If you are not listening, if you are not cooperating, what use are you to me? That is a real question. Answer it or you die."

"I am listening," said James.

"Good," said Kolokov, looking at the bald man and allowing himself a small smile of success. "You will call your friends. You will tell them to be in front of the Eternal Flame by the Tomb of the Unknown Warrior at the Moscow War Memorial in Alexandrovsky Gardens at ten o'clock tonight. They will have with them either a sizable package of diamonds or an even one . . ."

He looked at the bald man who stared blankly back.

". . . no, two million euros. Cash," Kolokov continued. "You understand?"

"Yes," said James.

James was having trouble breathing. Kolokov had smashed his nose, blocking off all air. James could only breathe through his swollen mouth.

"You know what happens if you try to escape again?"

"Yes."

"Are you hungry?"

"No."

"Thirsty?"

"No," James lied.

"I killed your companions because they would not tell me how to reach your friends, but you are cooperating. I have no reason to kill you. I am not a monster."

Kolokov lit a cigarette, pursed his lips, and added, "Now I think I will buy a bar in Zvenigorod. There is one whose bar I would gladly stand behind, within view of the monastery. Perhaps Montez and I could persuade the present owners to sell. What do you think?"

"Yes," said James.

"Yes? That is not a thought."

"You can probably convince the owners to sell," said James.

The bald Montez moved. Yes, like a big, dark click beetle after an hour of dormancy, he moved the right hand at his side and came up with a cell phone.

"Now, you make the call."

Montez flipped open the phone and brought it in front of James.

"The number," said Kolokov.

James told him the number, and the Spaniard pressed it into the keypad. Montez placed the phone close enough to James's face that he could speak into it. There was but one ring before the phone was answered. James gave the man who answered it a succinct message that ended with, "and bring with you either the last shipment of diamonds or two million euros."

"Yes," said the man.

"And do no try to free me," said James. "I am all right."

"We will not try to free you. We will bring the money or the diamonds."

Both were lies. James knew there was no

way two million euros could be obtained. Nor could they or would they try to raise the money. They could not deliver the diamonds. The diamonds had already been delivered to the woman in Kiev. The courier had been murdered and the murderer had stolen the payment.

There promised to be bloodshed at the War Memorial.

James hoped that the blood would be that of his captors.

"Are we going to have trouble?" asked Zelach, slouching through the door of the tiny grocery.

Behind the counter stood a black colossus of a woman wearing a red and white bandana on her head. She was serving a man and woman in their sixties. The man wore glasses so thick that Zelach could not see his eyes, only a blown-up distortion that reminded him of a mad doctor in some old French movie. Zelach would gladly have left the shop before Iosef asked a single question.

Iosef supplied all the energy for both of them. He smiled easy. Chatted. Got angry. Zelach did none of these things.

Iosef was looking for Maxim the Watchman. The grocery had been Maxim Groshnev's watch repair shop, which catered to mid-level Party members and the many people who had both reasonable and cheap watches that they hoped would keep telling them the time. But then, suddenly, there was no business. For a while the shop did well selling cheap American digital watches that looked like the real thing. But then even the market for cheap watches fell, and all Maxim had to count on were the secrets he paid for, traded for, and sold.

The woman in front of the counter picked up her cloth tote bag filled with groceries, grabbed the arm of the goggle glasses man, and moved around the two policemen and out the door.

"We are the police," Iosef said, approaching the woman who stood behind the bar, her arms folded, a defiant look on her face.

"I know."

"Do you know why we are here?" asked Iosef, who wore one of his most friendly smiles.

"You want to purchase oranges, cheese, and bread for a quiet picnic in the park."

Iosef shook his head no and expanded his smile, suggesting that her remark had been particularly witty.

"Maxim?" she said.

"Maxim," Iosef confirmed.

Four black men had stopped to look through the window at the contest between Sister Ann and the policemen. Everybody knew they were policemen.

Zelach was uneasy. In this neighborhood, violence had been done to both whites and blacks over the past dozen years. In this time men and women fleeing African tyranny or the consequences of their own criminal activity had encountered prejudice as their numbers increased. They acquired firearms as their people were targeted.

"Why?" Sister Ann asked.

"A purchase of information," said Iosef, picking up a huge bar of Czech chocolate from a box on the counter. The chocolate was covered in a silvery wrap and a simple white paper label.

Sister Ann looked at the candy in Iosef's hand. Iosef threw the wrapped chocolate over his shoulder in the general direction of Zelach who caught it cleanly.

"He is here," said Iosef, looking back at Zelach.

Zelach nodded.

"No, he is home," Sister Ann insisted.

"He has no home," said Iosef softly. "He does not want to be somewhere where he might be a target for those who have done business with him or heard about him. He carries a bedroll and thousands of euros and a sack of diamonds."

Maxim the Watchman was now one of the most successful fences in Moscow, a city within whose encircling border at least three hundred fences operated. Few, however, had the success of the Watchman. He supplied information to the police for the right to stay in business. It was the same reason he gave information to men of the Mafia.

Iosef took out a handful of rubles from his pocket and placed them on the counter.

"For the chocolate," he said, moving toward the door at the rear of the cramped store.

Zelach held the bar of chocolate awkwardly in his hand. The bar was too big for any of his pockets. Besides, it might begin to melt. He considered throwing the confection in the garbage but resisted the urge.

As Iosef opened the door, Zelach began slowly, carefully tearing the wrapper from the chocolate.

"You are here. Good," said Iosef genially as he went through the door.

The room was little more than a closet. A wiry old man with a bush of white hair was seated on a stool in front of a counter. Maxim, with pull-down enlarging glasses, was repairing a watch.

"Rebuilding," he said.

His voice was raspy, almost raw. He did not offer them a seat. There were no seats and there was no room for them. On a shelf above the work table was a monitor. On the monitor was the interior of the grocery. Sister Ann was looking up at the camera.

"I've forgotten your name," Maxim said. "But I know you are the son of Porfiry Petrovich Rostnikov. Are you more reasonable than your father . . ."

"No. I am Iosef, and this is Detective Zelach," said Iosef, no longer smiling.

"You are not wearing a watch," said Maxim. "I still have a few that I could give to you as a gift, were I allowed to present anything to the police that might be construed as a bribe."

"I know the time," said Zelach, nibbling at a piece of chocolate he had broken off.

He offered the chocolate bar to Iosef, who broke off a piece. It was bittersweet, delicious.

"You know what time it is without looking at a timepiece?" asked Maxim with a smile, looking at Iosef.

There was little Zelach might do that would surprise Iosef, who now watched for the latest hidden skill of his partner.

"It is 11:57 in the morning," said Zelach.

Maxim looked at his watch and then at Zelach.

"You are within two minutes," said Maxim.

"He is a man of many talents," said Iosef, offering the chocolate bar to the old man.

"Thank you," said Maxim, who cracked off a piece of chocolate, looked at what he had taken, made a what-the-hell shrug, and began to eat.

"Three men, black," said Iosef. "Two are tall. One is short, chunky, wears glasses."

"There are six of them. Sometimes they shop here," said Maxim.

"There are only three now," said Iosef. "Two are dead, one is missing. A Russian ten-euro gangster has him."

"And you want to know where you can find the last three?"

"Yes," said Iosef.

"It would be very dangerous to provoke these men, even if you had a little army. The tallest one is a little mad."

"We will be careful. Thank you for your concern. An address?"

"I don't know the address, but I can tell you the building."

"He won't know," said Patrice, playing with a sharpened pencil, turning it over and over between the long fingers of his left hand like a miniature baton.

Patrice, Biko, and Laurence were about to leave the small apartment. They could stand it no longer. Patrice had spent one year in a Botswanan prison on suspicion of smuggling diamonds from the mine in which he had been working. The suspicions were well founded. All small rooms felt like prison cells.

The others were not much better. While Patrice had a nervousness about him, Biko was calm, seldom moving unless it was necessary, and then doing so with often vicious speed and murderous efficiency. These two men were his fellow thieves, no more. Biko's real loyalty lay with his wives and children. For them he would die. For them he would kill even small children. He had no religion other than his family. He did, however, have a great respect for James Harumbaki as a leader who had made Biko's life comfortable. Biko had begun life in Sudan with nothing but the likelihood of starvation after the loss of his three sisters and his parents. Biko had been nine. He had no god or gods, no country. He knew he was not smart like James or even Patrice, but he was more ruthless than they. They counted on him for the actions they did not want to take.

Laurence was a survivor. He had joined his first group of mercenaries when he was ten. He did not know what they stood for or if they stood for anything. The leader of the small band was known as Justin. Justin had used Laurence as a sex object and a boy soldier. Laurence's one goal in life had been to graduate to bigger and bigger guns. He had succeeded. When Justin was killed by one of his own men after a drunken night, Laurence had joined another group and then another, and he was always used in some way. Chance had taken him to Botswana. Chance had put him in contact with James Harumbaki when both were waiting for a malaria injection at a free clinic. James took Laurence in. He did not abuse or take advantage of Laurence. And now Laurence had money in a bank, which he had never considered possible. He had not even known what a bank was until James taught him. And then James taught him to read and write English. Now Laurence was ready to kill or be killed if it could save James Harumbaki.

"I do not care if he knows," said Biko. "You give them to the Russian, he looks, then he tries to kill us and James Harumbaki, but we kill him first."

"We do not want James hurt," said Laurence.

"No," agreed Patrice.

Patrice's plan was simple. He had purchased twenty smooth, bumpy, small rocks, each milky white and crystalline. Light could be seen through the rocks if they were held up to the sun or a strong lamp. He had placed the rocks in a black miniature rectangular case the size of a laptop computer. The rocks nestled on a plush black velvet surface nestled into niches in the material. This was not the best way to pass real diamonds. That was best done by putting the diamonds in a plain canvas bag with a drawstring and stuffing them into a jacket pocket or up your ass. This display of quartz was designed for show and to fool a Russian.

"He knows nothing about diamonds," said Patrice.

"You are sure?" asked Laurence.

"I talked to him. He pretends. He speaks of pipes and carats but his words betray him. The Russian is a thug. Besides, we have no choice. We have no cash. We have no diamonds. I cannot reach Balta. I went to the club. He has not returned. He has missed shows for three nights. He is not bringing back our money or the diamonds."

"Then we find and kill him," said Biko. "We go to Kiev and kill him."

"We will, but we have no time now," said Patrice. "We need to rescue James Harumbaki."

We need to rescue him, Patrice thought, *so he can tell us what to do.*

"Balta will not be easy to kill," said Laurence, adjusting his glasses.

"Everyone is easy to kill," said Biko.

Patrice shoved the pad of paper upon which he had been pretending to make notes into his pocket and stood.

They headed for the door, Laurence in the lead. He stepped quickly onto the darkened landing on the third floor of the building. They were greeted by the pungent smell of curry, which Biko found mildly displeasing.

The stairway was narrow, barely wide enough for two people. Patrice led the way down followed by Laurence and Biko. Twenty-six steps from the ground level alcove, amid the odors of curry and the sound of distinctly Indian music, the front door below them opened.

The three men stopped. They were looking down at the two men who had confronted them in the cafe.

Fortunately for Iosef and Zelach, they

were a little more prepared than the Africans. The policemen had entered the building knowing that they might well find themselves in another gun battle. The Africans, on the other hand, while always somewhat alert, were not prepared for the sight of the two policemen.

Five men reached for handguns. Iosef fired first. Zelach fired at the same instant as Laurence. Biko and Laurence were at a disadvantage. Patrice stood between them and the two men below, who were now firing up at them.

There was a door on each side of the alcove. Iosef threw himself against the one on the right, which cracked on brittle hinges, sending the detective tumbling into a darkened room. There were two more shots as Iosef righted himself and moved to the open doorway. Then, the sounds of footsteps on the stairs. Something thudding, tumbling down. And there sat Zelach, as if he were a soldier taking a break after a long march, his weapon in his lap.

Iosef decided. He stepped into the alcove and turned his weapon upward. As he did, the body of Patrice took a tumble down the final three steps, almost knocking Iosef over. There was no one else on the steps. Biko and Laurence had retreated upward. Iosef kicked the fallen man's weapon across the floor.

"Zelach," Iosef called, aiming his weapon first at the fallen Botswanan and then up the stairs to the darkened landing.

"Yes," said Zelach. "I slipped. I'm not hurt."

At times, thought Iosef fleetingly, it is not a disadvantage to be a clumsy slouch.

"The stairs," said Iosef.

The music had stopped, but no doors opened.

"Yes," said Zelach, who got awkwardly to his knees and took two-handed aim up the stairs. "Is he dead?"

Iosef had leaned over the fallen Patrice, looked into his eyes, and gently felt for a pulse in the man's neck that he was unlikely to find, given the round, bleeding hole of darkness just under the fallen man's right eye.

"He is dead."

Unless they had barricaded themselves inside Apartment 4, where Maxim the Watchman had told them the men could be found, the Africans were gone. The question was: Where were they going?

Iosef went through the pockets of the dead man. There was a wallet with sixteen hundred euros and photographs of the dead man with an old woman and another man about the age of the dead man, whose name, Iosef now saw, was Patrice Dannay. Iosef turned the photograph over and found the people in it identified: Patrice — the dead man — Mother, and James Harumbaki, the man Iosef had seen running down the street, bleeding a trail of red.

Apartment 4 was unlocked, the door wide open. The fleeing men had paused or entered. Iosef motioned Zelach to one side of the door, just to be sure, and then he stepped inside.

The room was barracks bare, reminding him not only of the years he had spent in Afghanistan, but of the small neighborhood holding prisons of the Moscow Police.

There were six cots with a single pillow on each. All the cots were neatly made and covered with khaki blankets.

"There were only two who ran," said Zelach.

"I think," said Iosef, "the two who were here are now reclining in Paulinin's laboratory. One is dead at the foot of the stairs, and another . . . is unaccounted for."

There was only the one room. It was large enough if it had only been occupied by two people, but six had lived here with only the cots and a battered wooden dining room table with six white, one-piece plastic chairs.

Iosef holstered his weapon and went to the table, on which two items sat. Zelach in turn went to each of the beds, looking under them, pulling out small treasure after small treasure — a canvas army duffel bag, plastic carry-ons, and weapons, some automatic and others not so, but just as deadly.

Iosef was attracted by the box on the table. It was dark, leather, small, and open. It was lined in dark velvet, and someone had hurriedly grabbed the contents and torn the lining from the corner. Iosef pushed the lining over and reached down to pluck something from the box.

He placed the item on the table and next to it placed a sheet of paper on which someone had made a drawing of rectangular objects lined up.

"What do you make of this?" asked Iosef.

Zelach stopped his search and shambled to the table where Iosef pointed to the small rock. Zelach looked at the rock, picked it up, and looked some more.

"A diamond?" asked Iosef.

"No," said Zelach, "quartz."

"You are certain?"

"Yes," said Zelach.

"What is it worth?"

"Maybe a few rubles," said Zelach.

"Does it look like a diamond?"

"You asked if it was a diamond."

"Which means," said Iosef, "I would not know a diamond from a quartz."

"This means something?" asked Zelach.

"Maybe. Look at this."

Iosef pointed to the sheet of paper on the table on which were three penciled drawings, all quite well done. In the lower left was a drawing of a woman who looked somewhat like a rough version of the woman in the photograph Iosef had taken from Patrice Dannay's wallet. On the lower right was the name "James," printed in neat blocks on the six rungs of a ladder. And in the center of the page was a series of rectangular boxes, lined up head-to-head and extending into the distance.

"What do you make of that?" asked Iosef.

Zelach looked down at the sheet, pushed out his lower lip and said, "It's the War Memorial."

Iosef was about to say no, he could not possibly conclude that from this minimal sketch, but he knew better and said, "The War Memorial?"

"Yes. Each grave has dirt in it from each of the countries that fought on our side against the Nazis."

This Iosef already knew, but Zelach clearly

enjoyed presenting the information.

"What do we do now?" asked Zelach.

"We call Porfiry Petrovich," said Iosef.

CHAPTER TWELVE

Balta watched and listened.

It was cool, but pleasant enough for the tables of the coffee house to be set up out on the street. All the small round Plexiglas tables were taken, which suited Balta just fine. Balta looked at the beautiful Oxana who smiled as if she had a secret.

She was not alone. Balta admired Rochelle Tanquay's sleek, dark feline beauty. If everything worked out as he planned, Balta expected to be seeing a great deal more of the elegant Miss Tanquay.

Balta sipped strong espresso that was almost thick enough to require a spoon.

Oxana and Rochelle talked about the model's career, about the shoot in Paris and what it might mean to her. Oxana was delighted to listen to and take part in a conversation that was entirely about her.

There was a swell of laughter from a nearby table. A young man, who looked like a wrestler and wore a supposedly masculine two-day growth of beard, slapped the less-than-sturdy table, setting the cups and saucers into a jangling dance. The sound covered whatever Oxana was saying. Balta heard pieces of the model's words but not all. He was certain, however, that she had said nothing about diamonds. He really didn't expect her to.

Then the man who Balta had seen with Oxana in the park strode over, adjusting his tie when he saw Rochelle Tanquay. A smile showing remarkably even and reasonably white teeth appeared as Oxana made the introductions.

"This is Jan Pendowski," said Oxana. "Jan, this is Rochelle Tanquay."

"Oxana told me about you," Jan said, taking Rochelle's hand and holding onto it a bit longer than might have been considered polite.

"You are a policeman," Rochelle said, matter-of-factly removing her hand from Jan's grasp and reaching into her purse for a cigarette.

"I am a policeman," he said almost with apology.

He quickly removed a lighter from his pocket and extended it to Rochelle, who used it. She had offered a cigarette to

Oxana, who took it and waited for Jan to flick the lighter for her. He almost forgot. His eyes were on Rochelle.

Balta watched with amusement and saw a tinge of jealousy color Oxana's face.

"What kind of policeman are you?" Rochelle asked.

"I catch smugglers."

"Like people who bring fruit and cheap watches in their pockets?" Rochelle asked impishly.

"Like people who are inventive about bringing drugs into the Ukraine and even transporting gold and precious jewels across our country."

"Yes," Oxana said, trying to shift the conversation to another subject. "Jan, tell her about the perfect baby."

"The perfect baby?" asked Rochelle.

"A young couple is changing planes to head for Istanbul," said Jan with a grin. "They tell me the baby is asleep but they would be willing to move him gently if it is necessary to search his blankets.

"I say that there is no point in disturbing such a perfect baby. The couple thanks me. I examine the things they had brought in a basket for the baby. It is clear that none of the items, baby food, diapers, changes of clothing have been tampered with or are being used to hide anything."

"That's when . . ." Oxana prompted.

"That's when I knew," said Jan. "I took the baby from the young woman's arms, placed it on the table, and cut into its stomach with my pocket knife. An older woman watching from behind in the examination line screamed in horror."

At this memory, Jan Pendowski laughed.

"Artificial baby," said Oxana.

"Too perfect," said Jan. "So perfect that everything in the child's basket was untouched, new, absolutely clean in spite of the fact that the couple had been traveling most of the day. When I cut the baby open, out came the contents like a Mexican piñata exposing candy. The doll was filled with diamonds."

"Clever," said Rochelle, meeting the provocation of his eyes.

"I am not deceived by appearances," he said. "I have seen too much."

"I am certain you have many equally interesting stories," said Rochelle.

"Many," he said, unsure now of whether she was twitting him.

"Perhaps you can tell them to me when I have more time in Kiev," she said.

"Who knows?" said Jan as a waiter appeared with coffee for him and refills for

Rochelle and Oxana. "I may be getting to Paris in the not distant future."

"Be sure to look me up," said Rochelle.

"I will," said Jan.

Oxana watched the exchange with amusement and perhaps only the slightest hint of jealousy. Rochelle Tanquay was French. Rochelle was engaged in sexual teasing. Jan would gladly have jumped into bed or the back of his car with Rochelle, but without further encouragement, he would promptly forget her. Besides, if all went well, Oxana would have the diamonds and Jan would be dead before the end of the next day. All it took was resolve. Oxana had never killed anyone. She had come close on two occasions, both times as a result of being challenged by other models for work which was rightfully hers. Oxana was confident that with the proper incentive, and almost two million euros, she would have sufficient incentive to murder Jan, who was now outrageously suggesting seduction to another woman. He was a pig, a clever, handsome, and dangerous pig, but a pig nonetheless.

She admitted to herself that she was fascinated by both Jan's performance and Rochelle's. She enjoyed playing voyeur and even allowed herself the fantasy of rushing to Jan's apartment, undressing him, and making him spring to life if he had not already done so under the table. And yes, she also fantasized about seducing Rochelle before they left Kiev, though it was more likely that the clearly worldly Parisian knew more about making love to a woman than did Oxana.

"What is amusing?" asked Jan.

"Thinking about Paris," said Oxana.

Rochelle smiled.

"Paris will be good to you," she said.

Rochelle's eyes met Jan's. There was no denying the provocation. Jan considered how he would juggle being with Oxana and killing her and seducing the beautiful woman from Paris. It would be difficult, but he decided it would be worth the reward. And if Rochelle did turn him down, he would have one more night with Oxana.

With the diamonds now hidden in his apartment and two beautiful women from which to choose, life looked very good for Jan Pendowski. All that was left for him to do was rid himself of the two Russian police officers, one of whom, the woman, he had given fleeting consideration as a possible object of his attentions. He still might, though it could be a particularly dangerous effort.

Jan Pendowski sat back and glanced at a lean man in a jacket and open-necked shirt who had just risen from the next table. The man seemed vaguely familiar.

Balta had seen and heard enough.

Now he had a plan.

St. James's phone rang, the green one, the one reserved for Ellen Sten and the people in the field in Moscow, Devochka, and Kiev for the duration of the operation. The moment the situation was resolved to his satisfaction, the phone number would be changed.

"I am in Kiev," Ellen Sten said when he picked up the phone.

"Does Balta know you're there?"

"No."

"Good."

"I think he is planning to find the diamonds and try to sell them for himself," she said.

"Evidence?"

"You know his history. Do I need evidence other than his manifestly dangerous and psychotic behavior in the past? I plan to retrieve the diamonds when he has them and remove him from temptation."

There was but the slightest hint of reprimand in her voice. St. James had chosen

Balta for this assignment in spite of her warning not to do so. Balta was a ticking bomb good for a quick assassination and nothing more. She had but hinted at her reservations. It did not do to contradict St. James.

"Even with the money he got from the courier he murdered, he still wants more," said St. James. "He confirms my expectations about the human animal. I would have thought, however, that an assassin would have higher values than the majority of those on this planet."

"Shall I eliminate him when I have the diamonds back?"

"You have enough support to confront him?"

"Yes," she said. "Three men we have used before."

"Good men?"

"Very bad men," she said.

"Good," said St. James. "Keep me informed."

"I will."

He hung up, and so did she.

There were several reasons he liked Ellen Sten. She was efficient, did not try to steal from him, and did what she was told, presenting only limited and infrequent advice. There was but one reason he did not like Ellen Sten. Her sense of humor. This was particularly annoying to St. James, who had discovered even as a child that he completely lacked a sense of humor.

As long as Ellen Sten continued to eliminate or deal with his more sticky problems, he could listen to her attempts at wit.

This was Elena's first assignment following her almost two weeks in bed and another month of recovery while her arm returned to normal. She had been stabbed on a subway station platform when she and Iosef had attempted to arrest a crazy woman with a knife. The woman had plunged the blade deeply into Elena's shoulder. Following emergency treatment in the hospital, Elena had gone back to the apartment she shared with her aunt Anna.

The agreement had been certain and clearly stated. Elena and Iosef were to be married as soon as she was healed and back to normal.

It had been clearly stated, but it had not taken place. She had now been back at work for almost two weeks and neither she nor Iosef had again spoken of marriage. The decision to be silent had been mutually agreed upon. They had both hesitated and were still hesitating.

Elena checked her watch. Sasha was to meet her in the lobby of the hotel where they would compare notes and then meet the policeman Jan Pendowski. Then they were to go in search of Oxana Balakona.

Except that there was no need for the search. Elena knew exactly where the model was staying in Kiev.

The lobby was not crowded. Elena had no trouble finding Sasha seated in a blue cushioned chair with gilded arms and back. He looked up at her, and she could see that he had had little if any sleep. His hair was unruly. He needed a shave. For an instant she thought that Sasha's mother, Lydia of the loud voice, had been right. Her son might be better off in another line of work. He seldom looked happy. The best she had seen in months was a soulful self-pitying smile of resignation. His problems had taken on Jobian proportions. There were brief moments, even hours, of hope, as there had been the day before when they were coming to Kiev. Sasha had hoped that Maya would fall into his arms weeping with joy and agree to give him yet another chance and return to Moscow with the children. Such was not to be. He had told Elena very little of this, but it had been enough.

"So what is this news about a cafe you

mentioned on the phone?" asked Sasha.

Elena was sitting at the end of a sofa that matched his chair.

"I grew tired of the good Sergeant Pendowski telling us nothing. I found a modeling agency and tracked down Oxana Balakona and went to her apartment building. It was not difficult."

She paused, waiting for a reaction. None came.

"Are you not going to ask why I did not talk to Oxana Balakona when I found her?"

Sasha shrugged and ran a hand through his hair.

"Why did you not talk to her when you found her?" he asked.

"Before I could go up to her apartment, I saw Pendowski in his car outside," she said. "He was watching the building."

"And you decided to watch him."

"You *are* paying attention."

"Nothing could interest me more."

"I shall try to hold your interest," she said. "I assumed he was there for the same reason I was, to question Oxana Balakona. Before I could get to his car, he got out and went into the building."

Sasha was giving serious thought to either strangling or shouting at his partner. He was working out the script for when he saw his children and had another opportunity to talk to Maya.

". . . went into the building," Sasha prompted.

He opened his eyes wide to demonstrate that he was wide awake and fully attentive. The result, however, was exactly the opposite.

"I waited and watched," Elena continued. "He came out ten minutes later. I assumed he had confronted and spoken to her. Instead of getting into his car, Pendowski began walking. I followed him."

"Why?" asked Sasha, knowing that he was supposed to ask.

"His actions were odd," she said. *But not as odd as yours,* she thought.

"He walked for ten minutes to a cafe where Oxana Balakona and another woman were drinking coffee. He joined them and received a greeting of great familiarity."

Sasha looked up, touched his tongue with the small finger of his right hand, and then examined the finger.

"Ten minutes inside the building?" he asked.

"Ten minutes," she concurred.

"And she was not home."

"She was not."

"He entered her apartment and searched for . . ."

"The diamonds perhaps?" she said.

"Nothing suspicious about that — besides the fact that he did not inform us as he agreed to do if he discovered anything or found her."

Elena allowed herself not quite a smile but an inner satisfaction. She had engaged his interest.

"And then," Sasha said, "Pendowski goes to the exact cafe where Oxana is having coffee with another woman. He knew where she was, knew she wasn't home when he entered the apartment. What kind of embrace did they share?"

"Familiar," said Elena.

"They are in some kind of alliance," said Sasha.

"Precisely."

"The other woman. Who is she?" he asked. "What did she look like?"

"A model I think. Very elegant."

"Pretty?" asked Sasha.

Elena went into the canvas bag that served as purse, holster, and location for a collection of things edible and things forgotten. She came up with her digital camera, a gift from Iosef last year, on the anniversary of their engagement. She pushed a button three times and handed the camera to Sasha.

Sasha looked down at the image of Pendowski and the two women at the table.

"Pretty," said Elena.

"Very. I've seen her somewhere before."

He stared at the woman in the small rectangle.

"Can you make her larger?" he asked.

Elena took the camera back, made the adjustment, and gave it to Sasha.

"Yes," he said looking down. "I've seen her before."

"She's probably a model. You saw her in an ad or on television."

"No," he said. "I saw her in person."

"Where?"

"I don't know."

"Maybe we can learn a bit more," she said. "Pendowski awaits."

"I'll remember," Sasha said.

"Good," she said.

"Can you make a copy of the woman's photograph?"

"I'll have it printed in the morning."

Sasha seemed to have a burst of energy. He rose and shook his head to scatter the cloud that clung to him. For now, self-pity would have to wait. He could not and did not wish to ignore the call to play the game.

"Let us go," he said.

Elena rose to join him.

"To a few hours of professional evasion from our Ukrainian policeman. He is very clever, I think."

"I think so also," said Sasha. "I would not want it any other way."

Jan Pendowski allowed himself a grin, but it was a cautious grin. He was no fool, though he knew from experience that he could be fooled. He had never met a man, woman, or bird in the park that could not be fooled. So he was careful.

He would have preferred to meet Rochelle Tanquay in his apartment, but she had called and made it clear that, though he could name the place, she would come only if it were reasonably public.

Jan had made a suggestion and she had agreed on both a time and place. The conversation had been brief.

He had slipped her the note, in French, under the table at the cafe with Oxana sitting directly across from him. He had written it right in front of Oxana in his notebook and said, "Something I must remember to do."

He had been reasonably certain from the way the French woman's eyes had met his that she would not reveal the message to Oxana. Jan's goal was dual purpose. Seduction of course, but also possible business which might have to come first.

Now she approached with a smile, wearing a quite casual black dress with a fashionable white cashmere sweater tied around her neck. He had time as she moved to his table to consider what it would be like to watch her remove those clothes.

The dark bar was not crowded at this early afternoon hour. The sun was going down and the dim light from beyond the small amber windows cast long, soft shadows that were beginning to merge with the darkness. In a few moments, the man behind the bar, who was one of Jan's best informants, would turn on a few lights, though not enough to alter the mood. There were a few people in the bar: a furtive couple, the man in middle age, the woman quite young; a lone man who Jan looked at twice because the detective felt that he had seen him somewhere before; and an overly made-up woman in her sixties with two full shopping bags. The couple and the lone man who seemed familiar were drinking afternoon wine. The shopping woman was drinking a tall glass of sterner stuff.

Jan half rose as Rochelle reached the table

and placed her small handbag on the empty chair next to her. She sat facing Jan rather than next to him.

"A drink?" he asked in French.

"Wine."

The remainder of the conversation was in French.

A red-nailed finger touched the small earring in her right ear. The last of the sunlight caught a jewel and sent a brief flash of yellow-white. Jan Pendowski was a romantic.

Jan nodded to the man behind the bar, who had been admiring the policeman's companion.

"Small talk?" he asked.

"A little," she said. "It delays the scripted seduction you have planned."

"Good," he said. "Do you like Kiev?"

"Not particularly," she said as the bartender brought two wine glasses and a small bottle of his finest, which he poured with panache.

Jan was amused. He said nothing until the man had gone.

"He wanted to get a closer look at you," said Jan. "He does not usually provide such service. But I am sure you are accustomed to such attentions."

"Have I had men stare at me with less than brotherly intentions? Yes, and may it never stop."

They touched glasses.

"Ukrainian wine," he said.

"Not bad. Not French, but not bad at all."

"Are we finished with the small talk?" he asked sitting back.

"You are an intriguing man, if not a sophisticated one."

"My charm lies in my Polish stock. Earthy."

"And confident," she said, taking a second sip of wine. "I am not going to bed with you."

"Then we can come together on the floor."

"Your persistence is admirable. I will amend my statement. I am not going to bed with you tonight."

"Tomorrow morning?"

She laughed. He liked it. Her red lips opened and her white teeth spread. And she laughed.

"Perhaps," she said. "Normally I would expect some effort at seduction but Oxana and I must leave tomorrow, and it has been several months since I've been with a man."

"Honesty," he said. "I drink to it."

And he did. So did she.

"We will get back to that," he went on. "Do you make much money as a fashion editor?"

"Much? Let us say I do not have to concern myself with the cost of groceries. I get most of my clothing free from designers, and I put all my meals on the magazine's credit card."

"But you are not rich?"

"I am not rich. Is there a point to this?" she asked.

"Would you like to be rich?"

She tilted her head provocatively to one side and said, "No, I wish to gradually descend into abject poverty and end my days selling magazines behind a counter at the Gare de Lyon."

"Seriously," he said quite seriously.

"I would like to be rich."

"Someone at a jewelry shop in Paris, a shop whose name you would recognize, is waiting for a beautiful woman to arrive and present him with a package of diamonds. In exchange for the diamonds, the person in the jewelry shop will give the beautiful woman a wrapped gift box. Inside the gift box will be more than two million euros."

"You have these diamonds?"

"I have these diamonds. Oxana is supposed to deliver them to that shop in Paris, but I am confident she plans to keep the money."

"As a gift to herself?" said Rochelle.

"As a gift to herself, yes. She plans to keep the money and go somewhere, possibly New York or Singapore or Australia."

"I hope she does not plan to do this before the layout I have planned."

"Given our Oxana's vanity, I am confident she would not miss an opportunity to see pages of herself in your magazine."

"Why should you trust me?"

"You would be very easy to find and I think that while you wish to be very rich you do not wish to lose your identity and your world of Parisian fashion."

Her smile answered his question. He was sure he had her.

"I would not be at all surprised if Oxana plans to kill me to be sure I did not come after her. There are great advantages to her killing me."

"She would not have to fly to Singapore."

"Precisely."

He did not add that he planned to kill Oxana so that he could keep all the money and not worry about her threatening him with the revelation of his history of corruption.

"How much of this gift would be mine?" she asked.

"One-third, at least six hundred thousand euros. And there is a bonus."

She looked at him with curiosity.

"I will come to Paris, where we can celebrate."

"And that is my bonus?"

"That is my bonus," he said with a smile.

"And what of Oxana? She just accepts her fate and the loss of the six hundred thousand."

"She has too much to lose to complain," he said, finishing the last of his wine and pouring more for both of them.

It was a statement that did not bear close examination, and Rochelle Tanquay did not engage in even cursory examination.

"It is much less likely that a French woman who works for a fashionable and famous magazine would be examined by customs than a Russian national," he said. "The plan has many advantages."

"So I see," Rochelle said.

"To our success," said Jan. "And to tomorrow morning in my apartment, where I will give you the diamonds and we will have a *bon voyage* party."

They clinked glasses as Jan reached over to put his free hand on hers. She turned her hand palm up and held his.

The lone man drinking in the corner watched them and got up.

Jan had just enough time after he placed

Rochelle in a taxi. They had kissed as he opened the door, a kiss that suggested to him a passion that was to come in the morning.

He was pleased with himself. Certainly something could go wrong, but he had improvised his way through more than a dozen years as a policeman. He was confident that he could do it for at least the few more days he needed.

When he got back to his office, the Russians were waiting. He shook hands and slipped behind his desk in the small room. His wooden office chair let out a small screech as he leaned back.

"Found anything?" asked Elena.

"Promising leads on your model," Jan said, looking down at a pad on his desk as if trying to remember her name. "Oxana Balakona. I'm certain we will locate her within twenty-four hours."

"And the diamonds?" Sasha said.

Jan did not like the haunted way the man looked at him, but until proven otherwise he would assume that the Russian had seen too many ghosts, as had many who dealt with the violence of a big city. Certainly Moscow was still more violent than Kiev, though that might well change in the coming years as prosperity spread throughout the former Soviet states.

"If she has the diamonds, we will get them back for you," said Jan, confidently folding his hands on the desk and leaning forward with sincerity.

"Maybe she has turned them over to an accomplice," said Sasha.

Elena touched his leg with her hands out of the sightline of Pendowski. It was a warning that they were dealing with a shrewd adversary in his own country.

"I have a list of modeling agencies if you would like to share it with me," Pendowski said. "I can take half and you could take half. Speed up the search for Balakona, if you think you can find your way around the city."

"I am familiar with Kiev," said Sasha. "My wife was born here. I've been here many times."

"Your wife's family lives here?" Pendowski asked.

"And so does she," said Sasha.

Jan Pendowski nodded and said nothing. He knew all this. He had checked the background of Elena and Sasha for information he might use to slow them down or protect himself. Jan Pendowski knew where Maya Tkach lived with her two children. He knew where she worked. He knew the name of the man she was seeing, another reason perhaps why Tkach looked so ghostly.

"Here is a copy of the list of modeling agencies I made yesterday," said Pendowski. "Two sheets. You take the second. I've already started on the first."

He handed the sheet to Elena. Elena folded it evenly in half and placed it in her bag. She had no intention of calling on any agency on the list. Oxana Balakona had already been found.

The task had now changed. The one to watch was the policeman sitting across the desk.

"Then that is all for now," Elena said, rising.

"Dinner?" asked Jan Pendowski.

"No, thank you," said Elena. "We have a report to write."

"Sure? I know a small Mongolian restaurant where they make a yak dish like nothing you have ever eaten."

"A roast leg of yak sounds inviting, but not tonight," said Elena, now standing.

Sasha rose too.

"I will drive you back to your hotel," Pendowski said, also rising.

"We would appreciate that," said Elena.

"I will show you a few sights on the way. They will not be out of the way."

On the trip back to the hotel, Pendowski pointed out sights and kept up an engaging line of patter.

"We are in Andriyvsky Uzviz, a part of the Old Kiev Preserve. Once this was the shortest way to connect the princely Upper Town with the commercial Podil. Now it is a place for outdoor fairs and concerts. There are art galleries, shops, artists' studios. This is the place to come to find antiques and paintings. You should take some time to come back here. I will be happy to show you around."

"Thank you," said Elena.

In front of the hotel, he arranged to meet them in the early afternoon after they had spent the morning on their list. Elena and Sasha agreed. As he drove away, Elena said, "Perhaps we should watch him tonight."

"Tomorrow morning," said Sasha. "He seems particularly interested in our spending the morning looking for a modeling agency that is certainly not on the list in your pocket."

"Tomorrow morning," Elena agreed.

It was the third day. In two days, if the current team of detectives under Porfiry Petrovich Rostnikov had not made impressive progress in their investigation, they might all be looking at new and not very satisfying assignments.

She wondered, as they took the elevator up to their rooms, if it might be possible for Rostnikov simply to be reassigned to another department, or even another city, and bring his own team with him. She wondered about her relationship to Iosef. She wondered if she should call him. She wondered if maybe she should have accepted Pendowski's offer of roast Mongolian yak.

Chapter Thirteen

"You know this man, Lillita?" asked Porfiry Petrovich.

The little girl looked at old Boris sitting in the corner of the meeting room with his arms folded. He was bored. He had seen enough of little girls being paraded before him. He had told the one-legged policeman that the ghost girl was not one of the girls in Devochka.

Lillita was no more than ten. She was very thin, but not because food was unavailable. He had spoken to eleven little girls so far this morning, and all of them had been examples of baby fat or healthy fullness. This one was different. She had short, dull amber hair, a pinched, sad face, and moist eyes. Her lower lip jutted out just slightly in what may have been a pout. She wore a dark woolen skirt and a yellow shirt with buttons. She kept pulling up her sleeves, and they kept slipping down.

"Yes," she said. "That's Boris."

She had not bothered to look at the old man.

"You know what his job is?"

"He goes into the mine. He knows the mine. He takes people around."

"I am responsible for much more," said Boris defensively.

The girl shrugged. She didn't care. She had been doing her best to keep from looking at the plate of cookies on the table next to her.

Rostnikov had moved his chair in front of the table to be closer to the girls, but he was careful to gauge the distance so that he allowed plenty of space.

"Have a cookie," said Rostnikov. "Have two cookies."

The girl rose slightly from her chair and reached over to take two cookies.

"Spasiba," she said, holding the cookies lightly in her hand.

"You know about the dead people in the mine?" asked Rostnikov, reaching for two cookies.

"Yes."

"You knew Anatoliy Lebedev?"

"Old Lebedev," she said, watching Rostnikov eat a cookie. "I did not know the American."

"He was a Canadian."

"They are the same very much," she said, putting a cookie cautiously to her mouth.

"They might not agree," said Rostnikov.

Boris mumbled something, wanting to be heard but not wanting Rostnikov to know that he wanted to be heard. It was a very Russian way of making a point. And so, Boris had mumbled, "I will be dead and buried before he finishes talking to little girls and feeding them cookies."

Lillita Kapronopovich took a deliberate bite of her cookie.

"You think there is a girl with a lantern who wanders through the mine?" asked Porfiry Petrovich.

"Yes," the girl said.

"Who is she?"

"A ghost."

"Whose ghost?"

"You don't know?"

"I've heard, but I would like you to tell me."

"The ghost of a girl who died in the mine," she explained, "the old mine, when it first opened, the year my grandfather was born. They had little girls carrying lanterns and crawling into holes where adults could not go. The roof fell down and crushed her. Only her lantern was left. She haunts the mine now because she knows she should not have been sent down there. She knows. She tricks men into going into little spaces and then kills them."

"She makes the room fall?"

"She stabs them in the face," said the girl sweetly, finishing her cookie.

Boris groaned. He had heard twenty versions of this tale from little girls this day and most of them had gotten it wrong. Boris knew the true story, though he was not quite sure how he had heard it. He took it on faith that his version was the right one.

"I have two girls around your age at home in Moscow," Porfiry Petrovich said.

"You are too old to have little girls."

"They are not my children or my grandchildren. They and their grandmother live with my wife and me."

"In Moscow?"

"Yes."

"Is it really warm half of the year in Moscow?"

"It is," he said.

"I think I will live in Moscow when I get older."

"St. Petersburg is better," said Boris, and then added, "What am I saying? I don't want to be followed by little girls. Forget it. You are right. Moscow is better."

The girl gave Boris a tolerant look.

"Who told you the story of the ghost girl in the mine?"

"My grandfather," the child said.

"Where is he?"

"In his little room cleaning his guns. He thinks the Japanese are going to come and try to kill us all. He is a little crazy."

"I think I would like to talk to your grandfather," said Porfiry Petrovich.

"Why?" asked Boris. "She told you. He is crazy."

"I will humor him."

"Can I go now?" asked the girl.

"Yes, and take two more cookies."

She got off the chair and took two more cookies.

"Do I have to go back to school?"

"No," said Rostnikov. "You can eat cookies and drink beer and use bad words all day. You have my permission."

"You don't mean it."

She was smiling now.

"Well, no."

"Can I see your wooden leg?"

She was standing in front of his chair.

"If you show it to her," said Boris, "you will have to show it to all of them."

Rostnikov leaned forward awkwardly in his chair and pulled up the cuff of his left pant leg. The girl stared seriously and said, "Does it hurt?"

"No, we are becoming friends."

"Friends with a wooden leg?"

"It is plastic and metal."

"I see," said the girl, starting on her third cookie. "Friends? You talk to it?"

"Sometimes, but I was friendlier with my bad leg when I still had it, but if I wish I can always visit it."

"Your leg? Where is it?"

"In a laboratory in a lower basement of police headquarters in Moscow where I have my office."

"You are making a joke," she said, tilting her head to one side.

"No," said Rostnikov seriously. "It is best to keep old friends nearby, when possible."

Rostnikov let down his pant leg and Boris shuffled behind him.

"Can I tell my friends that you talk to your leg?"

"You have my permission."

"Thank you," she said and left the room.

Emil Karpo stepped in.

"Would you like a cookie, Emil Karpo?" Rostnikov asked.

"I do not eat cookies," said Karpo, who was dressed in his customary black.

Rostnikov knew his associate's diet quite

well, but it did not stop him from an occasional foray into the hope of temptation. Porfiry Petrovich Rostnikov firmly believed that the regular consumption of cookies was essential to the well-being of every reasonable Russian. Rostnikov ate a cookie.

"The little girl who just left here has a grandfather," Rostnikov said. "He cleans guns in preparation for an invasion by the Japanese. I would like you to talk to him about the places in the mine too small for all but little girls to crawl into. I should like to know where they are."

"There are not any such places," said Boris emphatically.

"But there is a ghost?" asked Rostnikov.

"The ghost is real, but do not tell anyone I said so. The small caves are not real, and you can tell anyone you like that I said so," said Boris.

"Enlightening," said Karpo.

"Hidden places, Emil Karpo. Hidden places," said Rostnikov.

Let the Moscow detectives find the covered cave, he thought. *I want no more of it. I want only for the killing to end. I will kill no more.*

But it makes no difference. I am surely going to be caught if I do something . . . Porfiry Petrovich Rostnikov will eventually figure it out. The question is, "How long is eventually?"

His choices were still narrow. He could gather everything he could get into a suitcase and make some excuse to be on the next plane out of Devochka. He had plenty of excuses open to him for short-term visits to Moscow. In Moscow he could disappear, and with the help of St. James he could leave Russia. But he was not certain that St. James would help him. His value lay in staying where he was, and the truth was that he did not want to leave. His life was here.

Even if St. James made him rich, it would not compensate for what he would have to give up. St. James would probably want the two detectives killed. He would have to kill them. Then what? More policemen? Maybe the next ones would not be so smart, or maybe they would and they would be looking for a ghost who had killed two policemen. It was not a good situation.

He made a decision. If either or both of the policemen decided to go into the mine, they would get a visit from the ghost girl and they would not leave the mine alive.

"So?" asked Iosef Rostnikov, holding the phone close to his ear to mask the sound of a building across the street being demolished by a huge wrecking ball.

274

He had watched the demolition for half an hour before making the call. There was something fascinating and satisfying in the sight of the massive ball swinging widely and then making an almost grateful loop into what remained of the wall.

Porfiry Petrovich lay in the bed fully clothed sans the leg, which kept him company within reach, on a chair. From the bed he could look through the window at a formation of clouds that looked like a laughing man reclining.

"They don't have the diamonds," Rostnikov said, watching the cloud slowly morph into something else he could not yet identify.

"They could have them and plan to simply give the people who have the hostage African the fake diamonds," said Iosef.

"Then they would not value the hostage's life very highly."

"But the kidnappers probably plan to kill him anyway," said Iosef. "They are likely to know that."

"There is little doubt of that. So perhaps your two Botswanans plan to start a small war at the War Memorial in the hope of saving their friend."

"Yes, I agree," said Iosef. "And you suggest?"

"Caution and backup. How is Zelach?"

"A man will be sure to meet at least once in his life something that is unlike anything he had happened to see before."

"Chekov?"

"Gogol," said Iosef. "Zelach is that thing."

"Be careful," said Porfiry Petrovich.

"I will be. Any other advice?"

"Marry Elena if she will still have you. You asked for my advice."

"I did," Iosef said. "Anything else I should know?"

"You have an uncle."

"An uncle?"

"He is here in Siberia."

"What better place for an uncle," Iosef said, knowing his father's sense of humor.

"You have cousins too. I will tell you more when I see you. Perhaps I can persuade him to visit Moscow if I do not have to arrest him for murder."

"He is a suspect, this uncle?"

"A suspect with definite credentials. Let us talk again after the war at the War Memorial."

Porfiry Petrovich Rostnikov hung up and reached awkwardly to place the phone back in its cradle on the night table.

He forced himself up, letting his leg hang over the side of the bed. He had a date with Viktor Panin to lift weights. Panin was also a suspect. There were few who were not. After lifting and showering, Rostnikov would meet with more little girls and Yevgeniy Zuyev, the mayor of Devochka, another suspect. The total number of suspects in the mining town was two hundred eleven men, two hundred eighteen women, and one hundred sixty-one school-age boys and girls. Somehow Rostnikov, who was slowly putting on his favorite gray sweatsuit, did not believe he would have to talk to all these people.

Speaking softly to his artificial leg, he put it on and decided he would wait for Emil Karpo's report on the grandfather who was preparing for invasion by the forces of Nippon.

It was not the girl Lillita's grandfather, Karpo discovered. It was her great-grandfather, Gennadi Ivanov. He was indeed alone in a small room into which he welcomed Karpo after the detective identified himself.

Karpo estimated that the man was at least ninety years old. He was surprisingly erect and tall, but so thin that he had to constantly adjust the thick suspenders over his sloping shoulders.

There was a bed in a corner, a dresser,

and a large table cluttered with the exposed insides of a rifle. Along one wall was a rack of rifles and a case of handguns behind glass doors.

"No ammunition," said the old man, offering a chair.

He sat on a bench that ran the length of the table.

"I will be given the ammunition when the Japanese come," he said. "At least that is what they tell me, have been telling me for tens of years. They do not believe the attack is coming. Their fathers did not believe. I wish they were right, but they are not. They were repulsed at Vladivostok by sea and in Korea by land in 1904. My father fought them off."

The old man wore a well trimmed white beard and a matching head of hair. He eyed the still-standing detective and made a decision.

"I know where they keep the ammunition. I can just walk over to Fedya Rostnikov's office, shoot the lock off, and arm forty men."

"But you have no ammunition to shoot the lock off," said Karpo.

The old man smiled knowingly, showing a mouth that had long since lost most of its teeth.

"Perhaps. Perhaps. Do you have any idea what this is?" he asked, pointing at the dismantled weapon on the table in front of him.

"A Mosin-Nagent rifle," said Karpo. "It fires a 7.62 × 54 rimmed cartridge. Five shot bolt action."

"Can hit a Japanese soldier at five hundred yards," said the old man. "This one was used in the war against Finland. Those Finns could fight. Better than the Japanese."

He picked up a small metal part from the table and squinted at it as he held it up.

"I am here to talk about the mine," said Karpo.

"Talk."

"There are hidden caves in the mine. Small caves that children can crawl through."

"Is that a question?" asked the old man.

"It is."

"Yes there are," Ivanov said, still looking at the small part as if it held a secret.

"Do you know where they are?"

"Three of them, but they have all been covered by collapsing walls. Children were killed. One ghost came from the crushed rocks and bits of diamond, the little girl with the lantern."

"You believe in the ghost girl?"

"I saw her twice."

"When?"

"I don't remember. I was a young man. It was just before we were warned for the first time that the Japanese might be on the way."

"You don't like the Japanese," said Karpo.

"I like the Japanese very much," said Ivanov, trying to take his eyes from the little machined part. "Very smart. Women are pretty. Children are beautiful. I just do not want them to take over all of Russia and turn us into Buddhists and slaves."

"Could you draw me a map of where the small caves are?"

"No one believes me about the caves. Why do you?"

"I did not say I believe you," said Karpo. "Nor do I not believe you."

"I'll draw it in exchange for a bullet for this gun," the old man said.

"You shall have it," said Karpo, reasonably confident he could provide the man with a bullet that would be guaranteed not to work or explode the gun in his hands.

"If I were not too old, I would take you to the caves," the old man said.

"I understand. There is a man named Boris who takes people into the mine. Could he find the caves using your map?"

"Boris? Stupid boy, but he knows the

mine. Yes, he can do it. Are you going in there?"

"I think so."

"Watch out for the ghost girl. If you hear her sing and you see her, your chances of being found dead are very good."

"It is a risk I will take."

"My bullet."

"I will get it for you."

"When is he coming home?" asked Nina.

Since her sister was two years older, Nina expected Laura to have answers to all of her questions, and she usually did.

"Soon," said Laura.

The girls were facing each other under the blanket on the makeshift bed on the floor. They were whispering in the darkness punctuated only by the light from the lamp-posts beyond the kitchen window.

"What is soon?"

"Three days," Laura said with confidence and no certain knowledge.

"What is he doing? Is he shooting some-one bad?"

"No. The creepy man does the killing."

"I like him," said Nina. "I do not think he is creepy."

"I do not think he is either, but other people do."

"Sarah and Grandmother Galina?"

"I do not know."

"I shall ask them. Will Porfiry Petrovich bring us anything from Siberia?"

"There is nothing to bring from Siberia," said Laura. "There is nothing there but snow and reindeer."

"When he comes back, he will fix Mrs. Dudenya's pipes."

"Yes," said Laura. "When I grow up, I shall be a plumber."

"When I grow up," said Nina, "I will be a policeman."

"Here is the list," said Fyodor Rostnikov, handing a printed sheet to Porfiry Petrovich.

They were seated on white folding chairs outside the apartment complex facing the mine, which was closed. It was a crime scene.

Porfiry Petrovich wore his lined overcoat and a black wool watch cap. Fyodor Andreiovich wore a dark blue pea coat and a black fur hat. In the summer, the temperature could reach ninety degrees Fahrenheit for a few days, but in the winter, which was approaching, the temperature averaged negative fifty-six degrees Fahrenheit. At the moment the temperature hovered somewhere around thirty degrees Fahrenheit, which meant that they both considered this a balmy day, nearly perfect for enjoying the afternoon.

Beyond the thick wall of trees that stretched as far to the left and right as Rostnikov could see were mountains and the Vitim River and Lake Baykal, the world's deepest lake. The city of Irkutsk was somewhere out there.

Porfiry Petrovich looked down at the short list of names Fyodor had given him. They were the names of all senior employees of the mining company who were allowed to enter the mine during the six-hour off shift, which was always between 11:00 p.m. and 5:00 a.m. In addition to the Devochka Council members, there were two resident mining engineers. It was a short list made even shorter by the murder of board member Anatoliy Lebedev.

"As you will see if you go to the mine . . ."

"I will go to the mine," said Porfiry Petrovich.

"As you will see," Fyodor went on, "there is a steel night fence which covers the only mine entrance. The door in the fence can only be opened with key cards."

Fyodor reached into the pocket of his jacket and extracted two large naval oranges.

He handed one to Porfiry Petrovich who nodded his thanks.

"And who provides these cards?" Rostnikov asked as he carefully began to peel the orange. It was firm and ripe. He brought it to his nose to smell. The world was suddenly engulfed in an orange miasma.

"I do," said Fyodor.

"And where were you on the shifts when the Canadian and Lebedev were killed?"

Fyodor allowed himself a knowing, if small, smile.

"Home, which, you will see when you come for dinner tonight, is over there: Building Two, ground floor. My children were sleeping. My wife and I went to bed just before midnight. I awoke in the morning at five-thirty as I always do."

"And your wife is a light sleeper?" asked Rostnikov.

This time Fyodor did allow himself a laugh, almost choking as he said, "She sleeps a sleep that would challenge a roomful of narcoleptics. Nothing wakes her."

Both men had a lap of orange peels and a ready orb of fruit. They had both separated the oranges into segments and were eating slowly.

"So I am the prime suspect?"

"One of several," said Porfiry Petrovich,

holding up the list and letting his eyes follow the slow walk of a man on the path to the mine.

The list was now covered with sticky fingertip tabs of orange. When he called Sarah later, he would tell her of the nearly perfect orange he had eaten in Siberia.

"During Lebedev's murder, I will now confess, I was with the person I thought might be the murderer of the Canadian," Fyodor said after a long pause. "I engaged him in conversation, tried to get him drunk, and wasted a night. It was I who got drunk."

"His name?"

"Your weight lifting partner Viktor Panin. I did not go to the mine. You can ask Viktor."

"And Viktor did not go to the mine?" said Porfiry Petrovich.

"He didn't even stop once to piss. The man must have a bladder as big as the giant Tunguska meteor hole near Podkamennaya. I do not know if he killed the Canadian, but he definitely did not kill poor Lebedev. We are having *shashlyk* for dinner in your honor. Come hungry."

It was Porfiry Petrovich's turn to smile.

"I shall arrive with a suitable appetite."

"Igor Sturnicki, one of the two engineers on your list, was in Barnaul visiting relatives. The other engineer, Mikhail Kline, was in the hospital with a broken leg."

"Could he walk on the leg?"

"It was and is in a cast from hip to ankle. It would be difficult to hobble to and into the mine to hide and commit a murder."

"You are sure the leg is broken?"

"A mine truck tipped on it. He will walk with a limp when he does walk again, which may not be for a long time."

"That leaves the rest of the council members," said Porfiry Petrovich.

"Yes. As you see, there are three more, our Chairman Yevgeniy Zuyev . . ."

Rostnikov remembered the thin, nervous man whose right eye seemed to wander while the left was fixed firmly on whatever object it was aimed toward.

"Magda Kaminskaya . . ."

Who, Rostnikov recalled, was short and overweight, with a definite wheezing problem.

"And Stepan Orlov . . ."

The image of a broad-shouldered man in need of a shave came to mind.

"Stepan, I'm afraid, is my candidate," said Fyodor.

"Why?"

"By a process of elimination," Fyodor said. "There is no one left to consider."

"Why have I not spoken to Stepan Orlov?"

"Because he has locked himself in his laboratory and put up a 'Do Not Disturb' sign."

"He does this often?"

"I have known him to do it."

"And what does he do in the laboratory?" asked Porfiry Petrovich.

"He is a microbiologist. He is supposed to be examining all evidence of insects, rats, and odd microbial-level life in the mines."

"And what has he found?"

"Among other things a species of blind white rats that have survived for hundreds of years in total darkness. He is a decent enough man when he is on the trail of some living creature, but when he has nothing under the microscope or scalpel, he is a surly creature at best."

"Anything else about him I should know before I knock at his laboratory door?"

"Only that he has enormously powerful arms and hands. We had an arm-wrestling competition last year. He finished second only to Viktor, and for a few moments it looked as if he might win."

"So he is your choice?"

"Yes, but Yevgeniy Zuyev is still possible."

"Orlov is your choice then?"

"Have you a better one?" Fyodor asked, wondering who he might have in mind.

Porfiry Petrovich Rostnikov did, indeed, have another suspect who might be better, but could well be overlooked. Sometimes, he thought, a person who looked and talked like a murderer was actually a murderer.

"What time do you want to go into the mine?"

"After dinner would be fine," said Porfiry Petrovich.

"Maybe we will encounter the ghost girl," Fyodor said, shaking his head.

"That would be very satisfying."

Fyodor reached over to take the orange peel from Porfiry Petrovich, who nodded his thanks. Rostnikov's peel was torn into eight pieces. Fyodor had managed to do it with only two curled pieces.

This, Porfiry Petrovich thought, *says something about each of us, but what it is that is being said is uncertain.*

"Shall we go see Stepan Orlov's laboratory?"

"Yes," said Rostnikov, starting to rise, his feet almost slipping on the crushed rocks.

Chapter Fourteen

Gerald St. James threw darts at the target across the room. The target was backed by a corkboard that covered almost half the wall to protect the paneling from the always-sharpened steel points. An open wooden box on his desk contained several dozen finely balanced darts, all neatly lined up.

Ellen Sten sat quietly in a firm red leather armchair near the floor-to-ceiling windows beyond which St. James could see the rooftop of DeBeers of London. She had flown in only hours before on St. James's private Astra/Gulfstram SPX. Ellen had not slept in more than fifty hours but, thanks to an intentionally slight overdose of Provigil, she was now awake and attentive.

St. James calmly balanced a dart over his shoulder and, with a snap of the wrist, sent it noiselessly across the room and into the target. The target was his own design.

He was not interested in keeping score or

hitting anything but the coin-sized black dot within a red circle the size of a baby's face. One should not get points for coming close. One did not get points in life for coming close. Gerald St. James's accuracy was uncanny.

Once, many years ago in Estonia, he had sat in a very damp cellar, wheezing and hiding from people who called themselves police. He had nothing to do but eat what was smuggled down to him by an old woman to whom he eventually had paid everything he owned.

In that cellar he had his knife. He kept it sharp against the jutting edges of the stone wall. For forty-one days he had thrown his knife, the knife with which he had killed the opium dealer who had tried to kill him.

That was long before he became Gerald St. James.

He had used the knife to kill the old woman. He took back the money he had given her and the bit more he found hidden in an empty grain jar in her kitchen.

Neither the boy he had been nor the man he had become ever showed anger or emotion of any kind, not that he did not feel them.

"So?" he asked, picking up another dart.

When he had exhausted his supply in the

box, he would get up and retrieve the darts. He considered this the exercise his physician had prescribed for him.

"The Moscow policeman Rostnikov," Ellen Sten said, "will discover our man in Devochka. He is capable. Our man has been careless."

"He will not talk," said St. James, hurling a fresh dart.

"You wish to take that chance?"

The chance was that their man would reveal how the diamonds were smuggled out of Devochka and turned over to the Botswanans in Moscow. There was no doubt now that the man who had contacted him, the Russian policeman named Yaklovev, knew about the operation, but he had no proof, no culprits to arrest and parade in court or use as chips to deal himself into a fortune. But the man had not indicated that he was interested in money. He wanted power. Others would not have believed the Russian, but St. James did. He understood. The Russian was a kindred seeker of power and approval. St. James did not intend to give him either.

Gerald St. James had carefully worked out the plan for the demise of his own network. It had outlived its usefulness and had become far too vulnerable. Devochka was only a small part of the St. James empire, a very vulnerable part. Devochka had become too elaborate. If and when it was reestablished, he would see to it that it was far more simple. As it stood now, the diamonds were smuggled out of Devochka by the regularly scheduled plane to Moscow. In Moscow, the diamonds were turned over to the Botswanans, who verified their authenticity and made arrangements to safeguard their transfer to a courier who would take them to the contact in Kiev, who, in turn, would get them to Paris, where they would be transported to London. It had evolved thus. It was much too awkward. It had all been set up by a member of the Russian parliament for a steep price. It had been early in Gerald St. James's expansion. He would never do something so full of unnecessary intrigue again. A simple transfer of diamonds to Ellen in Moscow and a quick flight on St. James's jet, and that would be that. The present system had to end, and so too did the contacts in Devochka, Moscow, and Kiev.

"No," said St. James. "Have him killed, but first have him eliminate any trace of what we have done in the mine."

"Cut off our access to the pipe?" she said calmly.

"The trickle is not worth the risk. We'll use our source to find another way to the pipe, but we'll wait a few years. Patience. Moscow?"

"The situation is a bit messy I'm afraid," Sten said. "Another of our Botswanans has been killed. This time by the police. That leaves two, plus the one the alcoholic Russian is holding."

St. James shook his head before throwing the dart in his hand.

"Situations involving the kind of people we deal with will often get messy."

"The Botswanans who are left do not know how to reach us. The one who is a hostage of the Russian . . ."

"Kolokov," she supplied.

"The Botswanan he has is our contact, correct?"

"Yes."

"And this Kolokov is proving himself an idiot."

"Yes," she said. "The two remaining Botswanans seem to be planning a rescue or an exchange. It seems the police know about the planned rescue. Shall we warn Kolokov?"

He looked at her and sighed.

"No," he said. "Let us not lose sight of our goal, which is . . ."

"To end our operation in Devochka, Moscow, and Kiev and eliminate anyone with whom we have had direct business contact so that it looks as if we were not involved."

"So that it looks as if we have been hurt by the murder and violence," he amended. "Messy. I wonder if they ever have problems like this at DeBeers?"

"I'm confident they do," she said.

He had at least fifteen darts left before he had to get up from his chair.

"Eliminate the enterprise," he said.

"Yes," she said.

"How difficult will it be to replace the Botswanans?"

"Not difficult. Expensive."

"You will have two years from the time the current enterprise is terminated till we have a new presence in Moscow. That leaves Kiev."

"Balta is behaving rather strangely," she said.

"Strangely? The man is mad," said St. James, deftly letting a dart fly and missing the red circle by at least a foot. "You know what he is doing?"

"I think so," she said. "With a man like that . . ."

"A man like that," St. James repeated,

remembering a time when circumstances had briefly made him a man like Balta, with a knife as sharp.

"He plans to find the diamonds and keep the money for himself," she said. "He has no intention I'm sure of turning over anything to the Botswanans."

"Who will not exist in any case. Talk to Balta."

"I doubt if it will do any good."

"I don't intend to reason with him. I intend to lull him into a sense of complacency."

"And then?"

"You will arrange to get the diamonds and the money and kill Balta. That will be the last step in our temporary closure of the Russian chain. The checkmate of Yaklovev and his Office of Special Investigations."

He paused, dart in hand, and sighed so slightly that only Ellen, who knew his every move, would have detected it.

"What is it?" she asked.

"What an asinine name. Balta."

Mounted on shiny dark stone and laid into notches along the path of gray blocks rested the thirteen honored rectangular polished coffins. The coffins contained not human remains but capsules of earth from the Hero

Cities of World War II — Moscow, Leningrad, Kiev, Minsk, Volgograd, Sevastopol, Odessa, Novorossiysk, Kerch, Tula, the Brest Fortress, Murmansk, and Smolensk. The name of each city stood out in large letters facing the path.

The memorial, the Eternal Flame, and the Tomb of the Unknown Warrior meant little to Biko and Laurence other than as possible places in which to hide while they waited for the coming of the Russians who had James Harumbaki.

Yesterday Patrice, before he was killed by the police, had wondered what they might do if the Russians came without their hostage. He had come to no clear conclusion. Biko and Laurence were even less equipped to deal with the problem. So they had concluded that they would arrive in the Alexandrovsky Gardens early, hide, wait, and when the Russians appeared with James Harumbaki they would spring out and fire, trying very hard not to kill James Harumbaki. If the Russians arrived without their hostage, they would try to bargain with the worthless stones Biko had in his pocket. They agreed that Laurence would do the talking, though his command of Russian was no better than Biko's.

But this was not to be.

First, there were uniformed soldiers in full dress and carrying rifles guarding the ground-level tomb, which was set back against a high wall behind the thirteen entombed capsules of earth.

They could be dealt with. They would have no idea what was going to happen, and both Biko and Laurence reasoned that in the bloody battle that was very likely to take place the death of a few soldiers caught in the crossfire would be marked as casualties of Moscow gang fighting.

But this was also not to be.

Biko and Laurence stood about forty yards from the memorial, off the path, behind a stand of bushes. They thought that this would be the direction from which the Russians would come with James Harumbaki.

And then, quite suddenly, to their left, down the path a dozen or so people quietly appeared, men and women, mostly in their twenties or thirties. All of them were carrying flowers. The group went silently past Biko and Laurence to the tomb and placed the flowers among others that had been put there during the day. The soldiers stood at attention.

Biko and Laurence waited behind a small brace of yellow-flowered bushes for the group to move away, but they stood silently, heads bowed.

Then Biko and Laurence heard something coming from their right. At first there was a distant murmur of voices. Then it became a chanting. Then dozens of people appeared, crowding the path, bleeding over onto the grass.

Biko and Laurence carefully moved farther back, where they were less likely to be seen.

They could not understand who these new, angry people were. There were boys in black shirts, bearded Russian Orthodox priests carrying crosses and icons, old babushkas crying out.

They descended on the small group that had laid out the flowers and began throwing stones, eggs, and condoms filled with water, shouting, "Moscow is not Sodom" and "Faggots Out." One screaming young woman with a bullhorn, her face turning red, screeched a tinny-sounding, "Not Gay Pride. Queer Shame."

"What is happening?" asked Biko.

"I do not know," answered Laurence as about twenty policemen in full uniform and wearing helmets with Plexiglas face covers appeared as if from the air, swinging batons at the black shirts, priests, and old ladies.

Surrounded, the twenty or so gays fought their way through the crowd with the help of the police and began to run, with the black shirts in pursuit. The police beat the attackers with clubs and pushed a dozen or so of them against the wall behind the tomb.

"We must leave and come back in an hour," said Laurence.

Biko agreed. If this crowd was attacking a small group of quiet homosexuals peacefully placing flowers on a tomb, what might they do to two black men who were carrying weapons?

As they eased away, above the shouting they could clearly hear the voice of the screaming woman on the bullhorn.

"Mayor Yuri Luzhkov of our beloved Moscow has said that any attempt by these people to lay flowers here is a 'desecration of a sacred place.' They should expect to be beaten."

"Russians are very crazy people," said Laurence. "I have known crazy people in Sudan, Ghana, but none as crazy as Russians."

Yes, thought Biko, *Africa is much safer.*

Sasha Tkach had just been through an early morning ordeal. His phone had rung just before six while he lay in the darkness of his hotel room, awake but unwilling to rise, shower, and shave. He would move when the glowing red numbers on his tiny travel clock, a gift from his mother, hit six and two zeroes.

"Sasha?"

It was the very last person whose voice he wished to hear.

"Yes."

"Do you know what your name means?" Lydia Tkach asked.

"You woke me to ask . . . ?"

"Aleksei, do you know?"

She almost never called him Aleksei, and when she did so it was intended to indicate a very serious subject of conversation. The problem was that Lydia thought anything regarding her only son was monumentally important.

"Defender of men," he said.

"Do you know what your name was supposed to be before your father, may he rest with the angels in a field of silver icons, insisted that you be called Aleksei?"

"You are a Communist and an atheist," he said, holding the phone a few inches from his ear to protect himself from his hard-of-hearing mother who, at the age of seventy, thought people could only be heard on telephones if they were shouted at. "You do not believe that my father is with any angels."

"I believe what the times dictate I should believe," she shouted. "That is how we survive. Your name was to have been the same as my father's, Kliment which means . . ."

"Merciful and gentle," he concluded.

"Merciful and gentle," she said, not heeding her son's words. "You were meant to be merciful and gentle."

"By God?"

"No, by me. Did you see Maya?"

"Yes."

"When is she coming home with the children?"

"She is not."

"Try again."

"I'm going to go see her and the children as soon as you let me go."

"Who is keeping you? It is time for you to stop being a policeman. I will bet that even now as we are speaking some criminal is planning to beat you or seduce you or stab you or shoot you . . ."

"Or drop a rock on my head or beat me with a wooden cross or . . ."

"You are mocking me."

"Yes."

"You are mocking your mother who is trying to save your marriage and your life," she said.

"I am sorry."

He was sitting up now, licking his dry lips with his dry tongue and wondering if perhaps his mother might not be right.

"Think about it."

"I will," he said.

"Now go get my grandchildren and your wife."

Before he could ask her how she got his cell phone's newly changed number, she hung up.

He should plan what he was going to say, how he would say it. It was difficult to convince himself that he would be fine if she gave him another chance. If he could not convince himself, how could he convince Maya?

What was it she had said? He was a lamb waiting to be shorn by any attractive woman. Some day the shears would slip and he would bleed and be standing shorn and suddenly naked.

He staggered to the bathroom, turned on the light, and looked at himself in the mirror. He was not growing more handsome with each passing day.

"Pathetic image that was meant to be Kliment, you must offer something meaningful. You must make a sacrifice that she cannot refuse."

His image looked back at him, letting him know exactly what that sacrifice must be. He hurried to shower, shave, wash, and dress so that he could see his children and present his gift to Maya.

Elena lined up the 5 × 7 photographs next to the fax machine in the Russian embassy.

They had two more days before the meeting that would determine the fate of the Office of Special Investigations.

It was a little before seven in the morning and she had a buttered roll and a cup of coffee perched on the table next to the machine. The roll and coffee had been provided by a junior diplomat who had worked through the previous night on a report dealing with the potential tour of a Chinese cellist who now resided in Kiev.

The junior diplomat, whose name was Machov, had told her that the fax machine would be in constant demand in less than twenty minutes when the rest of the staff started to come in.

The first photograph was of Jan Pendowski. The second was of the French woman named Rochelle Tanquay, and the third was of a thin, vacant-eyed man with a scarf around his neck who appeared to be following the Kiev policeman.

She faxed all three photos to Moscow. Later she would try to find a fax number for Porfiry Petrovich in Siberia. When she was finished, she put the photographs back in a folder in her briefcase and stood drinking her coffee and eating her roll.

She yearned for a sausage, even a small one. She had been watching her weight for months and she was sure, though he denied it, Iosef was also watching her weight.

He said that he loved her just the way she was, but when she pressed him about her size, he had admitted that she might be able to fit in clothing more svelte were she to shed a few pounds. Shed a few pounds. He had said it as if it were as easy as taking off one's shoes. "Svelte" was not a descriptive term for Elena. Full-bodied was much more accurate. Her bones would not allow for svelte as they had not allowed her mother, aunt, or grandmothers a leaner frame.

There was no way Elena Timofeyeva would or could ever look like Oxana Balakona or Rochelle Tanquay.

In half an hour she was due in Jan Pendowski's office for what she was certain would be a wild goose chase across Kiev in search of Oxana Balakona. She had agreed to let Sasha see Maya and the children instead of coming with her.

The primary problem with being alone to spend the better part of a day with Pendowski was that he was certain to make sexual overtures unless she did something forceful. She was not flattered by the possibility of his advances. He seemed to be in very good condition. He made that clear by wearing his sleeves rolled up to display his muscles and his shirt unbuttoned one button to show just a bit of chest. He was not an oaf, and she could see how some women might find him interesting. Elena found him wearisome, however. The man was a walking unsatisfied penis.

The one thing she had decided was that if he placed a hand on her once, she would remove it. If he placed a hand on her twice, he would hit the floor with a sudden and painful thud. She hoped, if that happened, there were many people around to watch, and that of the many people around to watch, police officers would be preferable.

She checked her watch and went looking for the junior diplomat to ask him if there was a place nearby, perhaps a cart or stand, where she could buy a sausage sandwich.

Iosef and Zelach were jostled forward by

the crowd, wedged in between two bearded priests wielding crosses like bludgeons and crying out against specified and unspecified blasphemy. Iosef wondered where these men had been for the almost seventy godless years of Communism.

It was difficult in the mélange of bodies to remain upright, to keep from getting herded by the police against the wall behind the tomb, and also to watch the two Africans, who were running from the scene.

The screaming woman with the bullhorn was at Zelach's side now, as the two policemen tried to make their way through the crowd to the grass beyond the path. Zelach reached up and turned a knob on the bullhorn, sending out a screech that brought winces to the faces of police, gay mourners, and the angry mob. Then the bullhorn went silent. The screaming woman had not noticed Zelach's move, but a babushka had and shouted, "That one. He turned it off." She was pointing at Zelach.

Iosef also shouted and pointed at a nearby tall black shirt.

"Him," he said. "I saw him too."

A few in the crowd reached for the protesting black shirt. Zelach and Iosef made a lunge through a small opening in the crowd and arrived in the open, just missing a baton swung by a particularly large policeman.

"Police," Iosef said, pulling out his identification and showing it to the large slashing policeman who was in no mood or condition to examine identification.

Iosef and Zelach ran. The large policeman turned back on the crowd.

"We are the police," Zelach said, panting.

"Policemen have been known to be injured by mobs and each other," said Iosef. "Which way did they go?"

"The mob? They are right . . ."

"The Africans."

"There," said Zelach, pointing.

"You see them?"

"They were heading for Red Square."

Iosef nodded and started in pursuit with Zelach right behind.

"They will get lost in the crowd," said Zelach.

"Two black men? One tall and thin, the other short and round?"

"It is possible."

"It is possible," said Iosef, who began laughing as they ran.

"Is this funny?" asked Zelach, barely able to keep up.

"Forgive me, Zelach. The Rostnikovs have a peculiar sense of humor."

Which, thought Zelach, *is better than hav-*

ing no sense of humor, which is the legacy of both sides of my family.

"There," gasped Zelach, trying to catch his breath.

Iosef saw them in the crowd, just about to hurry through the Metro station entrance.

"Slow, now," said Iosef.

It was a command Zelach has happy to hear.

Iosef was hoping that the two men they were trying to catch would also slow down. They had no reason to believe they were being followed. If the policemen hurried, they might be spotted. If they were too slow, they might well lose their quarry.

Biko and Laurence had to slow down. They had no magnetic Metro cards. They had to stop at the booth and pay their fares, pointing to the map of stations on the wall. Neither man commanded more than a short supply of Russian.

"Now what?" they both said at almost the same instant, walking toward their platform.

They walked through the palatial Metro station, past glittering statues and brightly painted ceilings, unsure of what their next step might be or how they might reconnect with the Russians who had James Harumbaki.

The loudspeaker announced the arrival of a train in Russian. It meant nothing to the two men, who were trying to decipher the name of the station on the wall. They were heading back to the only neighborhood in the city where they were likely to reach other Africans, particularly Botswanans.

They looked blankly at the station map and got on the first train that arrived, hoping that they had read the map correctly.

Their weapons were under their coats in leather and cloth slings designed by James Harumbaki. It was possible to fire simply by reaching under the coat, tilting the weapon, and firing while it was still in the sling. Biko had given serious consideration to doing just that when he saw the insane crowd moving in their direction in the park.

They were living in a nation of near madness.

Biko and Laurence sat in the almost empty late evening car of the Metro as far from others as they could. Across from them on a seat lay a German shepherd, asleep. There was no human who looked like an owner nearby. Laurence was particularly fond of dogs and wanted to move across and carefully offer his hand. The dog did not seem to belong to anyone. Maybe they could take it with them. Dogs had a calming effect on him, and he harbored a very slight feeling of guilt about the three times not long ago in Somalia when he had eaten the meat of scrawny dogs.

Farther down, three Russians were sprawled on the seat. They were drunk. One man had his head in the lap of a second. The third lay by himself, eyes open, about to slip to the floor.

As the car doors began to close, a large bald man holding a cloth to the back of his head got in, glanced at Biko and Laurence, and sat at the far end of the car.

The train moved out of the station, and a Russian voice announced the next station.

The bald man, Pau Montez, did not look directly at the Africans, and in the next car Iosef and Zelach sat doing their best not to be seen by the desperate Biko and Laurence.

"Do you know why I pace like this?" asked Kolokov without stopping.

James Harumbaki was not interested in the question but he waited for an answer. He was seated at a table, the chessboard before him. He was not tied, and he considered, since the large bald man was not present, that it might be possible to run across the room, throw open the door, dash through the house, and, once in the open, make a dash over the pile of rubbish and into the partial cover of the trees. He had gauged all this. It might be possible, but it was unlikely to succeed. James Harumbaki's legs were weak. One eye was almost closed. He felt slightly dizzy. And there were two others in the room, silent Russians, one of whom, though he looked quite out of shape, was close to the door. Better to wait for a more promising opportunity.

"Do you know why I pace?" Kolokov repeated, smoking as he walked a bit faster across the room.

James Harumbaki's lower lip was swollen where Kolokov had punched him.

The room smelled of sweat, tobacco, and sour dampness. James Harumbaki would have been sick to his stomach even if Kolokov had not punched his belly.

"No, I do not," said James Harumbaki.

"Because, it helps me think, think, think."

With each "think" Kolokov had tapped the side of his head with a distinct *thwack.*

James Harumbaki nodded his understanding.

"I am not surrounded by a council of great minds," Kolokov said, looking at his two cohorts who provided no response. "I would like to have at least one person I can count on to use his head for something besides a battering ram. You know what I mean?"

James Harumbaki croaked a "yes."

As a matter of fact, he did know what it was like to be surrounded by people who could not think. He wondered what resources Patrice, Biko, and Laurence were calling upon to replace his leadership. His life depended on what they were going to do and, while he did not doubt their determination, loyalty, or courage, he had no illusions about their intellect.

He smiled. Two gangs of incompetents led by a mad Russian and a Botswanan who really wanted to be a baker of fine cakes.

"This is funny?" asked Kolokov.

"No," said James Harumbaki. "I was just thinking that you are clearly correct in your assessment of the situation. We Africans smile at different things than do Russians."

Kolokov decided to ignore his hostage's reply.

James Harumbaki decided that he would have to control himself to keep from beating the Russian in six or eight moves when the man stopped pacing and decided to play another game of chess.

"All the great . . ." Kolokov began when the door opened.

The large bald man entered and said, "You will not believe this."

Kolokov had stopped pacing.

"I would believe that Putin has become a Jew," Kolokov said. "I would believe that the sun is about to stop shining. I would believe you have seen the ghost of Lenin. What can you possibly say that I would not believe? What are you doing here? You are supposed to be waiting for us at the War Memorial. You are supposed to be looking for the Africans."

"There was a demonstration at the War Memorial," said the bald man. "Faggots were putting flowers on the tomb."

"How patriotic," said Kolokov.

"Then there were lots of people. Men, boys, old women, priests. They came throwing eggs, water, stones. I got hit. Look."

He turned his head to reveal a bloody opening that almost certainly needed stitches and certainly would not be getting them.

"The police came."

"Yes, they beat the queers," said Kolokov, wanting the bald man to get to the point.

"No, they beat the others, the men, the women, the priests . . ."

"Yes, yes," said Kolokov. "Were the Africans there?"

"Yes, there were two of them. They ran away. I think some of the crowd was chasing them. I followed them. They got on the Metro."

"Where did they go?"

"To a bar, a bar full of blacks. I think they may have noticed me."

One of the other two men made a sound that may have been a laugh. The bald man gave him a warning look.

"How could they possibly notice you?" Kolokov said. "A big, bald white man with a gushing wound on his head. They must have had to employ very keen powers of observation honed from a hundred generations of hunting in the jungle. They will not be coming to the memorial to make the exchange."

"I have the phone number of the cafe," said the bald man.

Kolokov scratched his neck, and the bald man handed him a torn corner from a newspaper.

"You know the cafe they went to?"

The question was addressed to James Harumbaki.

"Yes," he said.

"You will call them and I will tell you a new place for the exchange," said Kolokov.

James Harumbaki said nothing.

"There is one more thing," said the bald man.

Kolokov had been leaning forward so that his face was only inches from his hostage.

"And what is that?" asked Kolokov, still looking at James Harumbaki.

"There were two other people following them. I think they were policemen."

Kolokov clasped his hands together, then clapped once and stood up.

"Go take care of your head," he said calmly. "We will all have a drink from the bottle of vodka which Bogdan, who laughs in the corner, will pour for us all. I will then play another game of chess with our valuable guest and decide how we will engage our endgame with his friends and the police."

He sat across from James Harumbaki.

"It will be interesting, and when it is over either we will have millions in diamonds or this will be the last game of chess for our guest."

It was at this point, as the mad Russian waited for him to set up the pieces on the board, that James Harumbaki decided that it was not the time or place to beat his captor.

The bodies of the two Africans had been

replaced on Paulinin's laboratory table by two bodies that had been flown in from some idiotic place in Siberia.

Rostnikov had called, inquired about the condition and tranquility of his leg, and asked that the examination of the bodies he had sent be done as soon as possible.

One reason, Rostnikov said, was that the Canadian government wanted the body of the younger man.

And that was why Paulinin had turned on the CD of Peter Illyich Tchaikovsky's *Rococo Variations for Cello and Orchestra,* switched on the bright overheads, scratched his head, adjusted his glasses, scrubbed his hands, and made a decision. In the privacy of his laboratory, he would perform a dual autopsy.

Before doing so, however, he consulted with the two dead men as he laid out his instruments.

"You do not mind?" he asked.

"No, why should we," said the old man, naked on the table. "We are dead. Are you not going to ask who killed us?"

"Would you tell me?" asked Paulinin, scalpel in hand, bending over the pale corpse of the Canadian.

"No," said the old man. "You will have to discover that for yourself."

"You agree?" he asked the Canadian as he made an incision to open wide the dark, almost blue, clotted wound in his chest, which had probably been the cause of death.

"Of course," said the Canadian in perfect Russian.

Paulinin paused, long, sharp blade inserted deeply in flesh, as a favorite cello solo called out from the shadows where the speakers rested. The beauty of the passage almost brought him to tears.

Paulinin knew full well that neither dead man could talk, that the conversation was completely within his mind. Often Paulinin would get carried away by his conversations with the dead and forget for a while that the dead could not really speak. He likened his experience to that of a writer who carries on conversations with characters who do not exist, or of people watching a movie who both believe and disbelieve that what they are seeing is really taking place.

"Of course," he said, pushing two fingers deeply into the wound, "one would have to be insane to believe that what was happening in a movie was really taking place, but at the same time, if the movie experience was working, the viewer would . . . what have I found?"

"What?" asked the Canadian.

"What?" asked the old man on the table behind Paulinin.

Paulinin took his bloody fingers from the wound, picked up a foot-long instrument with a pincer at the end, and inserted it into the wound where his fingers had been.

It took him a difficult minute or so of probing before he realized that he had pushed that which he sought into the auricle of the heart.

Tchaikovsky, orchestra, and plaintive cello urged him on.

He found what he was looking for and slowly, carefully, to keep from losing it, removed the long, thin instrument and held it up to the light. The object was small — tiny actually — a piece of metal with a determined clot of blood clinging to it.

He dropped the bit of metal into a kidney-shaped porcelain receptacle.

"What is it?" asked the Canadian. "It was in me. I have a right to know."

"He does not know yet what it is," said the old Russian.

"Let us know when you find out," said the Canadian.

"I will," Paulinin promised, "but before I examine it, I must probe the surfaces and recesses of your bodies for more treasures."

"We will not stop you," said the old man.

"I am certain you will not," said Paulinin, turning his attention and gleaming instruments on the old man.

"It is good to have a spotter who knows what he is doing," said Viktor Panin.

He was lying on his back on the bench in the well-equipped weight room. His hands were heavily chalked. Over his blue sweatshorts and a matching cutoff shirt that revealed his taut, full muscles, Viktor wore a leather harness pulled tightly to guard against hernia.

Rostnikov, wearing a full long-sleeved gray sweatsuit, stood at the head of the bench. The bar, with massive black disks weighing more than four hundred pounds, rested in the cradle of the matching upright thick round steel bars that straddled the bench. It was unlikely that Rostnikov, even with a rush of adrenaline, could hold the weight should Panin begin to falter, an eventuality that was quite unlikely.

"A spotter one can count on," said Panin, "gives one confidence."

Panin was looking up at the bar, gauging it, his strength, and his resolve, not seeing Porfiry Petrovich beyond that bar.

He placed both palms against the bar and worked his fingers around it. Rostnikov understood the meditative moment, the merging of hands, fingers, arms, body, mind, and the weight of iron — solid iron.

Viktor Panin closed his eyes, clearing his mind, took a deep breath, held it, and pushed upward, lifting the bar from the cradle and slowly bringing the crushing weight down toward his body. He stopped just short of his chest and exhaled. Then he lifted again, his arms steady, locking over his head.

Rostnikov had not seen anything quite like this before, though he had experienced something like the much younger man was feeling. It was a universal experience that Porfiry Petrovich was certain all who reached a certain level of truly heavy weights must feel.

Instead of resting the bar back on the cradles, Viktor Panin took another deep breath and brought the bar to his chest once more, still without a quiver in his arms. Then he slowly pushed the bar back to a locked arm position, exhaled, and placed the bar on the cradles.

"I've never done two repetitions with this much weight before," Panin said between short breaths, sitting upon the bench. "Your understanding inspires me, Porfiry Petrovich Rostnikov. Your turn now. I'll change the weights."

Viktor Panin got off the bench.

Rostnikov chalked his hands, beginning his necessary ritual of appeasing and praising his plastic and metal leg as he laid back on the bench.

"How much weight?" Viktor asked, moving to the bar.

"I think I will try this weight."

Viktor touched Porfiry Petrovich's arm.

"Good," the young man said.

"You have inspired me," said Rostnikov.

"Trust me."

"I will," said Rostnikov.

This the detective said knowing that Viktor could slip at a crucial moment, letting the four hundred pounds of steel drop, crushing Porfiry Petrovich's chest.

This the detective said knowing that he was putting his trust in a man who was still, in spite of an alibi for one of the two murders, a distinct suspect as diamond thief, smuggler, murderer, and keeper of the secret of the ghost girl.

Porfiry Petrovich Rostnikov, Chief Inspector in the Moscow Police Office of Special Investigations, had seen far stronger alibis crumble to dust.

Viktor Panin looked down at him, a smile of encouragement and confidence on the perspiring face of the younger man.

"When you are ready, Porfiry Petrovich."

Rostnikov closed his eyes and imagined the fleeting voice of Dinah Washington singing the first words of "What A Difference A Day Makes."

There were two days remaining until the Yak's deadline and the possible end of the Office of Special Investigations.

CHAPTER FIFTEEN

Six-year-old Pulcharia Tkach stood next to the sofa holding her four-year-old brother's hand. They were dressed in their school clothes, she in a blue blouse and skirt and knee-length white socks, he in a brown shirt and trousers that were slipping. Maya stood behind them protectively. The scene looked posed. It was posed.

Sasha was immediately depressed. He smiled as broadly and sincerely as he could and stepped forward to embrace his children.

Pulcharia looked up at her mother to be sure it was all right to hug her father. Maya smiled. Pulcharia let go of her brother's hand and rushed into the arms of Sasha, who bent to take her in. He could instantly feel the rapid beating of her heart against his chest, and, at least for an instant, his depression was replaced by a deep, painful sadness.

"Who is he?" asked Sasha's son, looking up at his mother.

"Your father," Maya said.

"I have a bug bite on my leg," Pulcharia said, still hugging.

"Where?" asked Sasha, reluctantly putting her down so she could show him.

He looked at her as she rolled down the sock on her left leg. She looked painfully like her mother.

"Here."

She pointed at a red bump.

"It itches," she said.

"Who?" the little boy insisted, now pulling at his mother's skirt.

"Your father," Maya repeated patiently.

"Oh. What does a father do?"

"What have you put on it?" Sasha asked his daughter.

"Mother put something on it that Erik gave her," said Pulcharia.

The Swede. Sasha could not stop himself from looking at his wife. Did her lips tighten? Yes.

"Erik is a sweet dish," said the boy, turning in a circle.

"Swedish," Pulcharia corrected.

"Your father cannot stay," said Maya. "He has to work, and you must go to school."

"School is cruel," the little boy said,

continuing to turn. "I have a new name."

"What is that?" asked Sasha.

"Taras. Taras. Taras."

The boy spun around madly.

"It is a Ukrainian name," Maya said. "He will get over it."

"He need not on my account," said Sasha.

"It was my sister's husband's idea," said Maya. "He thought it was funny. It is a Montagnard tribal name."

"I like it," Sasha lied.

"I told my friend Tula that you are a policeman and that you catch fish thieves and people who drink too much vodka and pee in the street," said Pulcharia.

"Your father catches people who do very bad things," Maya said. "He protects the good people of Moscow from the bad people of Moscow."

"Good peeeeeeople," the little boy said. "Bad peeeeeople. Taras. Taras. Taras."

"Your father will come back and see you again before he has to go back to Moscow and catch more bad people," Maya said.

Was this a sign of hope?

"I will be back tonight?" he said, making it a question and not a statement.

"Tonight," Maya said.

"For dinner?" asked Pulcharia.

"For dinner," Maya said.

Pulcharia smiled broadly.

"Will Erik be here too?" the girl asked.

"No, not tonight."

Pulcharia leaned toward her father and puckered her lips to be kissed. Sasha obliged.

"Taras too," said the little boy, who ran forward, perfectly balanced in spite of his spinning.

"Seven o'clock," said Maya.

"You are all very beautiful," Sasha said.

"Seven," Maya repeated.

The map which Gennadi Ivanov had drawn for Karpo lay flattened on the small table in Porfiry Petrovich's room.

Neither man had told anyone of the map drawn by the very old man who held a very old grudge against the Japanese. The two policemen could not trust the map or anyone in Devochka.

Rostnikov was sitting. Karpo stood.

"One of the many ironies of an artificial leg is that it is lighter than a real one," said Rostnikov. "I am unbalanced and have had to learn to compensate. Of course, I could ask the man who made my leg to add weight to it, but then he might add too much, and the surgeon would have to remove some of my right leg to get the balance right again."

"You are making a joke," said Karpo.

"I am," said Rostnikov, "but I am also making a point. Maintain your balance. Adjust to change. Do not seek perfection. There is no perfection."

"And you believe I seek perfection?" said Karpo.

"I know you do, Emil. Please sit. It is a strain to look up in a conversation and it destroys the illusion of intimacy."

Karpo moved to the bed and sat, his back upright. Rostnikov turned his chair to face him.

"There are those who believe you had no mother," said Rostnikov.

"Everyone has a mother," said Karpo.

"Well, the belief is not grounded in reality, but in perception."

"I find it difficult to believe that there are those who would engage in such curious perceptions."

"You may not know it, but there are those who find you a fascinating enigma. They do not know you as I do, Emil Karpo. I often think of you as my second son."

"I . . . thank you."

Rostnikov could not recall hearing even a touch of emotion in his associate's voice since the death of Mathilde. Only two events had shaken Emil Karpo's steel self-image: the fall of the Soviet Union and the death of Mathilde Verson. He had been devoted to both, and with their deaths had encased what little emotion he had previously displayed.

"Is there some reason we are discussing this now?" asked Karpo.

"Yes. I will tell you in a moment. My father was a good man."

Karpo had no response.

"What about your father, Emil Karpo?"

"You have read my file. You know the few facts of my history."

"This makes you uncomfortable."

"Perplexed."

"You never knew your father. Your mother and aunt raised you."

"That is correct."

"I think when we return to Moscow you might consider an attempt to locate your father."

"Why?"

"Closure," said Rostnikov. "You have a brother."

"Yes."

"When did you last talk to him?"

"Twenty-two years ago, on June four."

"And your mother?"

"Twenty-two years ago, on June four."

"And the reason for the events of that

momentous day in the history of the family, Karpo?"

"I believe you are mocking," said Karpo.

"Forgive me," said Rostnikov. "You are right. Mockery and irony are protective Russian responses that often prevail over consideration for others."

"On that day I told my brother, mother, and aunt that I could no longer see or talk to them because of their anti-Communist feelings and remarks. I told them that I would not issue a report on them."

"What do you think made you what you are, Emil my friend?"

"I do not know."

"Perhaps a meeting with your father, if he is still alive, would answer that question."

"Perhaps."

"Are you not curious?"

The pause was slight, but Rostnikov perceived it.

"No."

"Well, I am."

"You said this conversation had a particular point."

"It does," said Rostnikov. "In two hours, Boris will take us into the mine armed with this map. I am confident we will see the ghost girl and that someone will try to kill us to keep us from finding what is in at least one of the small caves on the map of our Japanese-obsessed friend."

"And you know who the person who will try to kill us is," said Karpo.

"Oh yes, and that is the point of my exploration of your familial relationships. I am very much afraid that the person who will attempt to kill us is my brother."

Each night the Yak allowed himself a single, full glass of a deep red Italian table wine before he went to sleep. He had one glass, and only one, a day unless he was with someone higher on the scale of politics or the law. If that person drank, so did Yaklovev. And that was the situation at the moment.

He was in the Taiga Restaurant, not far from the Bolshoi Opera. Across from him was a very smug General Peotor Frankovich in a blue suit and tie. The general's fat pink neck usually hung over the stiff collar of the uniform he liked to wear. The blue suit accented the roll of fat. Someone should tell him. That someone would not be Igor Yaklovev.

"We should be arranging for the transition," said Frankovich, holding his glass of wine, twisting it by the stem with thumb and finger.

They sat in a corner away from others. Privacy.

"Drink," said the general.

Yaklovev drank.

"There are still two days remaining," he said.

"If you insist," said Frankovich with a shrug. "I just thought a friendly dinner would be a good start to what is necessary. Of course the details will be worked out by yourself and your Chief Inspector . . ."

"Rostnikov, Porfiry Petrovich Rostnikov."

"Hmm," said the general, sipping his wine and then looking at it as if for imperfections. "We serve the same government for the good of the Russian people."

The last was said with no hint of sincerity.

"We do," said the Yak.

"There really is nothing that can alter what is inevitable," said Frankovich, reaching up to tug at his collar.

"Two days," the Yak said.

"There are no miracles, my friend," the general said.

The Yak was not hoping for miracles. There was a great deal Yaklovev had done and was still doing. Now, if only Rostnikov and his people could come through, the Yak would be ready to act. For now, he sat silently and drank his wine.

■ ■ ■ ■

Stepan Orlov, the microbiologist, looked up when Rostnikov entered his small laboratory. Orlov, a man of average height with wild, curly gray-brown hair, had unlocked and opened the door when Rostnikov had identified himself as a Moscow policeman.

The laboratory was spotless and neat. There were twelve small cages against one wall. Inside, animals scurried, trying to climb the metal walls or hide under wood shavings. One of the animals was making a squealing sound Rostnikov had never before heard.

Against one wall, on which there was the only window in the room, was a cot made military taut with a rough khaki blanket and a thin pillow. Three broad-topped metal tables forming a U sat in the center of the room with one wooden chair on rollers within the U. The table to the right of where Orlov now sat held a binocular microscope. The table on the left held a computer whose screen seemed to be pulsing between gray and white. On the center table was a large metal tray holding the second-largest rat Rostnikov had ever seen.

"You are admiring Rhazumi," Orlov said,

cleaning his glasses on his wrinkled white shirt.

"The rat."

"Big, is he not," said Orlov, reaching out to touch the nose of the dead animal that lay with its front legs together as if in prayer.

"I have seen only one bigger," said Rostnikov. "At the edge of the Moscow River. It was as big as a small dog."

"Yes," said Orlov, "but Rhazumi was blind. He lived for at least six years in the total darkness of the depths of the mine. And there are others. Their ancestors crawled down there when the mine was first opened and bred and adapted and consumed other small creatures and the detritus of humans. And at some point, they went blind. Survival of the fittest, in this case the blind. I think this species is unique in the world."

He looked with admiration at the dead animal. So did Rostnikov. Then he looked up at the window. The day was overcast.

"Is it cold out there today?"

"I have not been outside today," said Rostnikov.

"The temperature makes no difference to creatures who live and walk in darkness," said Orlov.

"Even the people?"

"Humans adapt by changing the environment, not by changing their bodies."

"I would like you to look at this map."

Rostnikov took out the rough map. Orlov took it.

"Gennadi Ivanov drew this," he said. "I recognize his mad scribbling."

"Yes," said Rostnikov.

"You want to sit? Oh, manners. Would you like a cup of coffee or tea?"

He nodded toward a table near the window behind him. On the table was a coffee maker that belonged to antiquity. The liquid beyond the glass was the color of a raven.

"No. Thank you."

"I avoid Ivanov," the scientist said. "Have not spoken to him in years. I used to talk to him about animal life he claimed to have seen in the mines, but he always brought the conversation back to the damned Japanese invasion."

"He still does."

"This map is not accurate," Orlov said. "I have better ones."

He reached into a drawer under the computer and came up with a folder, which he opened on top of Ivanov's map.

"Here."

He handed Rostnikov a sheet on which there was drawn a clear three-dimensional representation of the mine, complete with distances in meters in the same dark black ink used to draw the map.

"I understand there are small caves."

"They are marked with red dots. I have found some of my most interesting specimens in those tiny caves — insects, worms, bacteria. In one of those caves I made the discovery that will make me . . . a great discovery."

"May I ask what . . . ?"

"I lost my wife because of my work, because I have lived in this room, this cell of discovery. I eat in here, sleep in here. Through that door is a shower, sink, refrigerator, and toilet. I keep in shape. One hundred sit-ups, seventy-five push-ups. Look at my arms."

Orlov rolled up his sleeves to reveal truly massive biceps.

"I was told you beat Panin arm wrestling."

"Of course. Would you like to try me?"

"May I stand? I have an artificial leg and . . ."

"Yes," said Orlov. "Right hand or left?"

"Right," said Rostnikov, leaning over the table and positioning his elbow next to Stepan Orlov's.

"We do it only once," said Rostnikov.

"Once," Orlov agreed. "We begin when

you say 'ready.' "

"Ready," said Rostnikov, putting all he had into his thrust.

Orlov had not been ready for the instant "ready," but he did pull himself together and managed to stop his hand from touching the table, though there was no more than half an inch between the back of his hand and the shining metal. Before he could fully recover, Rostnikov, who had the advantage of leverage because he was standing, put his full weight into his arm and Orlov's hand hit the table.

Orlov began to laugh.

"No one has beaten me before," he said. "Now you . . ."

"You inadvertently allowed me an advantage."

"And that is how you work as a detective?"

"Whenever possible."

"I like you, Inspector . . ."

"Chief Inspector Porfiry Petrovich Rostnikov."

"Chief Inspector Porfiry Petrovich Rostnikov," Orlov repeated. "I will tell you my secret."

Rostnikov folded the map he had just been given and put it in his pocket. Orlov pursed his lips and touched the front paws of the dead rat.

"In the mouth of this creature," Orlov said softly, "there resides a bacteria, and that bacteria can do the supposedly impossible."

Rostnikov considered the possibility that the scientist might be every bit as mad about his bacteria as Gennadi Ivanov was about the Japanese invasion and his guns. Were there more who had been driven into small rooms of delusion in Devochka? Solzhenitsyn had written of such a Gulag phenomenon.

Orlov looked up.

"You are sworn to silence?" he asked. "I am still two years from publishing my findings."

"I swear to silence," said Rostnikov.

"I believe you. The bacteria can eat carbon. It can even eat diamonds."

With this Orlov folded his arms, adjusted his glasses, and smiled.

"Fascinating," said Rostnikov. "And what function can such a bacteria serve?"

"At this point," said Orlov, "it does not matter. It is not my task to find function. We came naked to the earth and converted what we found to all you see around you. We did it from nothing, from trial and error. A bacteria that consumes diamonds is a wondrous and amazing thing."

"It is," said Rostnikov.

"Even if the remaining diamond pipes run out, the mine must remain. I must remain. The bacteria and their hosts must be preserved, protected, and studied."

"That seems reasonable."

"You think me mad?"

"The dividing line between sanity and madness is not as clear as the lines on your map. In fact, I do not believe there is a line, only a vast area that, at least at its edges, touches us all."

"Gogol?" asked Orlov.

"Rostnikov," replied Rostnikov.

"We should wait till the night," said Pau Montez.

He had a square gauze pad taped to the back of his head. A tiny spot of blood had eked through it.

Kolokov was concentrating on the chessboard which James Harumbaki could see only dimly through his swollen right eye. His left eye was completely closed.

"I will consider your suggestion, but right now I am playing chess," Kolokov said, lighting his third cigarette since sitting across from his hostage.

James had decided not to beat the Russian in eight moves, though he could have. Kolokov played chess the way he played at being a gang leader: He was recklessly mediocre. James decided to stretch the game out and find a way to make his opponent think he was going to win. Then James Harumbaki would spring his trap and softly utter "checkmate."

"We will go when this game ends," Kolokov decided. "They won't be expecting us."

There was only one other gang member, Alek, in the room. He stood silently in the corner. He had survived by standing silently in corners out of Vladimir Kolokov's line of sight.

The other member of the gang, Bogdan, was standing in the doorway of an old apartment building that smelled of onions and people. He was watching the cafe in case the two Africans came out. Kolokov had sent him with the cell phone. He was to call if the Africans left the cafe and to follow them wherever they might be going.

Kolokov smiled at the chessboard and then at James Harumbaki. He was certain now to trap the African with his next move. He sat back, hands folded behind his head. He reeked of satisfaction with a cigarette dangling from the corner of his mouth.

"Checkmate," said James Harumbaki, moving his knight slowly and placing it neatly in the center of a black square.

The smile remained on Kolokov's face for a beat and then his hands came down and he leaned forward to look at the chessboard. It was indeed checkmate. James Harumbaki sat silently. Even had he wished to smile or display a look of satisfaction or regret, he would never make it evident on his battered face.

"Luck," said Kolokov.

"No," said James Harumbaki, thinking of his two comrades who had been brutalized and murdered by the fool across from him.

Kolokov's fists clenched.

"Do not kill him, Vladimir," the bald man said. "We need him. The diamonds."

Kolokov struck his captive with a closed fist. James Harumbaki's head spun to the side. He spit blood and a tooth on the floor. Even with his now further diminished eyesight, James Harumbaki was reasonably sure he could leap across the table, take Kolokov's gun, and shoot him. It was likely the bald man would have his own gun out by then, and James Harumbaki would be a dead man. It was tempting to consider making the move, but the likely result would be his widow and two orphans.

"Let us go now," said Kolokov, picking up his white queen and throwing it at James

Harumbaki.

The queen hit his chest and tumbled to the floor.

James Harumbaki longed for the moment when he would kill the Russian. He would probably have to kill the bald man first, but that, too, would provide satisfaction.

"Get up," shouted Kolokov.

James Harumbaki rose on shaking legs. He knew he could call on his body to respond when required. He had been tortured and beaten in Africa by better men than this Russian.

The Russian grabbed his arm and pushed him toward the door. The bald man went to the corner, opened a suitcase resting on a table against the wall, and revealed a cache of automatic weapons. James Harumbaki recognized the weapon that was handed to Kolokov, an AKS-74U Shorty Assault Rifle with a PBS silent fire device and a BS-1 silent underbarrel grenade launcher. James had seen the weapon used in Sudan, Somalia, and Rwanda. Patrice, Biko, and Laurence would be destroyed instantly along with others in the cafe or on the street unless they acted first. He hoped they understood that they must act first.

Both Kolokov and the bald man put on leather coats that had been hanging on metal hooks screwed into the wall. James Harumbaki watched the Russians hang the assault weapons on slings inside the coats.

"Now we go, black man," said Kolokov with a wild dancing grin. "We will have a talk with your friends and trade you for several handfuls of diamonds. And then we will destroy you and your friends and anyone, black or white, who gets in the way. And that will be the real checkmate."

"Why do we not just arrest them all?" asked Zelach. "The man in the doorway over there watching the two Africans and the Africans, too."

"We will," said Iosef. "But I believe something will happen very soon."

"What?" asked Zelach.

"The man in the doorway is waiting for someone," said Iosef.

"Who?"

"The bald man from the park and the Metro."

"When he comes, we arrest them all?" asked Zelach.

"We do. Meanwhile we stand here in our doorway, watching the two Africans through the window and the man in the doorway over there, who is also watching them."

Iosef had explained all this on the way

here. Zelach often required the repetition of data, not because he was stupid, but because it took time to sink in. But once Zelach put information into his memory, it remained there for eternity, ready for recall. He could relate accurately the details of an arrest made a decade earlier. He could relate it right down to the condition of the criminal's shoes and the exact nature of his crime.

"Do you think, Iosef Rostnikov, that he sees us?"

"No."

"Do you think there will be shooting again?"

"Possibly. Very likely."

Akardy Zelach went silent. He was not afraid, but he thought about his mother. Zelach's mother was, though few knew, a gypsy. She had settled in Moscow for her son's sake, so that he could be a policeman and someday marry a Russian girl and have children.

That day might yet come if Zelach survived long enough. He had once been shot on a case protecting Sasha Tkach. Zelach had survived after a long recovery. He might not be so fortunate the next time.

Now he stood in a doorway with the son of Porfiry Petrovich, wondering if his mother would rejoin her gypsy relatives should her

son be killed.
He wondered.

CHAPTER SIXTEEN

"Why was the ghost girl naked?"

Porfiry Petrovich Rostnikov asked the question as he and Emil Karpo walked down the long corridor on the first floor of the General Semyon Timoshenko apartment and office complex of Devochka.

"There was no ghost girl," said Karpo. "Whoever wrote that false report and put it in the files of Security Chief Fyodor Rostnikov made it up."

"Why?"

"I do not know," said Karpo.

Porfiry Petrovich's artificial leg made a slight clickity-clack sound on the polished concrete floor.

They moved slowly, their footsteps echoing.

Once, before they reached the cafeteria where they were to meet with Old Boris, a door opened. A woman, a bag in her hand and her hair tied in some kind of papered ringlets, stepped out, saw the two detectives, let her eyes rest for an instant on the gaunt detective clad in funereal black, and quickly ducked back through the door.

"He, or she, typed the report, including that colorful detail, and then, when we figured out that the entry was false, placed the typewriter on Fedya's bed. Why?"

"To make him appear guilty when we found it," said Karpo.

"He found it and told us immediately," said Rostnikov. "If making him look guilty was their goal, they accomplished quite the opposite."

They were almost there. Porfiry Petrovich could smell the food. If he was not wrong, it was cabbage soup. The food in Devochka was, he had discovered, surprisingly good. He glanced up at Karpo at his side.

"You think I am making this all too complex?" Rostnikov asked.

"You have historically demonstrated an intuitive ability in such situations."

"Thank you," said Rostnikov. "And you?"

"I have no intuition. I rely on reason alone and distrust reason only slightly less than I trust intuition. One can believe that he is acting with perfect reason only to be deluded by his own fallibility."

"And so I ask you to apply reason to the

crucial question of why the ghost girl was naked."

"Crucial?"

They were now immediately outside of the broad wooden door to the cafeteria.

Definitely cabbage, thought Rostnikov. He hoped they also had the small Georgian crackers that went so well with cooked cabbage.

"Yes," said Rostnikov. "The answer to the question of the naked ghost girl will tell us who our killer is."

He pushed through the door. Karpo followed.

Definitely cabbage.

There were six people talking, laughing, and smoking at a rear table in the cafeteria, which could hold perhaps three hundred people. It had originally been built to feed the workers and their families, but gradually the people of Devochka turned more and more to cooking and eating in the privacy of their own apartments. The irony, which did not escape Rostnikov, and which had been shared by Fyodor, was that the budget for the cafeteria had remained the same for almost fifty years. The cooking staff was obliged, lest they lose their funding, to spend their allotment on nearly gourmet-level food.

They moved immediately to the immaculately clean cafeteria line where they were the only ones waiting. The manager of the cafeteria himself gave both men an extra large serving of the cabbage dish.

"And so tonight we go into the mine," said Rostnikov.

Karpo nodded. He looked at the food piled on his plate and thought it a waste that should not be tolerated.

He had learned, however, that since the fall of the Communist state and ideology to which he had devoted his life, waste and corruption were rampant. He no longer thought that crime could be eliminated in the march toward a near-perfect state. No, the best that could be achieved was to hold the corrupt and the criminal at bay, to work without stop to keep the wall between lawful and lawless from falling under the sheer pressure of individual greed, gluttony, sloth, and occasional madness.

They sat. They ate slowly. They were well ahead of the dinner hour though they had been told that, even when that hour came, the cafeteria would not be overwhelmed.

"What have you noted about my reaction to the mine that might be relevant to our investigation?" asked Rostnikov, taking a large forkful of cabbage and meat. "This is very good."

"You have avoided going into the mine though you have had ample opportunity. And now, since we have but one day remaining till the deadline given by Director Yaklovev, you seem to have little choice but to descend if you feel it must be done."

"And why have I avoided the mine?" asked Rostnikov.

Karpo hesitated.

"I do not know."

"I think you do, Emil Karpo."

"You are afraid."

Rostnikov pointed his fork at his associate to punctuate the accuracy of his observation.

"Tunnels," Rostnikov said. "I have nightmares about them. I do not ride the Metro unless it is absolutely essential."

"I have observed."

"And the contemplation of what we will soon be doing makes me more than a bit uncomfortable."

The contemplation, thought Karpo, did not appear to affect the appetite of Porfiry Petrovich Rostnikov.

Karpo was about to say, "I am sorry," but Rostnikov anticipated and held up the versatile fork to stop him.

"I tell you this not because I feel the need

to cleanse my soul or mind, but to prepare you for what must be done should I literally or figuratively stumble in the lower depths."

Karpo knew better than to suggest that he go alone. Rostnikov would not forgo his responsibility.

With that, Boris entered the cafeteria, looked around, and squinted at the two detectives before he saw them and moved to join them.

It was evident to both detectives, and not for the first time, that their guide into the earth had very far from perfect vision.

Balta was ready, knife hidden, plan in place. There were no doubt other ways to accomplish his goal, but, he thought, each of us achieves satisfaction in his or her own way. Balta lived for the game. He had the cash he had taken from the woman on the train when he killed her with great efficiency and anatomical knowledge, which he hoped the police appreciated.

He knew the time Rochelle Tanquay was to be at the apartment of Jan Pendowski, the preening *babnik,* the lecher who had the diamonds. Balta would be there too.

Balta watched. Soon. Balta watched.

The knock at his door was gentle and right

on time. Jan Pendowski opened the door. Rochelle Tanquay stood there in a perfectly fitted tan suit, a silk scarf around her neck, her short dark hair brushed down in bangs. She looked, he thought, as if she had just stepped out of an ad for absolutely anything she wanted to sell.

She stepped in, and Jan leaned forward to gently clasp her right arm and kiss her. She did not resist. Her response was welcoming but reserved.

Jan closed the door and kissed her again. This time the response was even more welcoming. Both arms were around her now and his mouth was inches from hers. He could smell the scent of gardenia perfume.

His eyes made clear what he wanted.

"Shall we seal our partnership in bed?"

"When I see that you actually have diamonds, and this has not been an elaborate scheme to seduce me."

She said this with a smile.

"I am not devious," he said. "I say what I mean, and when I lie it is simple and direct. Simple and direct lies are the most convincing."

"I have never done anything illegal before," Rochelle Tanquay said, stepping back nervously. "Oh, small adventures. Cocaine. Deception in a game of cards with a lover, an Egyptian who could afford the loss, but . . ."

"The diamonds must be hidden carefully during your flight," Jan said.

"I know where I can put them. I fly around the world from Paris. I can go to a customs agent who recognizes me when I arrive. I've never been questioned."

"You know where to go in Paris?"

"Yes."

"I will meet you there after you get the money," he said.

"And Oxana?" Rochelle asked.

"Go ahead with your plan for her. Give her a magazine spread. She will be happy."

"But how will you tell her that she will not be carrying the diamonds to Paris, that she will not be sharing the money? I think it very likely that she may suspect me."

"I will take care of Oxana," he said, moving so close that Rochelle could see tiny flecks of green in his blue eyes.

"And now?" Rochelle said, almost purring.

Jan nodded and moved across the room to a small table holding a phone and the mail. The dark wooden table had curlicued legs like those of a delicate mythical animal.

"Antique, dated 1641 and signed by the maker. French. You should appreciate that.

Its authenticity has been verified by two dealers, who made substantial offers for it."

He slid the table away from the wall and stepped behind it.

"It was a gift to me from a very repulsive Tiblisi smuggler who was passing through Kiev with a substantial cache of drugs from Turkey hidden here."

Pendowski pulled a panel at the back of the table, which slid out to reveal a compartment in which rested a canvas bag tied with a leather thong.

"In exchange for the gift, I let him keep the drugs and be on his way after paying a slight toll in American dollars."

Jan held up the canvas bag. The contents were substantial enough to create a significant bulge.

He closed the compartment, pushed the table back against the wall, and stepped toward Rochelle Tanquay, opening the bag and tilting it forward to show the diamonds.

Rochelle reached out to take the bag, which he closed and tied. Then he held the bag over his head.

"First we seal our partnership in bed," he said, leaning so close that their lips were almost but not quite touching.

"Our partnership is dissolved."

The blade went smoothly and deeply

between two ribs and into his heart. Jan Pendowski's eyes opened wide in surprise. For an instant he did not know what had happened. He thought he might be having a heart attack. Both his father and one of his grandfathers had died young from heart attacks. But Rochelle had said the partnership was dissolved.

He stood looking at her, feeling no great pain, only the realization that he was no longer aware of his right arm and hand.

The second thrust, just below the ribs, made it clear to him what was happening.

He saw Rochelle, knife in hand, lean forward to kiss him quickly and then step back to avoid being touched by his blood as she thrust the blade smoothly into his neck. He went to his knees, clutching his throat. Blood seeped through his fingers. Breathing was impossible.

He slumped face forward to the now blood-soaked carpet as Rochelle deftly took the pouch of diamonds from his hand. Jan Pendowski made three urgent gasps for breath and died.

And then someone knocked at the door.

"And so we are gathered," said Iosef, looking at the strange quartet coming down the sidewalk.

The nervous man in a leather Mafia coat a bit too warm for the weather was smoking and clenching and unclenching his right fist. Behind him walked a very young man in a not-quite-so-fashionable coat, but a coat nonetheless. The substantial bald man they had seen on the Metro when they followed the two Africans was also wearing a leather coat, the uniform of the day for those with no imagination who wanted to hide weapons. Both Iosef and Zelach were well aware of what rested behind the leather.

The bald man had a tight grip on the left arm of a slight black man of no more than forty who wore no coat and displayed signs of having been beaten so badly that he belonged in a hospital. All four joined the man in the doorway who was watching the cafe.

Iosef watched the men in coats confer and talk to the man who had been hiding in the doorway.

"I think we are about to witness the gunfight at the OK Corral," said Iosef.

Zelach had no idea of what he was talking about. All he could think of was that they were probably about to face four heavily armed gangsters on one side and possibly a pair of armed Africans, maybe more than a pair, on the other. The two policemen were badly in need of heavily armed support.

"If we bring in backup at this point," said Iosef, "many people might be killed."

"If we do not," said Zelach, "maybe we will be killed."

"You are not afraid," said Iosef.

"No," said Zelach. "I was thinking about my mother."

Iosef turned his head away from the gathering in the doorway down the street and looked at Zelach.

"You are right," Iosef said. "I should have called for support."

"It is too late now," said Zelach, looking at the cafe.

The door had opened and the Africans named Biko and Laurence had stepped out. They were not alone. Five more black men carrying pistols and revolvers of various ilk were with them.

"Who do we shoot?" whispered Zelach.

"No one. I think they are going to shoot each other," answered Iosef.

The meeting was scheduled for tomorrow.

Yaklovev stood at the window in his office, looking down at the courtyard of Petrovka. He needed just a bit more to bargain with in the face of the potential loss of his control of the Office of Special Investigations. He was certain that with his connections he could find a reasonably prestigious and responsible position in the bureaucracy, possibly within the Kremlin itself. He was not concerned about what might happen to Rostnikov and the other detectives. But his current position and their investigative skills afforded him a perfect entree into the private lives, indiscretions, and crimes of politicians, business moguls, and even successful Mafia figures who wished for some degree of legitimacy.

No, he did not want to lose it now.

He went to his desk, pushed a button, and returned to the window. Below, a uniformed policeman had two German shepherds in tow and was heading for the gate beyond which stood a waiting police van.

The door opened, and Pankov came in.

"You rang for me?"

"You need not say that every time I call you," said the Yak. "Just come."

Yaklovev knew his statement would be ignored. The constantly frightened and nervous little man could not exist without frequent and ritualistic affirmation.

Pankov for his part was always startled upon entering the office to see the resemblance between Director Yaklovev and Lenin.

"I am going to get a call tonight from Chief Inspector Rostnikov. You are to be here and record it. Then you are to transcribe it so that I can, if necessary, edit it. Then you are to type it cleanly, make six copies, and have it in my hands by nine o'clock."

"Shall I bring it to your apartment?"

"No. I will be here till you have it done."

"It may take . . ."

"I expect it to take all night," said Yaklovev, watching as the dogs went through the rear doors of the van, which were then closed.

When he could no longer see the dogs, the Yak turned to Pankov, who stood, pad of paper and pen in hand, as close to the door as he could without looking ridiculous.

"You look particularly agitated today," Yaklovev said. "You are sweating. I would prefer that you not sweat when people come into the office."

"I wipe my brow and face constantly when no one is looking."

"I know," said the Yak, "but often someone is looking."

Pankov was startled into near panic. Did Director Yaklovev have a hidden camera in the outer office? Had Pankov done something he should not have done? He knew that the office and the offices of all the detectives were wired, because he was responsible for monitoring. He also knew that all the detectives were well aware that they could be heard. From time to time they made jokes at his expense and for his ears. Actually, only Iosef Rostnikov made such jokes.

"Pankov?"

"Yes."

"Pay attention. What is bothering you?"

"Will we all be replaced tomorrow, after your meeting?"

"If it is to be," Yaklovev said, "you would come with me wherever I were to be assigned. You are too valuable for me to lose."

Pankov was stunned. Never had he received anything resembling praise or reassurance from Director Yaklovev. Were he to be asked at that moment to get on his knees and kiss the feet of the Director, he would do so. Well, maybe not.

"Thank you," he said.

"Bring me the full file of General Frankovich."

"Now?"

"Now."

Pankov hurried out of the office and into his reception area office, where he experienced a rush of something that resembled comfort. He went to the locked cabinets in the room just to the right of his desk where files were carefully stored, updated, and indexed. The files were impressive, and Pankov kept them up to date, with every document uniformly lined up. Finding the thick file on General Frankovich took seconds.

What Pankov did not know, what no one but Igor Yaklovev knew, was that in a vault in a German bank not fifteen minutes from Petrovka, under a quite fictitious name, were other files, including one on General Frankovich. There was even one on President Putin himself. Yaklovev fully expected that Pankov's files were not only vulnerable but had probably been expertly penetrated. There was nothing in them that the Yak felt a need to keep from anyone with the ability and inclination to find them.

He moved back to his desk, sat, and waited for Pankov to return with the Frankovich file.

Later, when he grew hungry, he would send Pankov out to get him a sandwich. In the morning he would shave and change into the suit he had in the small closet behind him.

The Yak not only intended to survive, he was confident he could do so. Whether the same could be said of the detectives of the Office of Special Investigations would be decided in the morning.

CHAPTER SEVENTEEN

The pause was long. In the not great distance cars and trucks rambled, and the familiar construction sounds of discarded wood and rusted metal rattled down a chute and clanged onto the bed of a truck.

A lone car, an old Lada, came obliviously down the narrow street and stopped as a clutch of men on the left and another on the right stepped off of the narrow curb. The car came to a sudden stop. The driver, a man with many chins, pushed his head out of the window, displayed his angry pink face, and opened his mouth to shout. Then he saw the guns and the faces and registered the fact that he was being completely ignored.

There was no room to turn around. He backed up, trying to look over his shoulder. The car veered to his right and scraped a rear fender against a lamppost before successfully fading back the way it had come.

No one in the two groups now facing each other looked in the direction of the retreating car and the scratch of metal on metal.

"This is not going to be easy, is it?" called out Kolokov, stepping ahead of his three men, James Harumbaki behind him.

He was looking for someone to bargain with. No one emerged from among the six black men in front of him.

"Come. Come. Come," Kolokov said, pacing now. "The police will be coming and we will have to start shooting and you will not get our prisoner, who will be shot, and we will not get our diamonds and no one will be happy except Pau Montez, the bald man behind me, who likes shooting people and who has expressed a particular interest in shooting our hostage."

"Laurence," James Harumbaki called out hoarsely.

Kolokov spun around to look at his prisoner. The Russian smiled.

A small, plump young man stepped forward into the street. He stood no more than five paces from Kolokov who turned back to face him. The Russian noted that the young man did not appear to be in the least bit frightened.

"Die or trade?" asked Kolokov.

Laurence adjusted his glasses and said

nothing. He held up a cardboard box the size and shape of a large book. Kolokov held out a hand and Laurence took four more steps to hand the box to him.

From inside the doorway in which they had been standing, Akardy Zelach said, "When the shooting starts, who do we shoot?"

"If shooting is to be done," said Iosef Rostnikov, "there will be no need for our help in doing it. What is our assignment?"

"Diamonds," said Zelach.

"Diamonds," Iosef agreed.

Back in the street, Kolokov removed the lid from the box and reached in to pull out a small, almost round stone with a milky luster. He held it up as if he knew what he was looking at and motioned over his shoulder. Alek stepped forward. Kolokov handed him the stone. The man held it up and he too pretended that he knew what he was looking at. Then he nodded.

"We now carefully conclude our business," said Kolokov, backing away and putting the lid back on the box. "And no one dies."

The bald man pushed the stumbling James Harumbaki forward.

Kolokov handed the box to the bald man and held up his hands in a sign that this confrontation was over.

But it was not.

Before he even joined the line of black men, James Harumbaki, between swollen and torn lips, said, "Kill them."

The Africans fired first, but the Russians were quick to respond. Weapons were whipped out from under coats. Others were simply lifted and fired. It was not the bang-bang sound of television and movies, but a steady bap-bap-bap. There were no screams.

Iosef and Zelach watched as men flung their arms out, casting clattering weapons in the street. There was a pause, and then more firing. Neither side had moved forward or sought cover. Then James Harambuki's voice called out hoarsely as he pointed at Vladimir Kolokov,

"Do not kill him."

Two of the Russians behind Kolokov lay dead in the street. The bald man was also dead, but he sat with his back against the wall of a building. His eyes were open and he seemed to be smiling. Kolokov knelt, his right arm torn, bloody, nearly severed. He was blinking furiously.

James Harumbaki took a gun from the hand of Laurence and stepped in front of Kolokov, who spit blood and with his remaining good arm fumbled for a cigarette in his shirt pocket. He could not manage it, gave up, and looked at James Harumbaki, who looked down at him.

"I came very close," said Kolokov.

"No, you did not," said James Harumbaki. "Those are not real diamonds. I have a question. Answer, and you live if help comes to you in time."

"Ask," said Kolokov.

"Who told you that we had diamonds? Who told you where to find us when you took me and the two others you tortured and killed? Lie and you die. Tell the truth and you live."

Kolokov started an instinctive shrug but the pain was unbearable.

He was now surrounded by black faces looking down at him.

"A woman," Kolokov said. "I never met her. I think she was English. She called me, told me where you would be, that you would have diamonds, money."

"Where do I find this English woman?" asked James.

Kolokov shook his head.

"I do not know. I do not know her name."

The woman, whoever she was, had wanted to disrupt James Harumbaki's link in the chain from Siberia to Kiev, had wanted to destroy his operation and have him and his men killed. English. Gerald St. James was English, but why would he want to destroy his own operation?

"I believe you," said James Harumbaki, looking over his shoulder with his one, partially functioning eye.

Two Africans lay dead. A third was being tended to by Biko and another man.

James Harumbaki turned back to the kneeling Russian, who smiled through his pain and said, "We had some good chess matches."

"No, we did not," said James Harumbaki. "You may well be the worst chess player it has been my very bad fortune to face across a board."

And with that he held the gun up and put it to the head of Kolokov.

"You said you would not kill me."

"I am not," said James Harumbaki. "You are being killed by the ghosts of two good men who you tortured to death three days ago."

There were sirens now. Both directions. The police were coming.

"Three days? Was it only three days?" Kolokov asked as the bullet tore into his forehead.

Oxana Balakona could wait no longer. She

was to meet Rochelle Tanquay at the airport in three hours. Jan had stalled but she was going to his apartment to demand the diamonds. It was time. If she were going to hide and transport and trade them in Paris, she would have to have them now.

She took a taxi to his apartment. She also took a very small, flat, well polished gun in her purse. She had bought the gun for too much money from a man named Oleg, from whom she had purchased cocaine in the past.

If Jan stalled, balked, or backed out, Oxana was prepared to kill him. If she did not kill him today, she would have to at some point soon. She felt reasonably sure that she could fire the gun. She had never fired one before, certainly never killed anyone, but the diamonds were in the apartment, and the apartment was not large. She would have two hours to search for the diamonds before she had to get to the airport, where she had checked her bags the previous night.

This would be a successful day. She would make it a successful day.

The elevator in Jan Pendowski's apartment building was working. It did not always work. Oxana took this as a good sign. She went up to the fifth floor along with a very tiny, grunting woman clutching a large stuffed cloth shopping bag to her chest.

At the door to Jan's apartment she paused. She could not identify with certainty the sounds from within. A groan of pleasure, pain? Sex? With whom?

Oxana unzipped her small purse, looked down at her gun, and knocked.

"The woman in the photograph you took at the cafe," said Sasha. "I know who it is."

Elena had been following Oxana who had just gotten out of the taxi in front of the apartment building of Jan Pendowski when Sasha called on her cell phone.

"Rochelle Tanquay," said Elena, getting out of the taxi that she had taken to follow Oxana.

"Balta," said Sasha.

"Balta? Who is Balta?"

"A female impersonator," said Sasha. "A very good one."

"You go to see female impersonators?"

"Once," he said. "I went one time. Is that really relevant?"

"What is she . . . he doing here?" And then she answered her own question. "Diamonds."

"Diamonds," said Sasha.

"I will call you back," Elena said.

"Where are you?"

"The apartment building of Jan Pendowski. Oxana just went in."

"Wait. I am coming. I am not far."

Elena closed her phone and entered the building. She had no intention of waiting for a partner who cheated on his wife and went to see female impersonators.

"The tunnels have not been properly maintained," said Boris. "Not for thirty, forty years."

"I take no delight in hearing that," said Rostnikov, following the old man through the steel mesh gate that guarded the mine opening.

Emil Karpo watched as Boris closed and locked the gate behind them.

It was dark now. All three men wore yellow hard hats with mounted lights.

"You can turn your lights on now," Boris said.

Karpo and Porfiry Petrovich reached up and hit the switch on the hard hats that Boris had given them.

"The map in my head is better than Stepan Orlov's or that crazy old fool with the guns who thinks the Japanese are coming."

"This time we will use Orlov's map," said

Rostnikov, walking carefully toward an open-topped golf cart that sat in the middle of the wide tunnel. "Next time we will use yours."

"Next time," said Boris with a shake of his head. "I do not trust next times. You drive."

He was looking at Emil Karpo who obliged and got into the driver's seat. Boris got in next to him and Porfiry Petrovich sat in the back.

"Straight ahead," said Boris. "I will tell you when to stop. Lights on."

Karpo found the switch and turned on the single headlight, which, along with the lights from their helmet lamps, sent dancing beams ahead of them into the darkness. They started forward. Small green lights lined the ceiling of the shaft about four feet over their heads.

It was almost one in the morning, and the slow dance of head lamps and glowing green overhead lights made Rostnikov slightly sleepy. His eyes were closed when, a bit over two minutes later, Boris announced, "Here."

Karpo stopped the cart and they all stepped out. Rostnikov and his alien leg came last.

"Three tunnels," said Boris, turning his

head to each of the dark entrances.

"Which one did the Canadian go in?" asked Rostnikov.

Boris pointed to the one on the left.

"It does not go very far. There was a pipe there many, many years ago but it ran out."

"Why is it not sealed?" asked Karpo.

"Why?" said Boris. "Why should it be? No one goes in there."

"The Canadian went in there," Karpo reminded him.

"I told him it was pointless. He insisted. Americans do not listen," said Boris.

"He was not an American."

"He was a North American," Boris said. "The difference can be measured with the thinness of a single sheet of very fine paper."

"The ghost girl," Rostnikov prompted.

"Yes, that is the tunnel in which the girl died in 1936 or 1942 or 1957, depending on who tells the tale."

"And the other day," injected Rostnikov, "Anatoliy Lebedev, which tunnel did he go in?"

"I do not know. I found him out here. Right there, where you are standing."

Rostnikov turned his head downward. The beam of his hard hat revealed nothing, not even a stain of blood.

"I am going in that tunnel," Rostnikov

said, nodding at the tunnel on the left into which the Canadian had walked. "You two go in the other tunnels, the middle one first. How far does that go?"

"Maybe a quarter of a mile," said Boris. "Maybe . . ."

"Forty feet short of a quarter of a mile," said Karpo, looking at the Orlov map in his hands.

"Go in, to the end. Check the small caves marked on the map," said Rostnikov.

Karpo nodded his understanding of the order and started into the middle tunnel with Boris shuffling behind him. Rostnikov stood watching the light from the bouncing lamps on the hats of the two men slowly grow more and more dim as they moved away.

Rostnikov moved to the tunnel on the left and stepped in. It was definitely too small for the golf cart and not as flat as the tunnel out of which he was stepping. There were no green overhead lights glowing here. Only his lamp illuminated the dark tunnel.

He walked, his bandit leg protesting.

"The cave is not far," he told the leg softly. "Tonight I will clean you, oil you, dry you, and place you on a pillow on the bed."

This failed to appease the leg dragging along the rocky ground.

The small cave was exactly where the Orlov map showed it. Rostnikov removed the boards that covered it and peered inside. It appeared to be an empty space big enough for someone to fit in by crouching. On the floor of the cave, in a far corner, Rostnikov could see something crumpled on the floor. Rostnikov went down and awkwardly crawled forward until he could reach what he had seen. There was barely enough room for him to turn around and sit.

He did not bother to examine the walls for traces of diamonds. He knew there was no real chance of his recognizing a pipe of diamonds or even a real diamond among the stones next to him. What did interest him were the two empty candy bags. He picked up the first and smelled the inside. This was no ancient relic. It could not have been more than a day old, if that.

Rostnikov turned to his side and folded the two empty bags into his pocket. There was nothing else to see in the tiny cave. He began to ease himself out, this time feet first. Then he stopped. A light glowed outside the cave. Rostnikov pulled himself back inside the cave as the music began. It was a child's voice, high and plaintively sweet singing "Evening Bells."

". . . *tam slyshal zvon. f pasledni ras. I*

heard this sound there for the last time."

Rostnikov sang the next verse. His singing voice was not sweet, and he sounded not like a bell, but he could hold a tune.

"*I skolkikh nyet uzhe v zhivyky, tagda vesyolykh maladykh.* And how many no longer are among the living now, who were happy then, and young."

The singing of the child had stopped and was replaced by a deep male voice singing, "*I krepok ikh magilny son.* Deep in their sleep, in their tombs."

"You have a fine voice, Viktor Panin," said Rostnikov, "as does your son."

"How did you know?"

"That you were the killer, or that the ghost girl was a boy?"

"Both."

Panin was on one knee now looking into the small cave.

"The report of the naked ghost girl," said Rostnikov.

It was quite uncomfortable in the small cave. He shifted, but it did not help very much.

"Why would someone write a false report about a fifty-year-old sighting of a naked ghost girl? Answer: Because the person writing the report wanted me to look for a girl and not consider a boy. I met some very nice girls, but concluded that none of them was the girl."

"And me?" asked Panin.

"You," said Rostnikov. "When you killed Lebedev you left a very tiny piece of your knife blade inside him. On the blade was a faint trace of something my scientist friend Paulinin discovered. There were also faint traces of the same substance on the clothes and neck of poor Lebedev."

"What was this substance?" asked Panin.

"Chalk. Not the blue chalk next to the pool tables in the recreation room, but the white chalk of the workout room. I am sure I still have traces of it on my sweat suit. I know it takes a very long time to be absorbed by the skin or washed away. I made inquiries and found that you have a boy who is on the Devochka Children's Choir, a boy who, I am sorry to say, has great musical talent but is more than a bit backwards."

"I must kill you, Porfiry Petrovich," Panin said. "For my family."

"Well, I must stay alive for mine. How do you propose killing me? There is not enough room for you to get in here with me, and even if your son is very small I doubt if he could overcome me."

"I would not ask him to do that."

"Then . . ."

"I could shoot you."

"Too much noise. Karpo and Boris would hear."

"We would be gone by the time they got here," said Panin.

"Perhaps, but Emil Karpo is fast, and he will quickly be on your trail through the tunnel. One question," said Rostnikov. "You hid your son down here during the day before the gate was locked for the night."

"It was not difficult."

"And then he came out and opened the gate from inside."

"Yes."

"And the other ghost girls, over the many years before you were old enough to do this, before you had a son to do this? All the children of people, like you, who stole diamonds and smuggled them to Africans in Moscow?"

"Yes."

"Only you had no daughters, only sons."

"Now you know."

"Thank you. If you would help me out . . ."

"I am going to have to kill you, Porfiry Petrovich. Do you not understand?"

"It would be pointless. Emil Karpo is a very good shot and I believe he is some-where behind you, watching, at this very moment."

Just outside the small cave the darkness of the tunnel was illuminated by two sudden beams, one fixed on the kneeling Panin, the other on his son of no more than nine or ten, who stood in dress and wig, a thumb to his mouth.

"You tricked me," said Panin, with a deep sigh of resignation.

Rostnikov slid out of the cave on his back. Stones and pebbles tore at his jacket.

"We trapped you," said Boris triumphantly. "Do I get a medal? I would rather have that free trip to St. Petersburg and a job there."

"I will arrange it," Rostnikov said, accepting a helping hand from Panin who pulled him to his feet easily.

The child looked at his father and the three other men and began to sing again, but Panin stopped him by gently placing two fingers on the boy's mouth.

"There is one more thing you could tell us," said Rostnikov.

"No."

"I thought not," said Rostnikov, knowing that his jacket was torn and, if he were lucky, his back only minimally scratched.

"It is over?" asked Boris.

"Yes," Porfiry Petrovich Rostnikov lied.

■ ■ ■ ■

Oxana had a key to Jan's apartment.

Jan did not know this. It made no difference to Jan at the moment because the final few beats of his bleeding heart and faint pulse were marking the end of his life.

Oxana listened at the door. Nothing. She knocked. No answer.

She used her key. If luck were with her, she could search for the diamonds, find them, and deal with Jan later.

She stood in the open doorway trying to make sense out of what she was seeing.

Jan lay on the floor on his back. His shirt was covered with blood. Blood pulsed weakly from a black-red gash in his neck. Standing next to him, a pouch in one hand, a bloody knife in the other, stood Rochelle. She looked as composed as ever, as she said,

"Oxana, he called me, told me to get right over. He said you were in trouble."

Rochelle took a step toward Oxana.

"He had a knife," said Rochelle. "This knife. He told me to undress. He put the knife down and . . ."

"What is in the bag?" asked Oxana, taking the gun out of her purse and pointing it at the French woman.

"I do not know," Rochelle said, looking at the pouch as if she had no idea what it was doing in her hand. "He had it, and . . ."

"Put the bag on the floor. Put the knife on the floor and step back," said Oxana.

"What?"

"On the floor. Step back."

"Is there blood on my dress?" asked Rochelle.

It was Oxana's turn to say, "What?"

"I cannot go out covered in blood."

"Put the ba—"

Rochelle dropped the bag. Oxana watched it hit the floor and open enough to reveal three small glittering stones. When Oxana's eyes were fixed on the stones, Rochelle leapt forward and threw her elbow into the face of the startled model.

Oxana went down on her back, her jaw searing, throbbing with pain.

The door to the apartment was still open. It could not be helped now. Oxana would have to be killed quickly and the door kicked closed.

"Rochelle," Oxana gasped. "We can . . ."

"No, we cannot."

And then there was another voice, this time from the doorway, saying, "The knife, on the floor. Now."

Oxana turned her head, and Rochelle looked at the doorway, where Elena stood, weapon in hand.

Rochelle did not drop the knife. Elena fired across the room, through the window.

"Drop the knife, Balta," Elena said.

Balta smiled and dropped the knife. The woman in the doorway had her knees slightly bent, and she held her weapon in two hands. She was solidly built and rather pretty, not a beauty like Rochelle, certainly not a beauty like Oxana, who was certain that her jaw was broken.

Balta might have been able to dash the five steps across the room and plunge the knife into Elena, but it was a risk he did not have to take. He had a great deal with which to bargain.

Balta dropped the knife. Rochelle's voice was replaced by a somewhat deeper voice as he raised his hands and said, "You have me."

"Turn around," Elena ordered.

Oxana sat blinking her eyes, trying to understand her pain, Jan, and what was happening. Her gun lay on the floor next to the pouch leaking diamonds. Before she could consider what her possibilities might be, Elena kicked the little gun across the room.

"You too, get up," Elena said to Oxana. "Now."

Oxana managed to rise in agony.

"Together. Backs to me," said Elena.

Oxana looked down at the body of Jan Pendowski. Her knees were weak, not because of what she saw, but for the pain in her jaw.

Something clicked around her right wrist behind her. Oxana looked back to watch herself being handcuffed to Rochelle.

"*Ya ne pani'mayu.* I do not understand," Oxana managed.

"To begin, you stupid department store dummy," Balta said, opening his eyes wide, "I am a man."

Sergeants Moseyovich and Sworskov had gone to work doing what they did best. They closed off the street and called in the cleaning trucks and ambulances. Within half an hour the street was clean and empty, and traffic was moving again.

Three miles away, in the back room of a church that had been converted to a small museum of icons, sat Iosef Rostnikov, Akardy Zelach, a young portly man who insisted that his full name was Laurence, and a very badly beaten James Harumbaki.

They sat and said nothing while Iosef

listened to the call that had come on his phone. He had said,

"I understand."

And then he hung up.

"Christiana Verovona," said Iosef.

There was no reaction.

"She was murdered on a train coming from Kiev. She was carrying money just received from a model named Oxana Balakona for your diamonds."

Neither black man said anything.

"I know this because the man who killed Christiana Verovona just told a police officer in Kiev," said Iosef. "The officer has the money and the diamonds. I have been instructed by my Chief Inspector to let you get your passports, providing you have them, and escort you to the next airplane to Botswana. You will go as you are. Nothing but the clothes you are wearing. No money. You are never to return to Russia. If you do, you will be killed while attempting to rob an undercover police officer."

James Harumbaki considered asking "Why?" but he did not.

"You agree to these terms?" asked Iosef.

"We agree," said James Harumbaki.

Iosef had been informed by Porfiry Petrovich, who had been informed by the Yak, that it would be more convenient simply to get the Africans out of the country than to deal with the ramifications of their being in Russia.

"Good," said Iosef rising. "Then your stay in Russia is over."

Chapter Eighteen

The meeting with General Frankovich could not have gone better. Yaklovev had arrived armed with a report on the successful breakup of the diamond smuggling network that stretched from Siberia to Moscow to Kiev, and probably well beyond. He also had some audio tapes and a thick file discretely marked "Frankovich" which he placed next to himself at the conference table, where he sat next to the General. The directors of three other departments and a Kremlin representative were also at the table.

Yaklovev reported, was congratulated by the Kremlin representative and informed that the Office of Special Investigations had done an outstanding job. The Kremlin representative added that President Putin himself was going to send a letter of commendation to Yaklovev.

Throughout the meeting, General Frankovich said not one word.

Sasha appeared at the door of his wife's apartment one minute after seven o'clock. He brought with him a small yellow stuffed bear for Pulcharia and a picture book about airplanes for his child, whom he had resolved to call Taras until the bearer of the Ukrainian name grew tired of it.

Pulcharia opened the door. She wore a green dress he had never before seen. Over her shoulder she called out, "It is the policeman father." And then to Sasha, "Did you bring a gun?"

"No," he said.

She shrugged in disappointment and accepted the bear.

Sasha stepped inside as his daughter closed the door.

"Taras is here," his son giggled.

"I see," said Sasha, handing him the book.

Brother and sister, without a word, exchanged gifts.

"Come in," said Maya. "Dinner is ready."

There was to be no small talk in the living room, just conversation over dinner at the small table Maya had set up there. Taras, who constantly repeated his new name, rocked back and forth in his chair and smiled at Sasha, who smiled back and, from time to time without success, attempted conversation. Pulcharia played with her beet borscht, filling her soup spoon and dribbling it on a tender square of floating meat. The main dish was *sichenyky,* ground meat patties. For dessert, Maya had purchased a medium-sized *babka.* Sasha noted that nothing on the table was Russian. He noted, but he did not speak.

When they were finished, except for Pulcharia who continued to play with her food, Sasha rose to help clear the table.

"Stay, talk to the children," Maya said.

This was just the thing that Sasha did not want to do. He wanted to talk to Maya, to try again to persuade her. He did not wish to hear his son rock from side to side saying "Boyka" and his daughter creating a tepid volcano from a mound of floating beets.

Sasha grabbed some dishes and followed Maya into the kitchen alcove where he reached past her to place his stack in the sink.

"When?" he asked.

"We shall see."

"You mean never."

"I mean never."

"If I do not see the children regularly, they will forget me. If I do not see you . . . the Swede?"

Maya did not answer.

The children were no more than a dozen feet away, and Sasha had to admit that he was beginning to look forward to leaving the apartment. His children were perfect in the abstract, but not unflawed in reality. It depressed him. It made him feel guilty.

"You want to leave," Maya said, taking two dishes from Pulcharia, one of which tottered dangerously.

"No," he said.

She paused and turned to face him as Pulcharia headed back to the table.

"You are lying."

Sasha did not answer.

"If you cannot stand them for an hour, how would you stand them for many hours each day? You would make excuses to be elsewhere. It is what you did. It is what you would do."

"I love my children," he said softly.

"I know," she said.

"I love you," he said.

"I know that, too, but love is only the first part."

"You read that somewhere," he said.

"Come back in a year."

"You will have remarried."

"It is possible."

She suddenly came close to him and

kissed his lips. She smelled of sweet *babka*. He wept.

"And so?" asked Iosef, sitting at the desk in his cubicle in Petrovka.

"And so?" said Elena.

"What do you say?"

"Yes."

"Good. Then we marry on Tuesday. Your aunt has the papers and will preside. She is well enough?"

"Yes," Elena said.

She was sitting in the Kiev airport talking on her cell phone. Sasha Tkach sat across from her next to a man with huge eyes. Sasha did not seem to notice. He was busy looking at nothing.

"And that is it?" asked Iosef.

"I will see you in Moscow tonight," she said.

She hung up. So did he.

Iosef realized that he had failed to tell her that he loved her.

Pankov had spent the night in his sweat-dampened suit preparing material for the Yak's meeting with Frankovich. The temperature inside of Petrovka was notoriously uncertain. Last night it had been warm, hot even.

At some point while preparing this important material, Pankov suffered a stroke. His right arm began to twitch uncontrollably, the pen flying across the room and creating a black dot on the wall. Gradually, the tremor stopped. He felt as if he might pass out. When he was reasonably sure this would not happen, he resumed his preparation of the material. It was the third small stroke he had suffered in the past month. He had told no one, seen no doctor. With the other two incidents, as now, he had gone back to his duties.

Gerald St. James and Ellen Sten stood next to the window in his office looking through a steady, steaming rain at the top of the De-Beers building.

In his right hand, St. James held a dart. He rolled it between his fingers.

"Nothing to connect us?" he asked casually.

"Nothing. Those who could are dead or so well compensated that revelation would not be worth the reward we are giving them and their families. The network is ended," she said. "Do we start a new one at De-vochka?"

"We will wait a year," he said. "Maybe two. Then I will decide."

The primary value of the Devochka operation was a diversion. It brought in little, but kept authorities in sixteen countries from more closely examining St. James's larger operations in Australia, South Africa, and Botswana.

Some day soon he would sit at the table at DeBeers. When he sat, he would be Sir Gerald St. James. He was in the process of purchasing and bribing his way into the peerage even as he stood at the window.

"Loose ends?" he asked.

"The Africans will not talk. Balta already is talking, but is having great trouble getting anyone to believe him. The British police will certainly be informed through Interpol, and they may want to talk to you."

St. James made a sound signifying indifference and turned to place the dart on his desk.

Porfiry Petrovich sat in the office of his half-brother Fyodor. For fifteen minutes, they said nothing, just listened to a CD of recently restored early Louis Armstrong records.

"Panin will not talk," said Porfiry Petrovich.

"He is a good man," said Fyodor.

"A good man," said Porfiry Petrovich. "He

murdered two people, innocent people."

"There is that," said Fyodor, as Armstrong's trumpet played a plaintive six-note passage.

There was much that could be said, but nothing Porfiry Petrovich wanted to say.

His brother had conspired with Panin to smuggle diamonds and murder the Canadian Luc O'Neil and old Lebedev. Fyodor had provided an alibi for Viktor Panin for both murders. Fyodor had written the false report of the naked ghost girl and placed it in his own file. Then, when Porfiry Petrovich had figured out that the report was false, Fyodor had simply taken the typewriter and placed it on his bed where Karpo could find it, so it would look as if some incompetent killer were trying to implicate him.

These things Rostnikov knew of his brother.

These things Fyodor knew that his brother knew.

Panin had confessed to both murders. Fyodor had committed neither. That was sufficient excuse in the eyes of the law, but the eyes of a brother were very different. And Viktor Panin had not given up Fyodor Rostnikov, who promised to take care of Viktor's family.

"Time?" asked Rostnikov.

"A few minutes after two."

"I must go. The airplane is waiting."

Rostnikov rose. This time his leg cooperated fully.

Maybe it was the real beginning of a cordiality, if not a friendship, between man and man-made.

"I will walk out with you," said Fyodor, also rising.

"No," said Rostnikov.

Fyodor understood.

"There will be no more smuggling of diamonds from the mine," said Rostnikov.

"No more."

"Good."

That was all. No good-byes. Porfiry Petrovich left the room.

Back in his room in Moscow, Emil Karpo turned on the light, unpacked his bag, placed it on the shelf of his closet, and sat down at his desk to transcribe his notes into the latest black leather-bound journal.

Winter was coming. Cold comforted. The night wind rattled the single window.

After less than an hour, his eyes began to burn, and the neat block letters he wrote in dark ink began to blur. He would soon be needing glasses. It was inevitable.

A scratching sound at the door. Karpo

rubbed the bridge of his nose, wiping away the moisture that had formed in the corner of his eyes.

He did not hurry. The scratching did not stop. He crossed the room and, fingers of his right hand placed around the gun in the holster at his belt, opened the door.

The black cat limped in and moved to the cot.

Emil Karpo closed the door.

Paulinin had been particularly busy the past week. He had greeted, spoken to, and probed new bodies. He had to completely clean the laboratory tables each time a new arrival appeared.

For some reason that Paulinin did not wish to or bother to explore, he felt that something somber from Beethoven was in order. And so something somber for orchestra by Beethoven was playing now as he rubbed the bridge of his nose, scratched an itch on his cheek, and scrubbed his hands in the sink. The water was scalding hot. Paulinin wanted it that way.

And then he turned to the naked man on the table who had a particularly disruptive gunshot wound in his forehead. Paulinin had looked at the man's wallet. It contained no money. They never did. Someone along the line had made no effort to resist temptation. What did remain was a driver's license, which identified the dead man as Vladimir Kolokov.

Cymbals crashed behind Paulinin, who looked down at the dead man and said, "Let us see where you have been, Vladimir. From the look of your body, the tattoos of prison death, the scars of old and recent wounds . . ."

Paulinin reached down to explore the wound in the dead man's hand with a long finger.

". . . you are, like so many of those who pass through this room, definitely one of the people who walk in darkness."

ABOUT THE AUTHOR

People Who Walk in Darkness is the latest in Edgar Award winner and MWA's Grand Master **Stuart M. Kaminsky's** beloved Inspector Rostnikov mysteries. It was for a Rostnikov title, *A Cold Red Sunrise,* that Kaminsky won a Best Novel Edgar in 1989. In addition to the Rostnikov series, Kaminsky is the author of the Abe Lieberman, Lew Fonesca, and Toby Peters series. He lives with his family in Sarasota, Florida.

The employees of Thorndike Press hope you have enjoyed this Large Print book. All our Thorndike and Wheeler Large Print titles are designed for easy reading, and all our books are made to last. Other Thorndike Press Large Print books are available at your library, through selected bookstores, or directly from us.

For information about titles, please call:
(800) 223-1244

or visit our Web site at:
http://gale.cengage.com/thorndike

To share your comments, please write:
Publisher
Thorndike Press
295 Kennedy Memorial Drive
Waterville, ME 04901